SHADOWS OF WAR

ROBERT WESTALL was born in North Shields, Northumberland in 1929. After taking degrees in fine art from Durham University and London's Slade School, Westall worked as an art teacher and was also a freelance journalist and art critic for *The Guardian*.

It was not till later in life that Westall turned to fiction, having been inspired to become a writer after telling his son Christopher stories about his childhood during World War II. His first book, *The Machine Gunners*, was published in 1975 when he was 45; it was a major success, winning the Carnegie Medal, and has been recognized by critics as a lasting classic of children's literature. He would go on to publish over 40 books for young readers, including works that drew on his boyhood during the war, stories involving cats, and tales of the ghostly and supernatural. Besides *The Machine Gunners*, Westall is perhaps best known for *The Scarecrows* (1981), which won him a second Carnegie Medal and which his obituary in the *Independent* called 'one of the most searing and haunting child-eyed views of divorce yet to have been written', and *Blitzcat* (1989), which won the Smarties Prize. *The Watch House* (1977) and *The Machine Gunners* were also adapted for television serials.

After retiring from teaching in 1985, Westall worked briefly as an antique dealer, an experience that partly inspired his sole work of fiction for adults, the ghost story collection *Antique Dust* (1989). The first edition's jacket lists his hobbies as 'nosing round old buildings, studying cats and looking for the unknown' and notes that 'he has never seen a ghost but has not yet given up hope'.

Robert Westall died in 1993 at age 63.

Also Available by Robert Westall

Antique Dust
The Stones of Muncaster Cathedral
Spectral Shadows: Three Novellas

Robert Westall

SHADOWS OF WAR

VALANCOURT BOOKS

Shadows of War by Robert Westall
First Valancourt Books edition 2019

Published by Valancourt Books, Richmond, Virginia
http://www.valancourtbooks.com

ISBN 978-1-948405-36-2 (*trade paperback*)

Also available as an electronic book.

All Valancourt Books publications are printed on acid free paper that meets all ANSI standards for archival quality paper.

Set in Dante MT

CONTENTS

THE GERMAN GHOST

Ghosts? I only saw one once.

If it wasn't a ghost, it was something worse.

It was during my National Service in Germany. Keeping the world safe for democracy with a typewriter.

Nothing dashing or romantic; spent most of my time sitting in an office in Sennelager. Snug, though. The central heating worked right through those bitter North German winters. Installed by Germans of course.

You could especially forget romance. Lili Marlene had long since given up hanging round the lamplight by the barrack gate; gone to set up some posh brothel in Hamburg with mirrors on the ceiling. And on a corporal's pay I couldn't even compete with Turkish immigrant workers, let alone Yank top-sergeants. I settled for the YMCA ping-pong table, the NAAFI and the movies.

Snug. Till the chinless wonders at HQ BAOR had the great idea of holding an exercise in the middle of January. 'Exercise Topknot', which we immediately christened 'Exercise Top Nit'. Usual old story – Russian hordes pouring across the Elbe onto the North German Plain, and we were supposed to move into position to stop them.

'Move into position'. Sounds so simple. Reach your map reference point, camouflage your vehicles, dig your slit-trenches and put up your pup-tents. No Russki artillery pounding away at you; no MiGs strafing you at rooftop height. Just the endless winter fog that blankets the North German plain; the North German water that oozes into your slit-trench the moment you start to dig it; and the North German wind that drives sleet through every chink in your tent.

And it didn't help, knowing that the Russki hordes had far more sense and were no doubt toasting their stockinged feet round barrackroom stoves, and getting sloshed on cut-price vodka.

Or the fact that our vehicles were worn-out crap from the War. We had half-tracks from the Western Desert that couldn't manage five miles along summer roads without their tracks coming off or their engines dying of advanced emphysema.

And exercises are bloody *dangerous*. Blokes get killed. Not hundreds like in war, but they're just as dead. Squashed flat in their sleeping bags by tanks whose brakes have failed, having been parked for the night on a one-in-five slope. Killed by speed-happy army drivers trying to catch up with their convoys by driving their Humber thirty-hundredweights at ninety along the autobahn in a blizzard. Frozen to death in their pup-tents . . .

Stay alive; keep warm; have a brew-up. Those were my military objectives. After I'd been loaded into a canvas-topped three-tonner with my typewriter and filing cabinets, by a mob of foul-mouthed Jock linemen from Glasgow, who wondered loudly why I couldn't do my own loading.

At least I was with mates; they say while you have fags and mates the bastards can't grind you down. Nil carborundum. My main mate was Second Lieutenant Roger Pratt, of the Security Troop. Also National Service, and also a graduate. We'd done officer training together; only he'd passed out and got his little pip, and I'd failed through nipping off for a crafty weekend in London and leaving my rifle concealed (not very well) under my mattress. Roger envied me my two stripes, and leisurely dinners of eggs, beans and chips in the NAAFI. He said I was top of my pile of crap, and he was bottom of his, in the Officers' Mess. Everyone was bloody horrible to him, because he was National Service and wanted to be a poet when he grew up. The Army, above the rank of graduate corporal, does not recognize the existence of poetry. If the

CO had caught Roger writing his poetry he would have been court-martialled for being idle on parade.

Anyway, we set off into the fog of war; Roger's Land Rover and wireless CV truck in front, and my three-tonner behind. We were lumped together because we were both bloody useless, and nobody wanted us getting in the way. My only job was to type out Squadron Orders and file bumf from the War Office, and Roger's job was to listen in to the radio networks, to make sure that bored operators weren't sending each other the words of dirty songs like Eskimo Nell in Morse code. Roger and I reckoned that these dirty songs in Morse were our only chance of stopping the real Russkis, if they were invaded. By the time they'd been translated, and the Russian High Command had worked out what they were and stopped laughing, their whole campaign to conquer Europe would've ground to a halt . . .

Roger in front. Doing the map-reading. Roger couldn't read a map for toffee. He always got lost. Well, for God's sake, he was a poet, wasn't he? How could he make up his lines about 'the cathedral silence of the German mist' and read a map as well? And it was more than his pip was worth to ask any other British troops where we were. It would get back, with many a merry laugh in many an Officers' Mess, to our bastard of a CO. And then poor Rog would be for it.

That was where I came in. My degree was in German; I could ask German civilians the way . . .

But it suited me at the moment to sit by my driver in the warm cab with my own map. Probably half the division was lost by this time; the half who hadn't broken down.

Fog and flatness and old snow lying in ditches, and those endless bloody fir trees. Roger finally stopped and came back to me shivering in his officer's greatcoat.

'We're lost.'

'I think we're OK,' I said comfortingly. 'Just keep following this road till you come to a church on the left. We dig in by the church. The church is your map reference.'

'Do you think so?' he asked, trusting as a child. 'There's no sign of the rest of our lot . . .'

'It's them that's bloody lost,' I said firmly. 'Just look out for the church.'

We drove on; and, amazingly, a church appeared on the left. In the middle of a dense clump of pines, just right for us to hide our vehicles from air-observation by the Russkis, if there had been any Russkis and there hadn't been any fog. The church was an odd little place, with a tower with a sort of onion dome, the kind some Germans like. It had a graveyard too, full of rusting Gothic railings, tall tombs and long dead grass.

What it didn't have, which it should have had, according to the map, was a village attached. But I told Roger it was probably hidden by the fog . . .

Anyway, my blokes and his blokes were making ominous noises about dying of exposure and needing a brew-up. And his wireless ops said they were getting the divisional operators' dirty songs through loud and clear, which was all that mattered to Security Troop. And Roger was convinced that if we went any further we'd only get more lost, and probably end up exchanging fire with East German border guards.

So we drove our vehicles in under the pines, and covered them with camouflage netting and dead branches; and dug our slit-trenches and watched them fill up with good old muddy German water . . . The tea was strong and tasted great.

Two hours later, our squadron commander turned up in his Austin Champ, with the sergeant major sitting alongside. Unlike the CO, who was a miserable old bastard, our major was a real hero. Western Desert campaign, and a DSO at El Hamma. One of those blokes who has everything. Bright. Handsome as Errol Flynn, though he had to shave twice a day or his jowl went black. Real charm, even with the meanest squaddie; must have been a killer with the ladies. And he actually loved what he called 'real soldiering'. No matter how wet and cold he was, and even when one of his three-tonners was upside down in a ditch at midnight, he loved it all. He roared in now, driving himself like a maniac, with his terrified driver in the back cuddling his enthralled Labrador.

'You're out of position, Mr Pratt,' he bawled at poor Roger.

Roger turned pale. 'By how much, sir?' he quavered.

The major laughed wolfishly, 'About a hundred yards.'

Roger wiped his face with relief. He'd been expecting about ten miles . . . a hundred yards was nothing in this man's army.

'This church is the old Marienburgerkirche. The new one's just down the road. Nearly fooled us as well, didn't it, sar'nt major?'

'Yessir.'

'This is actually a better position. More cover. Other place was a damned public football pitch . . . which is no doubt why you chose this, Mr Pratt?'

'Yessir.'

The major smiled wolfishly again. Loving every moment, like a boy on holiday. The sar'nt major only managed a small frozen smirk. He was an old hand, only months from demob, and you could tell he felt the cold. He was wrapped up in everything he could lay his hands on, including a balaclava that must have been left over from the Murmansk campaign of 1919.

The major made a small alteration on the map strapped to his thigh, glanced keenly at our slit-trenches full to the brim, the pup-tents starting to flap loose in the wind. Then he looked at the church.

'Church looks all right to me – why the hell did they want to build a new one? And the graveyard's very untidy – that's not like the Hun . . . Still, carry on, Mr Pratt.' He zoomed away, splattering us all with mud, but especially Roger's new greatcoat.

We brewed up again, using a fire-bucket of sand soused

in petrol. Another old Western Desert trick, but in that wind nothing more modern would work.

After that it just got murkier and more boring. Rog's operators kept logging the dirty song transmissions from the warmth of their CV, which had the luxury of closable doors. In my truck, I tried to knock out Squadron Orders with hands turning blue inside fingerless mittens. A few dispatch riders roared up, plastered with mud from head to foot so that bits of drying soil fell off their faces when they grinned. Like the major, they were loving it, breaking all speed limits to carry vital messages like:

'Amendment to Army Council Instructions. For "Army Spotting planes – aircrews" read "Army Spotting planes – airscrews".'

Roger kept me company in the cold, because I was the only one he could share his innermost thoughts with. The only thing the rest of his troop ever discussed was who was the greatest centre-forward England ever had.

He kept looking over the tailgate and shivering.

'Funny-looking old church. Don't blame them for building a new one up the road.'

'Graveyard's full up, I expect. Standing room in the aisles only.' I wasn't feeling like a philosophical discussion. I was trying to work out who to put on orderly corporal tomorrow, and deciding it should be Masher Higgins because I hated him, and being twenty-four hours on orderly corporal the day you come off an exercise is a fate worse than death.

'Don't say things like that,' said Roger, with a poetic quiver. 'There's an awful lot of tombs. By the end, the dead must have outnumbered the living congregation . . .'

He dropped over the tailgate, and went and walked all round the building. When he came back, he looked less cheerful than ever.

'There isn't even a slate missing from the roof. But the windows are all dust and cobwebs. You can't see a thing inside . . .'

That was a mistake. He'd sort of given permission to

inspect the church. And the idle ones in our mob, the runners and drivers, including that notable loony Spud Malone, left with nothing to do, had climbed the churchyard wall, and were wading through the long sodden grass between the tombs, and kicking at the rusty iron railings around the graves. I heard Spud yell something about Dracula and the next minute he was trying to bury his teeth in Taffy Williams' neck. Which was his mistake because Taffy, who's a big lad, punched him in the gut, and they both fell inside a set of grave railings.

'You'd better have a word with them,' I said to Roger.

'Oh, it's just high spirits. They're bored. They've got to let off steam somehow.'

By that time, they were letting off steam on a life-size marble angel, which by some quirk of the sculptor's art, was *remarkably* well endowed.

'Wouldn't mind a crack at you, darlin', when I get through the Pearly Gates,' said Taffy Williams, embracing her.

'Get your skiving hands off her,' shouted Spud Malone. 'I saw her first. Din' I, darlin'?'

The statue rocked alarmingly on its base, with a sharp grating sound.

'I really do think you ought to have a word with them, Rog. You know what the Germans are like about compensation . . .'

'It's all right. They're moving on.'

You must think we were a right pair of seven-stone weaklings, a second lieutenant and a full corporal, just letting them run amok, without opening our mouths. The trouble was, they were Regulars, and we were only National Service. To a Regular, stripes on a National Serviceman aren't worth the cloth they're sewn on; and a National Service pip is pure fancy dress. And we were a long way from the regiment. Rub up Regulars the wrong way, and they're quite likely to thump you one, and cheerfully do a month in the glasshouse afterwards. It was all a matter of pride. To them we weren't real soldiers at all.

We went on watching, hoping their boyish enthusiasm would find a new course, like an argument about whether Newcastle United should really have won the FA cup in 1922, followed by a fist fight.

Then they noticed the tall black marble tomb with classical columns down the front, and a gilded urn on top . . .

'It's the entrance to a crypt,' shouted Spud. 'Look, these doors open. They're only fastened by a chain.'

'Halloo, Drac,' bawled Taffy Williams, hammering with his fists on the metal doors. 'Howzabout dropping down to the local bloodbank for a pint?'

They hauled savagely on the doors, making the chain rattle and echo, harsh and sharp, through the dense pine trees. There were shouts.

'Bodies down there, in lead coffins.'

'Get the crowbar from the Land Rover.'

I muttered, 'Roger, for God's sake. If this gets back to the CO . . .'

He rose to his feet, with the pale resolution of a Christian martyr . . .

But he was too late. There was a new figure, standing between the church and the tomb. A figure all in black; in a kind of long black skirt. The sort some priests wear, with lots of little cloth buttons down the front. His head was bare, his hair was snowy white, and his dark eyes were blazing.

'Cripes,' said Roger. 'The priest. That's torn it.' We watched in horror.

'What's he saying to them?' asked Rog, after a bit.

'British scum. Murderers of German children. Defilers of German womanhood. Who won't even respect the dead . . .'

'It's lucky none of them speak German,' said Roger. 'They might thump him.'

'I don't think so. They're bloody paralysed. Even Malone.'

And indeed, I'd never seen our mob so totally cowed. They just stood like little children, while the harsh high German voice echoed and re-echoed through the grove of pines.

'We'd better go over and apologize,' said Rog. 'I think he's going to complain to the authorities. You interpret, right?'

We jumped out of the lorry, and made our way awkwardly through the long wet grass and tomb railings. We really had to look where we were going, or we'd have gone arse over tip. So I was only able to look at our German once we'd arrived. But I saw him quite clearly in detail, starting with his cracked black shoes, his greasy cassock, with what looked like fag ash in its folds, though it might just have been white dust.

I saw his white hands clenched by his sides, whiter at the knuckles; his droopy-folded neck; his white face marbled with little veins; his yellowing false teeth, as he opened his mouth to blast us in turn; and his fanatical dark eyes, that seemed to look right through your skull. I dropped my own eyes quick but the harsh voice went on and on and on.

Then I watched his cracked shoes stalking away, pressing down the wet grass.

'What did he say to me?' asked Rog.

'He said you weren't fit to be an officer. In the German army, you would have been shot.'

'I expect I would,' said Rog unhappily. 'Do you reckon he *is* going to make a complaint?'

'I never bet on certainties.'

I've never spent a more wretched night. OK, it was cold and wet and pitch dark. But I'd been cold, wet and in the dark plenty of times since I'd joined this man's army. And we were all safely inside the trucks. It would have been certain death in the tents, most of which blew down by morning.

Roger and I settled in the cab of my truck. The three drivers were in the cab of the CV, and the rest were in the back of the CV with the operators, who stayed on the air all night. And who no doubt were gossiping between themselves, making out that Roger and I were a pair of queers shacked up together.

We had greatcoats and blankets, and we could run the

engine for a bit of heat, if the cold got too bad. We'd had three brew-ups with something stronger in them, and there were plenty of doorstep corned beef sandwiches. But the tea had tasted like ditchwater, and the sandwiches like cardboard, and the cold just kept worming its way in under the doors, through the gaps round the clutch and brake pedals. It seemed more than ordinary cold. When we did run the engine, we didn't seem to get hot air, just petrol fumes.

And that was before Spud Malone went for a pee.

First thing we knew of it was when a dark figure ran slap into our cab, and began scrabbling at Roger's door like a mad thing. Roger grabbed his torch and shone it, and there was Malone's white distorted face. Lit from below by the torch, it looked like something out of hell.

All of a shake, Roger wound down the window.

'What's the matter, Malone?'

'Aah went for a pee in the churchyard. An' he was there watching me.'

'Who?'

'That nutter in black. I was half finished, and he was suddenly there alongside me. Made me piss all down me trousers.'

'Serve you right,' said Roger snappishly. 'Why did you have to go in his churchyard? You could've gone anywhere. You could be on a charge for that.'

'Thanks for nowt,' shouted Malone. 'He's not *human*, that feller. You can't hear him coming. He's still watching us now. Over there by the churchyard wall.'

Malone's teeth were chattering. I'd never heard teeth chatter like that before.

Roger switched on the truck's headlights. They showed the churchyard wall, the tops of the tombs, the pines. Was that a white face watching us? Or just a trick of the headlights? Whatever it was, when I looked again, it was gone.

And we couldn't keep the headlights on all night, without risking running down the battery.

'He's an effing Nazi nutter,' shouted Malone. 'I'd like to bash his face in.'

But the moment Rog switched the headlights off, he was frantically scrambling into the safety of the other cab.

In spite of all the tea we'd drunk, nobody else ventured far from the trucks that night. They came out to pee against the truck wheels in twos and threes, with the headlights glaring. The thought of that creep suddenly appearing at your shoulder while you were relieving yourself was totally unnerving.

In between, Roger worried about the complaint that would go to the CO in the morning.

'He's bound to complain now. He's a fanatic. Staying up all night to watch what we do . . .'

We didn't get a wink of sleep till dawn.

We were less than a credit to Her Majesty's Forces.

Roger was a very *variable* coward.

As the darkness totally retreated, about eight o'clock, and he sipped his first brew-up of the day, his fear of ghosties and ghoulies and things that go bump in the night retreated, to be replaced by a growing fear about what our dear Commanding Officer was going to do to him, on receipt of a complaint.

The Germans were terrible in those days: they would lodge a complaint if you dropped a fag packet in the street. They would throw long-dead chickens and piglets in front of our convoys, so they could claim we'd run them over and get compensation.

After we got the message from HQ that we were pulling out at noon, Rog spent half an hour trying to shave in lukewarm water, then announced he was going down to the village to make a full and abject apology. He was even thinking of offering them a few Deutschmarks for their organ fund appeal, if they had one. I refused to contribute. Second lieutenants got more pay than corporals; though not much more.

But I went along to interpret. What had we got to lose? Mind you, I wasn't exactly looking forward to it. Having my lugs burnt off by the priest, then getting back to camp and getting my lugs burnt off again by the CO. And maybe losing a stripe, and the seven and sixpence pay that went with it.

The village was just round the first bend in the road; a neat tidy little place; very German, no litter. The new church was a modern brick job, with strange geometrical windows and a flat roof, and the priest's house was right next to it. We walked up the neat garden path like two prisoners going to execution.

The door was opened by a plump smiling little housekeeper, whose rosy face belied the gloom of her black dress. I explained what we wanted.

'Come in, come in,' she said. 'Father Koenig is just back from saying Mass. He is having his breakfast. I am sure he will want you to have coffee with him. Go through. I will fetch more coffee.' She pointed through to a door.

Roger knocked, and a voice with a mouthful of food called, 'Komm!'

He was sitting in front of a bowl of steaming coffee, with his snowy-white napkin tucked into his dog collar, and he looked up with a beaming smile.

A little round balding man, with rimless glasses and a very sweet expression.

Not the same bloke at all.

He said, in near-perfect English, 'Come in, gentlemen. I am always delighted to entertain our NATO allies. You must join me in some coffee.'

He got to his feet and shook hands with us both. His hand was warm and soft.

The housekeeper bustled in with fresh coffee as we sat down, then he said, 'What can I do for you gentlemen?'

Well, that was a bit of a facer, I can tell you. Roger blurted out a garbled version of events, and said he was sorry for what we'd done in the churchyard.

The little man frowned, baffled, and looked out of the window towards his new church.

'But you haven't been near my churchyard . . .'

'Not this one,' said Roger. 'The one up the road.'

The little priest went a shade paler. His hand, holding his coffee spoon, began to tremble. Then he stirred his coffee with endless, needless vigour, and watched himself doing it, intently.

'The *old* churchyard! Was any harm done to the tombs?'

'No. They only rattled the door of the black one. But the grass is a bit trampled . . .'

'So,' said the little man, still stirring, and a bit breathless. 'What is a bit of grass between allies? Nobody goes to the old church now. Even the relatives of those buried there are now dead.'

'The other priest seemed pretty narked . . .' said Roger, starting to relax a bit.

'My friend, *what* other priest? There *is* no other priest. There is only me, and I work alone. This is only a small village.'

He sounded so jovial, so reasonable. So why were beads of sweat breaking out on his smooth-shaved upper lip?

'Him,' I said, pointing. For I had caught sight of him, behind the little man's shoulder. The same black cassock and cracked black shoes; the same dark fanatical glare.

The little priest swivelled in his chair, very reluctantly, to follow my pointing finger. Then he turned back to us, and tried another smile. But it was as faltering as a creaky old theatre curtain going up.

'The photograph? That is Father Schalken, my predecessor.'

'Well he's still hanging round the church, and he's *very* angry.'

'My dear young man! That's impossible. He . . .' The little man faltered, and turned again to stare out of the window.

'He what . . . ?' I asked. I think I knew already, but I had to know for certain. I'd have gone mad, if I hadn't known for certain.

'He was killed twelve years ago. In the bombing of Hamburg, while caring for the injured children. His body was brought back here and buried in . . .'

'The black tomb? The tomb with the urn on top?'

The little man nodded wordlessly.

'God, a ghost . . .' said Roger, shattered, and yet not entirely displeased. It's the poet in him.

'He *wasn't* a ghost,' I said. 'He can't have been. I saw the grass bending under his feet, as he walked away.'

The little man still tried to smile. But his face seemed to fade away, behind the smile. His rosy cheeks faded to a network of little red veins, in a dead white face. As if he himself was the dead man, hovering on the verge of dissolution, frantically still trying to go on existing. He opened his mouth three times to say something. Then he fainted clean away, where he sat.

The housekeeper heard our yells for help, and came bustling in and took charge of him. As she loosened his collar and chafed his hands, she kept up a babble of German about the good father working too hard, and being under strain . . .

Roger and I got out, as he started to come round. I don't think either of us wanted to harm him further.

We got back to the trucks. I had never heard Roger give orders to break camp so decisively. And none of the Regulars gave him a moment's trouble. I had never seen men work so hard and fast. In twenty minutes we were setting up on the public football pitch by the new church. Right bang on the map reference this time. Again, nobody grumbled.

I remarked on this to Taffy Williams, my driver, once we were settled.

'It was that old geezer,' he said. 'He watched us right to the end. He might have thought he was hidden, but *I* saw him, among the trees.'

I didn't say a word. I didn't want to panic a whole army.

ADOLF

I first met Adolf when I was going to the off-licence for my dad's lager. He was standing at his front door, half-way down Tennyson Terrace. I remember walking down that dark, little side-street, and there was this one front door open, and a band of light lying across the pavement. Something made me think it was a bit odd, so I crossed the street to get as far away as possible. But as I crept past, a harsh voice called out,

'Boy!'

I didn't like the voice, or the bossy way it called. But I'm nosy (it gets me into trouble, sometimes), so I turned back and went across.

I couldn't see much of him, 'cos his back was against the light. But he stood very upright, and from his voice and the smell of him close-to, I could tell he was old and a foreigner.

'What's your name, boy?'

'Billy Martin,' I said grudgingly. I didn't want to tell him even that much.

'Billy Martin? *Gut!*'

He seemed to come to some decision and said, 'Will you go to the shop for me, Billy Martin? The offie?'

I didn't want to be bothered, but somehow I felt it would make more bother to say 'no'.

'Yeah. Why not?'

'*Gut*. Here is my list. And here is money. Be quick, please – I have not eaten yet.'

It made me feel like I was his *servant*. I'd have liked to have said 'no' then, all right. But I'd said yes, hadn't I? So when he put two bits of paper in my hand, I just took them. It wasn't until I'd walked to the next street-lamp that I saw one of the bits of paper was a fifty-pound note. That shook me, I can tell you. I mean, the temptation to run off with it was pretty strong. People shouldn't be allowed to tempt kids like that! I mean, giving a fifty-pound note to a total stranger!

But I'm not the sort to look for trouble. Not on a Thursday night, when I'm looking forward to a can of lager, and Anneka Rice's bum in *Treasure Hunt*. So I was determined to see he got his change down to the last penny. I was that angry with him, see?

When I got into the offie, I found it was easier said than done. His list was all in funny spiky writing. He wanted seven eggs, for some reason best known to himself, and there was that funny bar across the figure seven. I was still scratching my head when Jack Simms, who runs the offie, said,

'Old Adolf got you running errands for him? Give it me, I can read his writing.'

That's how I found out his name was Adolf.

I got Jack Simms to write down the price of everything and total it up, and I counted Adolf's change carefully before I left the shop. Put it in my right-hand pocket, and Dad's change in my left.

'Don't want no trouble,' I explained to Simms.

'He's a funny old bugger,' said Simms, agreeing.

When I knocked at Adolf's front door, I heard him call out, 'Come. It is not locked.'

I didn't like that. I'd rather have handed over the stuff in the street. Felt a bit like a fly walking into a spider's web. But I'm big for my age, and he was an old man. I told myself not to be daft.

His front room was big and brightly lit and stunk like a paint factory. Adolf was sitting in an old wooden rocker, with a big black cat on his lap. I put the carrier full of groceries on the wooden table beside him, and put the change in his hand and waited. He checked the groceries carefully, then checked the list and counted his change. Then he said *'Gut'* and looked up at me. He had very pale blue eyes, bulgy. They seemed to look straight through me.

I dropped my eyes first. But I remember I noticed his long nose and little white moustache, and the white hair combed hard across from the right. He was very wrinkly. Then he said, '*Gut*. You are an honest child.'

'I'm not a child. I'm fourteen.'

'Children always wish to be grown up before their time. It was the same in the Hitler *jugend*.'

I didn't understand the word then. But it made me uneasy, the ugly, foreign sound of it. So I said,

'Gotta be going. Watching *Treasure Hunt* with me dad.'

'Do you not wish a reward for your work?'

The sarky way he asked made me mad. 'We British don't take money for running errands. Had to go to the offie for me dad anyway.'

'How righteous! The British are always righteous. It is always the *foreign* football fans who start the fights.' You could tell he hated us British like poison, so I just turned on my heel to walk out.

And then I saw the painting he had done. It stood on an easel next to the door. You could tell from the smell that it was still wet. Great thick dabs of paint. Should've been a right mess, but it wasn't. It was a view of our town square, from high up, with the parish church. Really good. The crowds of little people were only rough dabs of paint, but they seemed to be walking, when you looked at them.

'That's smart,' I said. 'The people are really walking.' It just burst out of me.

He made a noise behind me like a snort of disgust. But you could tell he was a bit pleased, really.

Then he said,

'I need shopping on Tuesdays and Thursdays and Saturdays. Will you go for me? I will pay you fifty pence for each trip.'

I stared at him.

'I myself cannot do it. I have a stiff leg.' He wasn't asking for sympathy. Just telling me. You could tell he hated having a stiff leg. So I said OK. It wasn't any bother. I go most nights for Dad anyway.

And his paintings interested me. I could see other ones now, stacked against the walls. All local scenes, buildings and people. All good, but they made Cromborough look as if the sun never shone – as if there was always a big dark thunderstorm hanging over the town. As if something terrible was going to happen, like the end of the world or something.

'Do you sell them?' I asked.

He smiled a sour smile. 'When I was young, I wished only to be an artist. But my father wished me to be civil servant. My father thought being civil servant was the greatest thing in the world. And then came my fight – my fight against evil. Now I am old, yes, I paint to stay alive.'

His eyes no longer looked straight through me. They were dreamy, far away, as if he was looking at Mount Everest or something. Gave me the creeps. So I said, to bring him back to earth,

'You shouldn't give total strangers fifty-pound notes. They mightn't come back with the change.'

He smiled; a really sneaky smile. 'I have watched you, boy. You come down this street every night at quarter to eight, and you return at eight. I know from the name on your carrier bag that you have been to the offie. If you had not come back, how long would it have taken the *polizei* to find Billy Martin? I am not a fool, and now I have proved that you are not a fool. I have no wish to be served by fools . . .' He held out a fifty-pence piece. 'Here is your first night's wages. Do not tell me there is any boy who cannot use fifty pence?'

I took it. It was warm from his old wrinkled hand. I didn't really want to take it. Felt I was selling my soul, somehow. But I took it and ran, though I was glad when it was spent and gone.

I was late for *Treasure Hunt*. And my dad was dying for his first mouthful of lager.

The next night I called, I'd made up my mind not to go in. But when I got back with his shopping, he said slyly,

'I have made a new painting, for myself alone. Do you not wish to see it? Many in this town would like to see it . . .'

It was enough to get me in.

He pulled a drape off the picture on the easel. It was in his usual style, and yet different. It was of our local Job Centre. Now, by sheer fluke, our Job Centre is much too posh for the job it does. Used to be the Railway Hotel, when we still had a railway. All marble columns and a gilded dome on top, but the gilt's half worn off now. But it still looks far too grand, and Adolf had made it look grander. And very posh and cosy inside, what you could see through the windows.

It's unfortunate that the Social Security people park their cars in front, because they're pretty posh cars, D and E reg, which can't cheer up the poor old dolies as they queue up for their Giro.

And Adolf had made the cars bigger and posher than they really were . . .

He'd painted the little figures of the dolies, going in looking totally fed up and coming out looking even more fed up, like they already knew where their money was going, and were still up to their eyebrows in debt. It was really very clever; he'd told the truth, but made it look so much *worse*.

'I didn't know you cared about the dolies,' I said. Because I couldn't think what else to say.

'I know them. Because I have been one. Long before the war. I left home, because I could not bear to become civil servant. I went to Vienna to become artist. But I became day-labourer instead, to stay alive. I stood in line every day, while the rich men in their fur collars inspected us like cattle. If they liked the look of us they hired us, and we knew we would eat that day. But the money was gone before night. Why should the poor think of tomorrow? What does tomorrow offer the poor? When they have money, they eat and drink till it is gone. That is when I dreamed of my fight. To give the poor a steady wage, to make them prudent. To give them good food and strong bodies. To make their lives joyful, not endless drudgery.'

He had that dreamy look on his face again. It still gave me the creeps. So I said,

'Britain's not like that. Britain's not as bad as that . . .'

He looked at me with those pale, bulging, blue eyes. 'You are patriotic, because your father has money. But why should the poor be patriotic and wish to serve their country? What has their country ever done for them?'

I didn't like it. Didn't seem right. He was sort of turning the world upside down. And worse, he was starting to make me see things the same way. I didn't want any part in his fight. My dad makes a decent living going round repairing tellies; my mum works in our school canteen. We run a good car, and go to Marbella or Gran Canaria for a fortnight every year. And I'm going to get my GCSEs and work for Austin Rover as a tech. apprentice . . .

But if this old bugger started talking to the dolies . . . I was suddenly glad he had a stiff leg and couldn't get out of the house much.

'Gotta go now,' I said suddenly. 'My dad'll want his beer.'

'Ah, beer,' he said, still dreamy. 'I remember the *bier-kellers* – men would meet and sit and talk out their grievances, and plan to put the world right. Now they drink their beer at home, and watch the *verdammt* television.'

I just went.

Looking back, after his terrible end, I often wondered what I thought he was, in the beginning, just a funny old foreigner I suppose, who could paint pictures good enough to sell. He was certainly well off for a pensioner. His terrace-house was newly painted, and the high privet behind his railings neatly cut. His was the only house to have kept its front gate. And he kept himself very neat: grey trousers and a grey cardie and grey slippers. And he didn't smell – only of paint.

Why didn't I mention him to Dad? Because Dad's more the practical sort: a good bloke to have around if the car breaks down, or if you want new fence-posts putting in that won't fall down in a couple of years. But he's not a great bloke for talk. He always switches off discussion programmes on the telly – calls them 'talking-shops'. And he calls MPs of all parties 'big-mouths' and never votes at elections. And my mum is just interested in the garden and bus-trips with mobs of other women in her spare time. I sometimes wondered what would happen to the world if no one was more interested in running it than my mum and dad.

Certainly Adolf was keen on world events. He had this telly with teletext in the corner of his studio, and every so often he would click on the news headlines and look at something that President Bush or President Gorbachev had done and mutter 'Foolish, foolish' to himself. Once he said to me about Afghanistan,

'The Russians have no sense of history. You British failed in Afghanistan; the Russians should have learnt your lesson. They have thrown away a division of good soldiers. Any nation like Afghanistan, that lives only to fight, *cannot* be beaten.'

Other times he would be more cheerful. Offer me strange dark coffee that he said was 'Genuine Viennese coffee – you will not get better in Vienna today.' It wasn't bad – I got to quite like it.

Sometimes he would get me to talk to his pets. He had two cats. One was a great fat tabby that he called Hermann. The other was the sneaky black one that would sidle up to you, friendly-like, then suddenly bite you. He called that one Heinrich. And he had a red-and-blue parrot, on a stand in the corner, that looked as old as the hills, like any other parrot. He said he called that Josef (with an 'f' he insisted) because when it spoke, it told nothing but lies. It talked a foreign language I couldn't understand. But no wonder. I gave up even French in the third year – I'm on the technical side, like Dad.

He talked to them all, like they were human. I expect he was lonely. I think, apart from me, he had no one else who he could really talk to. Though there was a cleaning woman who I never saw, who he called Little Eva.

I would ask about his pictures. He would chat away about the people in them. How when busy people met, they would talk half-way down a street, but idle people always stood around on street corners. How observant old ladies were, peering through their net curtains. 'They have lived their lives,' he would say. 'Now they can only live through the joys and sorrows of others.' There was usually an old lady peering out somewhere in his pictures, if you knew where to look for her.

There was only one picture he would never talk about. An odd picture of an old-fashioned railway-carriage, parked in the middle of a forest. He said only one thing about it ever, and he was pale and shaking with rage at the time. He said that railway-carriage was the most evil place in the world. The sorrows of all mankind were born in that railway-carriage.

He looked quite insane for a moment, then he changed the subject.

One night, though, he grabbed me in before I had even done his shopping.

'You must see my new picture that I have painted. I have caught the *truth*.' His hands were quivering as he grabbed my shoulders.

God, it was a *horrible* picture. Of some Middle Eastern country, because the buildings had flat roofs and were painted in pale colours.

What was left of them. Because they'd been blown to buggery. And underneath the fallen walls, little kids in what had been white nightshirts were lying dead. Just a head sticking out here, and a hand sticking out there. It was all the more horrible because it was highly detailed, not his usual slabby style. There seemed to be a crumpled newspaper photograph pinned to the corner of his easel, as if he'd been painting from it, but it was so covered with oil-painty fingerprints that you couldn't see what it was of any more.

'Who are they?' I asked, feeling quite sick.

'Palestinian children. The Jews did that. The Jews have learnt their lessons well. *They* invade without warning, now. *They* shoot unarmed protesters. *They* torture their prisoners, to make them confess. They conquer, they oppress. They have become the Chosen of God, the Master Race.'

Funny thing was, I couldn't tell whether he was condemning them or approving of them. He just seemed crazy with excitement. 'That is the *truth*,' he kept on yelling. 'I have caught the *truth*.'

'But it's not all like that,' I shouted. 'The whole world's not like that. Not my mum and dad. Not *Britain*.'

'Oh, no,' he said. 'The British are not like that. The British do their evil far away, where they do not have to look at it. Like Dresden.'

'What you mean, Dresden?'

He grabbed my shoulders again. Hard. 'Do they not teach you about Dresden at school? How strange! Then I will teach you.' He forced me to sit down.

'Dresden was the prettiest town in Germany. A historic town, all made of old timber. No factories, except the one where the beautiful Dresden china was made. And in 1945, Dresden was full of women and children, fleeing from the Russians. A hundred thousand of them.

'And your fine RAF sent a thousand bombers and blew Dresden to pieces. Then they dropped incendiaries to set the wreckage on fire, so that those who were buried alive were roasted alive. All to please Stalin, when the war was already lost and won. That was Dresden, which they do not teach you at school.'

'Let me go,' I shouted and then ran out of the house, wiping the spit of his rage off my face as I went.

I never went back. As far as I was concerned he was a nutter, a dangerous old nutter.

But I couldn't get what he'd said about Dresden out of my mind. So finally I went and asked my history teacher. He didn't say much, just that there was a book about Bomber Command in the school library. I got it out at lunchtime and read it.

It admitted that Dresden had been bombed in 1945. It said it was a strategic rail-centre, and that the bombing had been in support of the advancing Red Army. And that was all.

I closed the book and thought thanks for nothing. That night I dreamt that I was in Dresden, roasting alive. I woke up rigid, in a cold sweat, and couldn't get back to sleep again. But somehow I knew that old Adolf had been right, and the British book was telling lies.

Jesus, you ever had that feeling? If you find one book telling lies, you wonder if all the other books aren't telling lies as well. There I was, reading all those books for GCSE, like a good little boy, and they might *all* be lies. I had to ask somebody, but *who*? Mum and Dad hadn't even been born when Dresden was bombed.

In the end I went back to my history teacher. Told him about the two versions of Dresden. He looked annoyed, yet shifty at the same time.

'You must use your own judgement, Martin. That's what we're here for. To teach you to use your own judgement, using primary sources and documents.'

'Like *what*? How do I find out how the Germans felt about the war?'

'Look, old lad. You mustn't get carried away. We're not even *doing* the Second World War for GCSE. You've got exams to pass this summer. Concentrate on those. You've got your career to think of . . .'

Christ, I hate it when they go on like that. I mean, they encourage you to think for yourself, then when you do, they get upset. So I went on yelling, 'Where's the book the Germans wrote?'

Maybe he just wanted to get rid of me. I don't think he reckoned I'd ever find the book (and no wonder). So he just said, with a nasty, half-hidden grin,

'Hitler wrote a book called *Mein Kampf*. That was what started the Second World War.'

I looked for it in the school library. It wasn't there, of course. I asked the librarian, and she gave me a funny look and said, 'I hope you're not thinking of joining the National Front, Billy Martin.'

That should have warned me that I was living in the Red Republic of Cromborough, run by the Loony Left. But I just went down to the public library, and they hadn't got it on the shelves either. Fortunately they've taught us to use the microfiche system at school, so I sat down at the microfiche and went through all the non-fiction slides till I found 'Authors HA-GE'.

No 'Hitler, Adolf.' No *Mein Kampf*. Not a single copy in the whole Red Republic of Cromborough.

So I filled in a request card. *Mein Kampf* by Hitler, Adolf. I didn't know the publisher or the date, but it was hardly *Little Noddy Rides Again*. I gave the card to the woman on the inquiries counter with the last fifty-pence piece I'd had off old Adolf. The woman read the card and nearly went mad.

'Oh, you cheeky little idiot,' she shouts. 'Is this your idea of a joke? Wasting my time and the library's request cards?'

'I really want it,' I said. 'Honest!'

Up comes the Chief Librarian, a fat bloke with spectacles.

'What seems to be the trouble, Mrs Seddon?'

She gave him the card, tight-lipped. He read it, tight-lipped, then tore it up and gave me my fifty pence back, with a slam into my hand, as if he would have liked to clonk me one. Then he said,

'Go away, or I'll call the police.'

I knew there was no point in arguing. When they get that look on their faces . . .

But as I told you before, I'm nosy. And the more people

don't want me to know something, the more I want to know it. And I knew where to go. The dirty second-hand bookshop in Wythenshawe Street. A huge old place, full of shifty-looking blokes fumbling the stuff on the shelves. I've been chucked out dozens of times, once the owner's finished serving somebody else. He always asks me what book I want, very sharp, and then says he hasn't got it, quick, without even looking on the shelves.

Anyway, this happened as usual. But when I said *Mein Kampf* he went a bit thoughtful, and his eyes got that greedy glint. He'll sell anybody anything for money.

'Gotta copy. But it's seventeen pounds to you.'

That was a facer, because I only had twenty-one pounds in the Post Office, saved up for our next trip to Gran Canaria.

'Can I sell it back to you afterwards?' I asked.

'Give you ten pounds for it. If it's still in mint condition.' Greedy sod.

'Let's see it,' I said, in case he was pulling a fast one, and selling me something written in German.

But it was in English, translated in 1937. With a foreword very respectful towards Hitler. And lots of pictures of Hitler striding around wet streets in a belted raincoat, looking like he's worried and going to give someone a piece of his mind. A big fat book, like an encyclopaedia . . .

So I gave the bloke fifty pence deposit, and he said he'd put it by till the end of the week. But I drew out the money next evening, and picked up the book on the way home. My mother noticed me carrying it and asked what it was, but I'd got a bit wary by that time and said it was just a schoolbook for homework.

Well, once in my bedroom, it was a revelation. I suppose it would've been boring to any other kid, 'cos Hitler certainly didn't have a style like James Bond. But it was all there.

All the things *my* Adolf had said. About wanting to be an artist, and his rows with his father, who wanted him to be a civil servant. (He was terribly respectful about his father, even though they had had all those rows which made him leave home.) And about being a day-labourer, and the plight of the poor, and his fight against evil, which in German was *mein kampf* – my fight.

What a facer! And then I began looking at the pictures of Hitler: those bulging eyes that looked straight through you; that little moustache: that hair brushed across hard from the right. Just like *my* Adolf. And when my Adolf had criticized Bush or Gorbachev, he'd spoken about them like he was their equal, like he understood what their problems were . . .

God, I knew about the Nazi war-criminals hiding in Brazil and Paraguay, and the trial of Eichmann and that John Demjanyuk. And people saying there were war-criminals still hiding out in Britain.

But could Hitler really have escaped from the Berlin bunker and be living half-way down Tennyson Terrace?

I didn't get much sleep that night, I can tell you.

I kept it to myself for a week. Who could I tell? I thought of telling Dad. But he was watching *Tomorrow's World*. I thought of telling Mum, but she was busy getting the tea. I thought of telling my history teacher, but I knew he'd just take the piss out of me, and I'd be the laughing-stock of the staff room.

Which is why, in the end, I told Gaz Higgins. Which was my big mistake. Gaz is the brightest kid in our class. He's got an open mind. Trouble is, he's also got an open mouth. If you want everyone in the school to know something, tell Gaz Higgins it's your most precious secret.

Anyway, he didn't laugh at me. He got quite excited, especially when I mentioned my Adolf's paintings. He's quite keen on art, 'cos he wants to be a famous cartoonist with the *Sun* when he grows up, and get to chat up the Page Three birds. He said he had an old colour supplement at home, full of Hitler's paintings.

He brought it to school next day. God, they were the same kind of paintings. Pictures of grand big buildings in Vienna done with the same broad brushstrokes, and with the same dark sky all thunderclouds, and a feeling that something terrible was going to happen. Only the young Hitler hadn't been so keen on painting little people scurrying around – there were hardly any people in *his* pictures at all.

'It's him,' I said. 'He still paints the same.'

'I'm not surprised he came to England,' said Gaz. 'He lived in Liverpool a bit before the war. His cousin kept a boarding-house there – his name was Alois Hitler. I saw a play about it on the telly.'

The bell went for afternoon school then, and we didn't say much more because he had double-art and I had double-history. He didn't say much more to me about it ever, really.

But he must have said plenty to other people. Considering what happened afterwards.

I first noticed it, going down to the offie one night. I always slunk past on the other side of the street now, frightened Adolf would spot me. Though it wasn't a Tuesday or a Thursday or a Saturday night . . .

But even from the other side of the street, by the dim light of the next street-lamp, I could see people had been daubing on Adolf's garden wall. A couple of small swastikas.

Next night the swastikas were bigger. And by the end of the week, N F symbols were appearing.

By the next Monday night, someone had aerosolled WAR CRIMINAL and KILL THE JEWS and a star of David in yellow.

By the end of that week, I began to notice groups of kids hanging round in twos and threes. Not local kids. Punks with four-packs of beer, shouting weird things at the house and kicking each other with their big boots. As if they were waiting for something to happen. More every night I passed.

There was never any sign of Adolf, but that didn't seem to discourage them. I began getting very worried, because whatever Adolf had once done, he was now a lame old man, and those punks and skinheads aren't funny, once they get their eye on you.

But I didn't know what to do. There was still nobody I could talk to about it.

Then, on the Wednesday night, my dad was sitting reading through the news in the local paper, on his way to the car ads. And he stops and says,

'That big-mouth Harrington's really done it this time.'

'What's he done. Dad?'

Harrington was a far-Left Labour councillor and Dad's real pet hate. Every week Harrington finds some reason to get his name in the paper. Everything, to Harrington, is 'a public scandal' or 'a creeping threat to the underprivileged of Cromborough.' If he gets really stuck, he'll make a round of the public lavatories and make a fuss about *them*.

'He's gone too far . . . he's gone off his chump properly. He reckons there's a top Nazi war-criminal living in Tennyson Terrace, and he can't even spell incognito properly. Two ts. Pig ignorant, that man. I hope the bloke does him for libel . . .'

My heart sank into my boots. 'What's the war-criminal's name, Dad?' I quavered.

'Doesn't give it. Even he's not *that* big a fool.'

'Dad,' I said, taking a deep breath. 'I know the bloke he means. I think it's Adolf Hitler hisself.'

'Yewhat?' shouts Dad, for once paying full attention to something other than motor cars.

So I told him everything.

'Jesus Christ, our Billy,' says Dad, 'ye're more barmy than old Harrington. Where have you got all this rubbish from? Hitler was old when he died in 1945. If he was alive now he'd be a hundred and five or something. How old's this bloke down Tennyson Terrace?'

'Dunno,' I said. 'Pretty old. All old people look alike.' But I knew I'd been a total idiot. My Adolf was nowhere near that age. 'About as old as Grandpa, I think.'

'Christ, Billy, your Grandpa's only *sixty-eight*.'

Then I told Dad about the daubing on Adolf's wall, and the skinheads and punks who were hanging about.

'This is serious,' said Dad. 'We're going to have to get this sorted, afore something worse happens. Where's me coat?'

'Aw, Dad, leave it. It'll blow over.' I was scared of facing Adolf again, after what I'd done. 'He's a nasty old sod. He can look after himself. He's as sharp as a wagonload of monkeys.'

'You're coming wi' me,' says Dad, grabbing me. 'I've got no money to pay for a case of libel. You're going to go down there an' apologize. Then we'll put things right wi' the newspaper.'

Just then Mum comes in from her Townswomen's Guild choir practice. 'There's trouble brewing down Tennyson Terrace,' she says. 'A whole mob of skinheads. I was scared to walk past the end of the street . . .'

'C'mon,' shouts Dad as he whizzes out the front door. I was never so proud of him in my life. Or so ashamed of myself.

As we turned the corner of Tennyson Terrace (and me mam came too, though she didn't look like she wanted to), we heard the skinheads shouting 'A-DOLF A-DOLF A-DOLF' in that awful rhythmic way they have. And then, beyond the huddled crowd, there was a sudden flare of yellow light, and the crash of glass.

'They're throwing petrol,' shouts Dad. 'Go home, Renee. Go home quick an' ring the police.' And my mum doesn't argue.

There's three more flares and crashes before we reach the back of the crowd. I think they must have thrown one through the studio window, because it was all alight inside. It must have caught easily, with all that oil-paint. The front door was alight as well, with burning petrol dribbling down the doorstep. Only the upstairs was still dark.

My dad tore through the skinheads, shoving them left and right. I was scared they'd beat him to a pulp, but all their eyes were feasting themselves on the burning house. I don't think they even noticed Dad, no more than if he was a fly, no matter how much he cursed and pushed them.

And there wasn't another grown-up in sight: not even a face in any of the neighbouring windows. Cowering bastards!

But it meant Dad and I were right at the front when old Adolf pushed open his upstairs bedroom window. Smoke trickled out past him and you could see a bit of flame-light already flickering behind in the bedroom doorway.

He only shouted one thing. I'll never forget it. He shouted, 'Even if I was Hitler, am I any worse than you?'

Then the smoke got to his lungs, and he doubled up coughing, and we never saw him again.

Then we heard the police sirens coming from three different directions at once. And all those skinheads took to their brave British heels.

It was all in the local paper the following week.

HOUSE OF WAR-HERO PETROL-BOMBED.

Police are seeking the gang of skinheads who petrol-bombed, last Wednesday night, the home of Warrant-Officer Adolf Krainer, late of the Polish Air Force. Warrant-Officer Krainer, who is recovering in a Leeds hospital, had lived in Cromborough since being invalided out of the air force in 1945 with a thigh wound sustained while bombing Germany. He flew sixty-seven missions and was awarded the Air Force Cross for nursing his Lancaster home on two engines after his last mission to Dresden.

In his early days in Cromborough, he was a founder member of the Polish Club and chairman of the Anglo-German Friendship Society, which arranged exchange-trips for schoolchildren between Cromborough and Dresden. He was well known as a painter and exhibited in London and Leeds.

In recent years, he increasingly lived the life of a recluse.

His home was gutted, in spite of the best efforts of Cromborough Fire Brigade.

When recovered, he will live with friends in Leeds.

'He was never quite right in the head,' said old Simms to my dad in the offie. Since the fire Dad's walked down with me to collect the lager, 'cos I'm nervous now. Not of skinheads, but of Adolf Krainer's burnt-out house, watching me.

'Never normal,' continued Simms, 'not since he first came to the town. Always going on about Dresden, and all those little German kids who were burnt alive. Made your flesh creep to hear him. That's why he started the Friendship Society, but it never cured his guilt.

'Always going on about the Treaty of Versailles in 1919 – reckoned the Germans got a bad deal in that railway-carriage at Fontainebleau. He said it sowed the seeds of the Second World War.

'He even saw good in Hitler. Many's the night I've heard him defend Hitler and that book *Mein Kampf* in this very shop – I thought sometimes some bloke would knock him flat for it.

'In fact,' went on Simms, lowering his voice, 'I reckon he read that *Mein Kampf* too often, when he was sitting alone. It sort of took him over. He even got to look a bit like Hitler in the end – the way he combed his hair, and that little tash. Did you ever meet him?'

'No,' said Dad hurriedly, with a worried look at me. 'No, I never did.'

'War does funny things to people – years after,' said Simms. 'Old Krainer started off fighting Hitler, and ended up thinking he *was* Hitler. I'm glad I was only on the anti-aircraft guns meself – outside Lowestoft . . .'

Dad and I picked up our lager and left.

The blank windows of the gutted house of Adolf Krainer seemed to follow us like eyes, the whole length of Tennyson Terrace.

DADDY-LONG-LEGS

Granda's house was much too close to Hitler.

The only people in Garmouth who lived closer than us were the lighthouse-keepers on the end of the piers. All there was between us and Hitler was the North Sea. On sunny evenings I used to watch the little white fat clouds blowing eastward, and think that by morning they would be looking down on places in Norway and Denmark and Holland where grey soldiers strutted around doing the goose-step in their jackboots, and people crept about in fear of a hand on their shoulder. I even worried about the clouds a bit.

We were on a tiny headland that jutted out into the mouth of the Tyne. Not worth defending, the soldiers from the Castle said, as they laid their long corkscrews of barbed wire inland from us. There was a checkpoint a hundred yards away up the pier road, where sometimes, with bayonets fixed to the rifles on their shoulders, they demanded to see our identity cards. But usually they let us through with a wink and a thumbs-up, because they knew us.

The Old Coastguard House, they called my grandfather's house. It was really only a white-painted cottage, with a little tower one storey higher than the roof. The tower had great windows, watching the Tyne on the right, the bay of Prior's Haven on the left, and the Castle beyond, and the North Sea in front. My granda had stuck great criss-crosses of sticky tape over the windows, to save us being cut to bits by flying glass if a bomb fell near. He had scrounged a lot of sandbags from the soldiers, in exchange for the odd bottle of my grandmother's elderberry wine. The soldiers were very keen on my grandmother's elderberry. They said a nip of it was as good as a tot of whisky when you were freezing on guard duty of a winter's night. My granda filled the sandbags with soil from the garden, leaving a great hole which filled with water when it rained in winter. My grandfather considered keeping ducks on it, but he thought the firing of the Castle guns would scare them witless during air raids, and besides, the pond dried out completely in summer. A pity, because the ducks' eggs would have helped the war effort.

My grandfather built up the sandbags round the windows of the cottage, till we looked a real fortress. Of course he couldn't sandbag the tower windows, they were too high up. But nobody was supposed to go up there during air raids.

I think people worried about us, stuck out there on our little headland. They offered us an Anderson air raid shelter for the garden; but Granda said he preferred our cellar, which had walls three feet thick. They offered to evacuate us altogether. But Granda said he wasn't going to run away from bloody Hitler, into some council house. He would face Hitler where he stood; and he ran up the Union Jack on our flagpole every morning to prove it. He and I did it together, standing to attention, then we saluted the flag and Granda said, 'God save the King', without fail. Grandma said we should take it down during air raids, as it would make us a target. Granda just made a noise of contempt, deep in his throat. Otherwise, though, Grandma was as keen on the war effort as we were, collecting in the National Savings every Tuesday morning, knitting comforts for the troops, keeping eggs fresh in isinglass, and bottling all the fruit she could lay her hands on.

I remember I'd just got home from school that December night. The cottage looked dark and lonely, and my guts scrunched up a bit, as they always did when I passed the checkpoint and said ta-ta to the soldiers, who always called me 'Sunny Jim'. Granda would still be at work down the fish quay, and Grandma would be finishing her shopping up in Shields. There would be a lot to do: the blackout curtains to draw, the lamps to light (for we had no electricity) and the ready-laid fire to set a match to. Grandma had left some old potatoes in a bowl of water, which meant she wanted me to peel them for supper and put the peelings in the swill bucket for Mason's pig . . .

I had just lit the last lamp, in the kitchen, and was rolling up my sleeves to tackle the potatoes, when I saw the daddy-long-legs come cruising across the room. It was a big one, a whopper. It looked nearly as big as a German bomber, and I hated it as much. I mean, I love bees and ladybirds, but daddy-long-legs hang about you and suddenly scrape against your bare skin with their scratchy, traily legs. Given half a chance they get down the back of your neck. It was long past the season for them, but this one must have been hibernating or something, and been awakened by a sudden warmth. I backed off and grabbed an old copy of Granda's *Daily Express* and prepared to swat it. But it had no interest in me. It made straight for the oil lamp, and banged against the glass shade with that awful persistent pinging. And then suddenly it went down inside, between the shade and the glass chimney. I could still hear it pinging and see its shadow, magnified on the frosted glass. God, it must be getting pretty hot down there . . .

I squinted down cautiously between the shade and the hot chimney. It was hurling itself against the chimney, mad to reach the flame. Silly thing, it would do itself an injury . . . Then I noticed that one of its long crooked legs had already fallen off. As I watched, another broke off. But still the creature hurled itself against the chimney. Another leg went, then another, and there was a stink of burning that was not paraffin. Then it fell against the chimney with a sharp sizzle and lay still at last, just a little dirty mark. There was a tiny wisp of smoke; the stink was awful.

Feeling a bit sick, because it had been a living thing, I went back to peeling the potatoes.

It was then that the siren went. I ran to the door, slipped through the blackout curtain and went outside to look for Granda and Grandma. It was quite dark by that time; but I heard a distant tiny fizz, and the first searchlight came on at the Castle. A dim, poor yellow beam at first, but quickly followed by a brilliant white beam, so bright it looked nearly solid. High up, little wisps of cloud trailed through the beam, like cigarette smoke. Then another beam and another. Four, five, six, all swinging out to seawards, groping for Jerry like the fingers of a robot's hand. Then more, dimmer, search-lights, up towards Blyth. And more still, across the river in South Shields. It made me proud; we were ready for them, waiting.

But in the deep blue reflected light, which lit up the pier road like moonlight, there was no sign of Granda or Grandma. I could see the two sentries on the checkpoint, huddling behind their sandbags, the ends of their fags like little red pinpoints. They'd be in trouble for that, if this raid was more than a false alarm. You can see a fag end from five thousand feet up, my Granda says . . .

But otherwise, the pier road was empty. And there was no chance of them coming now; the wardens would force them down some shelter, until the raid was over. I was on my own. I felt a silly impulse to run up and join the sentries, but they'd only send me back into cover. And besides, it was time to be brave. I checked the stirrup pump with its red buckets of water, in case they dropped incendiaries. Then I did what I was supposed to do, and went down the cellar to shelter.

But there was nothing to do down there. By the light of the oil lamp, trembling slightly in my hand because it was so heavy, all I could see was Granda's three sacks of spare pota-toes, and the dusty rows of Grandma's bottles of elderberry. This year's still had little Christmas balloons, yellow, red and blue, fastened over their necks. They were still fermenting. Some of the balloons were small but fat and shiny; others looked all shrivelled and shrunken.

I should sit down on a mattress and be good. But it was cold and I couldn't hear anything. I mean, the Jerries might be overhead; they might have dropped incendiaries by this time, the cottage roof might be burning, and how would I know? When he was there, in an air raid, Granda kept nipping upstairs for a look-see. As the person in charge of the cottage tonight, so should I. Or so I told myself.

I crept upstairs. Nothing was on fire. Everything was silent, except for some frantic dog barking on and on, up the town.

And then I heard it; very faint, far out over the sea. *Vroomah, vroomah, vroomah.* Jerry was coming. You could always tell Jerry, because the Raff planes made a steady drone. But Jerry's engines weren't synchronized, Granda said.

And as I went on listening, I knew there was more than one of them. The whole sea was full of their echoes. My stomach drew itself up like a fist. I wasn't scared; just ready. Your stomach always does that.

Then the whole blue scene turned bright pale yellow. The earth shook, and the universe seemed to crack apart like an egg. The Castle guns had fired. I waited, counted under my breath. Seventeen, eighteen, nineteen. Four brilliant stars out to sea burnt black holes in my eyes. They were in a W-shape, and everywhere I looked now there were four black dots in a W-shape. Then the sound of explosions, rolling in across the water like waves. Then the echoes going away down the coast, off every cliff, fainter and fainter.

The guns fired again. People were rude about those guns. They said they never hit anything; that they couldn't hit a barn door at ten yards. That the gunners should get their eyes checked. But, tonight . . . There was suddenly a light out to sea, high in the air. A little yellow light where no light should be. The Jerries never showed a light, any more than we did.

But this light grew. And now it was falling, falling. Like a shooting star, when we say that it is the soul of someone dying.

And I knew what it was. We'd hit one. It was going to crash. I leapt up and down in tremendous glee.

Burn, bastard, burn. We'd had too many folk killed in raids for us to love the Jerries any more.

It never reached the sea. There was such a flash as made

the guns look like a piddling Guy Fawkes' night and a bang that hurt my ears. But I could still hear faint cheering – from the Castle, from across the river; very faint, in South Shields. Then there was just a shower of red fragments, falling to the water.

But the rest of the planes came on. The guns went on firing. They were nearly overhead now. There was a faint whispering in the air, then a rattle on the pantiles of Granda's house above me. I ducked down into the cellar entrance. It seemed especially silly to be killed by falling *British* shrapnel . . .

I didn't poke my head out again until it was quiet. Far up the river, the bangs were still lighting up the sky. The red lines of pom-pom tracers climbed so slowly, so lazily. Then the whooshing flicker of the Home Guard's rocket batteries. And the tremor of the first bombs coming, through the soles of my shoes. It was Newcastle that was copping it tonight . . . we could do with a break.

It was so peaceful, to seawards. Just the faint blue light from the searchlights, which could have been moonlight . . .

And then, by that light, I saw it. White, like a slowly drifting mushroom.

A Jerry parachute. I could see the little black dot of the man, under his harness. He was going to land in the water of the harbour; he was going to get very wet, and that would cool his courage, as Grandma always said. He might drown . . .

The parachute collapsed slowly into the water about two or three hundred yards out. Ah well, they'd pick him up. The picket boat on the defence boom that lay right across the river. It would be full of armed sailors. I was just an interested spectator.

But for some reason, the picket boat continued to stay moored to the far end of the boom. There was no sound from its heavy diesel engine. Come on, come on! The bloke might drown . . . Or he might come ashore and do anything. Myself, I hoped he drowned.

But I watched and watched, and that boat never stirred. Maybe they hadn't noticed the parachute; maybe they'd been following the raid up the river, like I'd just been doing... Maybe the Jerry wasn't drowning; maybe he was swimming ashore at this very moment.

And we were the nearest bit of shore.

I decided to run for the sentries. But at that moment, a second wave of bombers droned in. The shellbursts overhead were churning the sky into a deafening porridge of flashes. I could hear the shrapnel falling, rattling on the roof again. I daren't go out. I'd seen what shrapnel had done to one of Granda's rabbits, old Chinnie. I had found her. The roof of her hutch was smashed in, and the floor, and Chinnie lay like a bloody cushion, blue Chinchilla fur hammered into the ground in a mass of wooden splinters and fluff . . .

I hovered piteously from foot to foot. Oh, please God, send him to land somewhere else. South Shields, the rocks below the Castle . . .

I thought at first it was a seal in the water. We get the odd seal up the Gar; they come in for the guts from the fish-gutting, when they're really hungry – even though the Gar is an oily, stinking old river. Sometimes they bob around out there and stare at the land, the water shining on their sleek dark heads.

But seals don't have a pale white blob where their face should be. And seals don't rise up out of the water till their shoulders are showing, then their whole bodies, the gap between their legs. They don't haul themselves out of the water and begin to climb the low soily cliff.

Oh, God, let the guns stop, let the shrapnel stop! But a third wave was vrooming in overhead, and a piece of shrapnel suddenly smashed our front gate into a shower of white fragments.

Suddenly, I made up my mind that I would rather be smashed to a bloody pulp by British shrapnel than be in the power of the Swastika. Holding my arms above my head in an absolutely hopeless attempt to protect myself, I ran for the smashed gate.

As I went through it, a very big, very strong hand grabbed me. I think I squealed like a shot rabbit my father had once had to kill with a blow to the back of the neck. I think I kicked out and bucked wildly, just like that very rabbit, fighting for its life. My efforts were equally useless. The huge hand carried me back to the front door and flung me inside. Our little hall was filled with a huge gasping and panting. Our front door slammed shut. The hand picked me up again and carried me into the living room and threw me on a couch. And for the first time, I saw him.

He was huge, black, shining and dripping water all over Grandma's carpet. He trailed tentacles from his body with little shining metal bits on the end. And he did look like a seal, with the leather helmet almost crushing his head in so that only his eyes showed, and his pale long nose, and his mouth, gaping like a fish's.

'Others?' he shouted. 'Others?' He stared around him wildly, then seemed to remember something suddenly and felt, groped at, his shining, dripping side. And pulled out something black with a long tube . . .

I recognized it from the war magazine that my father used to buy me, before he joined the Raff. It was a Luger automatic pistol, with a twelve-shot magazine. All the Jerry aircrew carried them.

He tore off his leather helmet as if it suddenly hurt him. It made him look a bit more human; he had fair hair, quite long, a bit like our Raff types, which surprised me. Funny how you can still be surprised, even when you're almost wetting yourself with terror . . .

'Others?' he said a third time. He was listening. It made him look like a wild animal, alert. Then I twigged what he was getting at. Was anybody else in the house? Then he grabbed me again, shouting, *'Raus, raus!'* and dragged me from room to room by my hair.

When we had searched everywhere, even the lookout tower and the cellar, he brought me back and threw me on the couch again. He listened to the outside; the raid had quietened. But he was still shaking. Then he fell into Granda's chair, and we stared at each other. I didn't much like the look of him at all. He had green eyes, too close together. My Granda always says never to trust a man who has eyes too close together.

Then he pointed the gun at me (I think he enjoyed pointing the gun at me) and said, 'Food!'

What could I do but lead him to Grandma's larder? And get him our only half-loaf from the enamel bread bin. And the butter dish from the top shelf, with our tiny ration of butter and marge, mixed together so it would last longer. I began to cut a thin slice, but he pushed me aside into a corner with the gun-barrel, then put the gun down and smeared the whole half-loaf with all the butter and marge and began to wolf it down, tearing off huge chunks. I noticed he had very large white teeth, a bit like tombstones. When he had gulped it all down, he poked me into the larder with the gun again, and went along the shelves to see what else he could find. He found our little cheese ration and swallowed it in one mouthful, just tearing off the greaseproof paper with his large teeth, and swallowing so fast you could tell from the gulp he gave that it hurt him. He found a quarter-jar of jam and began to eat it with a spoon, his gun in his left hand now. Then three shrivelled apples, which he stuffed into a pocket of his dripping suit. Didn't they feed them, before they came on a raid? Were all the Germans starving, like our propaganda used to say, back in the phoney war?

How did I feel? I felt the end of the world had come, the worst had happened. That I, alone, in Garmouth, was already under the Nazi jackboot. That I was now already inside the Third Reich. He might do anything to me . . .

And yet nothing was changed; the fire still burned on steadily, making steam rise from his suit, as he sat by it. There were Granda's old pipes in their rack, and a twist of tobacco in its silver paper. There was Grandma's knitting still in her chair. The world had turned insane.

And then I began to worry about Granda and Gran. Soon, the raid would be over. Soon they would come walking down the pier road, and straight into . . . Granda might try and do something; he was as brave as a lion. The German would shoot him. Then he might shoot Gran too . . . But what could I do? Nothing. Even when the noise of the raid stopped, there was no point in shouting. The sentries on the checkpoint would never hear me. And then he would shoot *me* . . .

He was watching me now.

'Derink!' he said. 'Derink. Derink!' He made a drinking motion with his free hand.

Like a slave, I crept into the kitchen. A slave of the Third Reich. I got our half-bottle of milk from the cooler on the floor, put it on the kitchen table, and turned to get the tea and sugar canisters and the teapot . . .

'Derink!' he shouted again, and swept them all off on to the floor in his rage. The milk bottle broke and the milk and fragments went everywhere. 'Derink!' He raised his hand to his lips again, and threw his head back. I could tell from the shape his fingers made, that he meant he wanted a bottle. He pointed down the cellar. '*Wein . . . vin . . . wine!*'

He must have noticed the row of bottles, Gran's elderberry, when he searched the cellar. I took up the oil lamp and went down for some. He didn't follow me; only stood by the cellar door, listening to the outside.

The long rows of bottles glistened in the lamplight. They were arranged by year. Gran kept her elderberry a long time . . .

And then it came to me. Gran's elderberry . . . people laughed at it because it wasn't proper wine. But it was strong stuff. She gave the curate from the church a glass of her old batch once, and he liked it so much he'd accepted a second . . .

He was so drunk by the time he reached Front Street that

he fell off his bicycle. Elderberry gets stronger every year you keep it. This year's – 1940 – still fermenting, wouldn't do him any harm. But 1939 . . . 1938 . . . I picked up two bottles of her 1938, dusted them with my hand, and carried them upstairs.

He gave a quick, wolfish grin. *'Wein? Ja! Ja!'* He couldn't get a bottle open quick enough. Pulled the cork out with his strong tombstone teeth and spat it out, so it bounced on the hearthrug. Then he raised the bottle, threw back his head and the sound of glugging filled the room. It was already much more than the curate ever had.

He stopped at last to draw breath. His wolfish grin was wider.

'Wein. Ja. Gut!' He seemed to relax as it hit him. Stretched his legs out to the fire. Then he had a long think and said, quite clearly but slowly, '*Englander* not our natural enemy are!' He seemed quite pleased with himself. Then he took another swig and announced, '*Englander* little *Brüders* . . . broth . . . brothers are.' He put down the bottle for a moment, and reached out and patted me on the shoulder. Then he picked up the bottle again and offered it to me, indicating that I drink too.

I made a right mess of it. I didn't want to drink, get drunk, and yet I had to. Otherwise he might suspect I was trying to poison him . . .

So I drank, and it went down the wrong way, and I sprayed it all over the place and went into a helpless fit of coughing.

He threw back his head and laughed as if he thought that was hilarious.

'*Wein* . . . not . . . little *Brüders ist*. Big men . . . *Wein*.' He drank some more. The bottle was half empty by now. The more he got, the more he seemed to want. And, oddly, the better it made his English.

'English little *Brüders* . . . but Europe is corrupt . . . we must make a new order . . . then . . . happy!'

I just waited patiently. Time was on my side now.

It began to have an effect on him. He began to slump deeper

into his chair. But the hand with the gun kept playing with it twitchily. I was dead scared it might go off. And he wasn't grinning any more. He looked at me solemnly, owlishly.

'*Prost* . . . drink toast. To Rudi! *Mein Kamerad!*' More wine glugged down, while I waited. Then he said, in a small hopeless voice, 'Rudi *ist tot* . . . dead. *Und* Karli, *und* Maxi, *und* Heini. *Alles* . . . *tot*.'

And then, unbelieving, I saw a tear run down his face. Then another and another. He put his face in his hands and sobbed like a woman, only worse, because women know how to cry properly. He was just a gulping, sniffing, revolting mess. I reckoned that any minute I'd be able to snatch the gun from where it lay. But I didn't know how to use it . . .

'*Kamerad, Kamerad*,' he moaned; comrades, comrades. He was rocking in his chair, like a woman rocking a baby.

And I just waited. Then he began to sing, like a lot of drunks do. Something about '*Ich habe einen Kamerad*'. It was horrible. It embarrassed me so much my toes squirmed inside my shoes.

But I went on waiting.

Finally he stopped, a stupid look of alarm growing on his face. He tried to get up and failed, falling back heavily into the chair. He tried again, pressing down with his hands on the chair arms. And since he had the bottle in one hand, and the gun in the other, he didn't make it again. The hand holding the bottle opened, and the bottle fell to the rug with a dull clunk and rolled towards me, spilling out a trail of dark elderberry.

Slowly, at last, like a very old man, he managed to lever himself to his feet, and stood swaying above me. I thought he was going to shoot me then. But he decided not to; perhaps he remembered he had sent me for the wine – his little slave labourer.

Instead, he made a wavering track for the door, crashing into every bit of furniture on the way, hurting himself and gasping. Suddenly he reminded me of something. And I remembered what it was. The daddy-long-legs, in the oil lamp. Like it, he had come flying in; like it, he was dashing himself to bits. I almost laughed out loud. Except that pistol was wavering all over the room.

Then it suddenly went off. Even in the middle of that raid, the noise was deafening. A panel of the door suddenly wasn't there, and the air was full of a Guy Fawkes smell, and the smell of splintered wood. That piny, resinous smell.

Then the gun went off again. He cried out, and I saw blood pouring from a tear in the leg of his wetsuit. And then, with a wild yell, he was out of the front door and the wind was blowing in.

I think I ran across to replace, of all things, the blackout curtain. We were trained so hard to keep the blackout; it was second nature. But as soon as my hand was on it, I heard a yell and a big splash from outside. I knew what had happened. He had fallen into our sandbag hole – the hole we had thought of using for a duckpond.

I ran to see. He was just a series of sodden humps, face down in the water. He didn't move at all. Suddenly a mass of bubbles rose and burst where his face would be, under the water. It was unbelievable. I mean, that hole was only about seven feet across. There wasn't a foot of water in it.

And yet I knew he was drowning. As I watched, one hand came up out of the water and clawed at the side. But it couldn't get a grip, because the sides were steep and slippery. His head turned, his face looked at me and then fell back, and more bubbles came from his mouth.

Soon, any minute now, he would move for the last time; then he would be dead. One dead murderer; one dead Nazi thug.

What made me jump into the hole beside him? Try to lift him out and fail, for he was far too heavy for my eleven years? What made me force my legs under his head and lift his face clear of the filthy, muddy water, so that he could groan and choke and breathe and mutter to himself in a language I would never understand. *'Freund, Freund!'* His big hand wandered round my body, till I grabbed it and held on to it.

'Freund, Freund.'

And that was how we stayed, while the returning bombers droned back over us, and the guns fired intermittently, and the shrapnel sang its awful song to earth.

And that was how Granda and Gran found us, and stared at my mudstained face, after the all-clear had gone. By the light of the fires from the burning docks at Newcastle.

'God love the bairn,' said my gran. 'What's he doin' wi' that feller?'

Granda took a careful look. 'Reckon that feller's a Jerry. Run for the sentries up at the wire, Martha.'

I had nothing to say. I was so cold I could not move my jaws any more. But I kept wondering why I did what I did. He was a murderer. Maybe he was the pilot who dropped the bomb that killed my mother at Newcastle, when she'd just nipped down to the shops for a box of matches to light our fire.

That's when my dad joined the Raff. To get revenge on the bastards who killed my mother.

So why couldn't I just let him lie there and die? I thought a lot about that. It wasn't because he'd ever been nice or likeable; it wasn't even because he'd cried for his dead mates. It wasn't even because if I'd let him die, *I* would have killed him. It was a heroic thing to kill a Nazi in those days. Everyone would have thought me a hero.

No, it was just that he was still alive. And I didn't want him dead in Granda's garden. I mean, if he'd died, he'd still be there, to me. Even if Granda filled the duckpond in; which he did, a few days later, shovelling soil from all over the garden into it, furiously. Saying it was a danger in the blackout.

His name was Konrad Huess. I know because he wrote to me after the war, to thank me. Sent me lots of photos of his wife and kids. I was glad, then. For his wife and kids. But I never replied. I was too mixed up.

I still am.

GIFTS FROM THE SEA

The next bomb was the closest yet. Its slow, descending screech got louder and louder and louder.

Brian began to count under his breath. If you were still counting when you reached ten, you knew it hadn't blown you to pieces. He stared at the curving white wall of the shelter, the candle flickering in its saucer. The last things he might ever see on this earth . . .

Seven, eight, nine . . . the bunk he was lying on kicked like a horse. The candle fell over and rolled round the saucer, still burning, and starting to drip wax on to the little table. From the top bunk, his mother reached with a nearly steady hand and set it upright again. They listened to the sound of falling bricks as a house collapsed, the rain of wood and broken slates pattering down on the road and thudding on to the earth on top of their shelter.

'Some poor bugger's gotten it,' said Mam.

After the all-clear had gone, they climbed out wearily into the dawn and saw which poor bugger had gotten it. Number ten was just a pile of bricks. Eight and twelve had lost their windows and half the slates off their roofs. The road was littered. A big black dog was running around in circles, barking at everything and everybody. An ambulance was just disappearing round the corner of the road, and a crowd of people were breaking up, where number ten had been. Dad came across, filthy in his warden's uniform. Mam stared at his face silently, biting her lip.

'It's all right, hinny.' He grinned, teeth very white in his black face. 'They were in the shelter. We got them out. They're not hurt. But she cried when she saw what was left of her house.'

'She kept it like a little palace,' said Mam. 'She was that proud of it.'

Dad looked up at the sky, the way the German bombers had gone.

'Aye, well,' he said, 'the RAF lads got one of the buggers.'

They trailed round to the back door of their house. The kitchen seemed just as they'd left it; only a little jug with roses on it had fallen on the floor and broken into a hundred fragments.

'That was a wedding present,' said Mam. 'Your Auntie Florrie gave us that.' She bent down wearily and began picking up the pieces.

But it was when they opened the front-room door that they gasped. The windows were still whole, and the curtains intact. But everything else was just heaps of whiteness, as if there'd been a snowstorm.

'Ceiling's down,' said Dad. Brian stared up at where the ceiling had been. Just an interesting pattern of inch-wide laths, nailed to the joists. Dad ran upstairs and shouted that the bedroom ceilings were down too.

'Eeh, what a mess,' said Mam. 'How we ever going to get this straight?' Brian could tell she was on the verge of tears. 'Me best room. Where can I put the vicar now, if he calls . . .'

'Just thank God you've still got a house to clean, hinny,' said Dad gently. 'But,' he added, looking at Brian, '*you'd* better go and stay at your gran's, till we get this lot cleared up.'

An hour later, still unwashed, still without breakfast, Brian was on the little electric train down to the coast. He had Mam's real leather attaché-case on the seat beside him, with a change of underpants, pyjamas, a hot-water bottle and his five best Dinkie toys. He felt empty and peculiar, but excited. An adventure; you couldn't say he was running away like those evacuee kids. Gran, at the coast, was nearer the Jerry bombers than home. It was more like a holiday; no school for a week. And even more like a holiday because he was setting out before most kids were up. The train was full of men going to work in the shipyards. Blackened overalls and the jackets of old pinstripe suits; greasy caps pulled down over their eyes as they dozed. Everybody grabbed a nap when they could these days. But they all looked like his dad, so he felt quite safe with them.

He turned and looked out of the window, down at the river far below. Greasy old river, with brilliant swirls of oil on it. Packed with ships, docked three-deep on each bank. Big tankers; the rusty grey shapes of destroyers and corvettes. Already some welders were at work, sending down showers of brilliant electric-blue sparks, like fireworks in the dull grey morning.

Britain can make it, thought Brian. Britain can take it. He often heard Mr Churchill talking inside his head, especially when he felt tired or fed up. It helped.

The man beside him spoke to the man opposite. 'Aah see Gateshead's playin' Manchester City on Saturday.'

'Andy Dudgeon'll hold them.'

'City's good . . .'

'Andy'll still hold them.'

Brian was last to get out. At Tynemouth. He walked down empty Front Street, sniffing the smell of the sea that came to greet him. *Just* like being on holiday. A Co-op cart was delivering milk. Brian felt so good and grown up, he almost stopped and told the milkman all about being bombed. But only a kid would've done that, so he only said good-morning.

Gran gave him a good breakfast. She cut her toast much thicker than Mam, and always burnt the edges in an interesting way because she toasted it with a fork on the open fire. It tasted strongly of soot, but there was a huge lump of butter in the dish that made up for it. He didn't ask where the butter had come from; he'd just be told that Granda knew a feller who worked down the docks.

After breakfast he helped Granda hoist the Union Jack on

the wireless-mast in front of the row of coastguard cottages on the cliff. An act of defiance against Hitler. Granda ran it up the pole, broke out the tightly wrapped bundle with a vigorous tug on the rope. The flag fluttered bravely in the wind. Granda said 'God save the King' and they both saluted the flag. Then Granda said 'God help the workers', but that was just a joke. They always did it the same, when he stayed with Granda. Then Granda went to work, and Gran got out the poss-tub and the poss-stick, it being Monday morning, and started thumping the washing in the water as if Fatty Goering was somewhere down there in a midget submarine.

Washing day was no time to be in the house. Wet washing hung in front of the fire, steam billowed, the windows misted up and even your hands felt damp. Brian got out, followed by a yell that twelve o'clock was dinner-time.

Everything was still terribly *early*. Brian felt hopelessly ahead of himself. Still, he had plenty of *plans*. First he called at the school, to stand grandly outside the railings and watch the local kids being marched in, and feel *free* himself. Then he went on to tour the defences; the sandbagged anti-aircraft pom-poms on the sea-front. He spent a long time hovering from foot to foot, enjoying the guns' shining, oily evilness, till a grumpy sentry asked him why he wasn't in school.

Then he headed down the pier. The pier was like a road, running half a mile out into the grey of the sea. It was like walking on the water. It was like walking into the wide blue yonder, like the song of the American Army Air Corps. It was like playing dare with the Nazis, across the sea in Norway. It was even better when waves were breaking over the granite wall, as they were today. You tiptoed along, listening for the sound of the next wave, and if you were lucky you just managed to duck down behind the wall before the wave broke, and stayed dry. Otherwise you got soaked to the skin, all down your front.

He dodged successfully all the way, feeling more and more omnipotent. At the far end he stood in the shelter of the enormous lighthouse and watched an armed trawler put to sea. It came speeding up the smooth water of the estuary, and then pitched like a bucking bronco as it was hit by the first sea wave. The wind blew its sooty smell right up to him, with the smell of grilling kippers from the galley chimney. Soot, salt, wind, spray and kippers blew around his head, so that he shouted out loud for joy, and waved to the men on the deck; and one of them waved back.

And then he suddenly felt lonely, out there so close to Hitler. Getting back to land was harder and scarier. The waves might creep up behind your back; so might a German bomber. They'd machine-gunned the lighthouse before now; they would machine-gun anything that moved, and most things that didn't. He took much longer getting back to shore, running sideways like a crab, looking back over his shoulder for waves and Germans.

At the end of the pier he met a dog, on the loose like himself. A big Alsatian, all wet and spiky-haired from swimming in the river, and thirsting for mischief. It shook itself all over him, then put its paws on his shoulders and licked his face all over with a long, smooth, pinky-purple tongue.

Then it stood by the steps down to the rocks and barked encouragingly. Brian stood doubtful. It was good fun going round the tumbled rocks at the base of the Castle Cliff, but dicey. The cliff was brown and flaky and crumbling; there'd been falls of rock. When his dad was a boy it had been called Queen Victoria's Head because, seen sideways, it had looked just like the profile of the old Queen on a coin: nose, chin, bust, everything. Then the cliff had fallen and the Queen was gone, and now the cliff looked like nothing at all.

The boulders at the foot were huge and green with seaweed, with narrow cracks in between, where you could trap and break your ankle. And if you trapped your ankle or broke it, and you were alone except for a dog that didn't know you, you would just have to lie there till the tide came in and drowned you and swept your body out to sea. Nobody else walked round Castle Cliff rocks on a weekday . . .

The dog barked, insisting. Brian looked at the line of damp on the rocks, and decided the tide was still going out.

He followed the dog out on to the rocks, waving his arms wildly as he leapt from boulder to boulder, and his hobnailed boots slithered on the green weed and only came to a crunching stop in the nick of time, as they met a patch of white barnacles.

But almost immediately he was glad he'd come. He began to find things brought in by the tide. First a glass fishing-float, caught in a veil of black, tarry net. He scrabbled aside the net; underneath, the float was thick, dark green glass, half the size of a football. He dropped it inside his shirt, where it lay cool and damp against his belt, because he had to have both hands free for the rocks. Mam would like the glass float for her mantelpiece; it would help make up for the damage the Nazis had done to her house.

Then there was a funny dark piece of wood, about as big as an owl. At some time it had had a bolt driven through it, for there was a dark round hole, like an eye, at one end. It had been burnt too. It had ridged feathers of damp, blue-black, shiny charcoal. Brian looked out to sea, remembering ships bombed and burnt and sunk by the Nazi bombers, within sight of the shore . . .

But the sea, and the grinding rocks, had worn the lump of wood into the shape of folded wings and a tail, so that when he held it out upright in his hand, it *did* look like a bird, with a round dark eye each side of its head. The dog thought it looked like a bird too. It ran up, barking frantically, and neatly snatched the bird from his hand with one slashing grab. Then it discovered it was only wet wood and let it drop. It barked at it some more, then looked at Brian, head on one side, baffled.

He picked it up and held it out at arm's length again, waggling it to make it look alive. And again the dog thought it was a bird, and leapt and grabbed. Then dropped it, shaking its head vigorously, to get the sharp taste of salt out of its mouth.

He threw it for the dog, as far towards the sea as he could. It hit a boulder and leapt in the air with a hollow clonk. On the rebound, the dog caught it and slithered wildly down a sloping rock, ending up with a splash in a deep rock-pool. It brought the piece of wood back to him, and shook itself all over him, soaking him anew.

The fourth time he threw it, it clonked down a crack in the rocks and vanished out of sight. The dog tried to get down after it, but couldn't, and stood barking instead. Brian was suddenly sad; he would have liked to have taken it home and given it to his dad. His dad might have set it on a base and varnished it and put it on the mantelpiece. His dad liked things like that. As he stood, he heard the cautious voice of his dad inside his head telling him to be careful, or he'd be a long time dead. It made him check on the state of the tide, but he was sure it was still going out.

But he explored more cautiously after that. Found evil-smelling cod's heads from the fish-gutting, hollow-eyed like skulls, with teeth sharp and brown as a mummified alligator. He sniffed at the stink of rotting flesh, was nearly sick, and sniffed more gently a second time, till finally he could stand the smell without being sick. It was part of toughening yourself up for the War Effort . . .

And then he found the patch of limpets, clinging to a rock. He hovered again. Limpets were his great temptation. They clung to the rocks so hard, you might have thought them stuck there for ever with glue. But he'd found out long ago they weren't. Under the shallow cone of the ribbed shell was a sort of snail, which clung to the rock with a great big sucker-foot. If the limpet heard or felt you coming, it put on maximum suction and you'd never get it off the rock. But if you crept up quietly, you could get the blade of your knife under it before it knew you were there, and you could flick it off upside down into the palm of your hand.

And there it was, all pale soft folds, gently writhing in its bed of liquid, all beautiful with its two eyes coming out on stalks, like snails' eyes . . . It somehow gave him a squishy feeling, like the photos of semi-nude girls at the Windmill Theatre in London, which he snitched out of *Picture Post* after his parents had read it, and which he hid in an old tobacco-tin of his father's, under a pile of his own *War Illustrateds*.

He took his fill, till the feeling wore off, and then he carefully chose a smooth wet patch of rock and put the limpet back on it, right way up. He tested it; the limpet had resumed its grip on the rock, but only feebly. When the tide came back in, the waves might knock it off, and whirl it round and smash it . . . He felt somehow terribly, terribly guilty and wished he hadn't done it. But he could never resist, till afterwards.

The dog barked impatiently, summoning him on, not understanding why he was wasting the wonderful morning. He scrambled on after it, trying to stop worrying about the limpet.

They came round Castle Cliff at last, safe into King Edward's Bay. Little, snug, a sun-trap his dad had called it, when they came down for the day before the war. Chock-full of bathers then, deck-chairs, ice-cream kiosks and places where you could get a tray of tea for a shilling, and a shilling back on the crockery afterwards.

Not now. Totally empty.

And divided into two halves by the wire; huge rolls of barbed wire, stretching like serpents from cliff to cliff. Inland of the wire, the beach was dead mucky, full of footmarks, dropped fag-ends, rusting, broken bits of buckets and spades. People still came here for a smell of the briny, even in wartime. Holidays-at-home . . . the government organized it . . . fat girls in their pre-war frocks, dancing with each other in the open air on the Prom, to the music of the local army band in khaki uniform; pretending they were having a hell of a good time, and hoping one of the band would pick them up afterwards . . .

Seawards of the wire, the beach was clean, smooth, pure,

washed spotless by the outgoing tide. Sometimes the waves, at the highest tides, passed through the wire. Nothing else did. For there were notices with a skull and crossbones, warning of the minefields buried under the sand to kill the invading Jerries, or at least blow their legs off.

Unfortunately, the dog could not read. It went straight up to the wire and began to wriggle through, waggling its hips like a girl trying to catch a soldier's eye. Brian shouted at the dog, leaping up and down, frantic. Feeling responsible, feeling he'd brought it here. Forgetting *it* had brought *him*.

The dog took no notice. It finished its wriggling and leapt gaily on to the clean, wet, flat sand. It became sort of drunk with space and wetness and flatness, tearing round in ever-increasing circles, cornering so sharply its feet slid and it nearly fell on its side. Brian waited terrified for the small savage flash and explosion, braced to see large, furry, bloody bits of dog fly through the air, as if they were legs of pork in a butcher's shop before the war.

But nothing happened. The dog changed its tactics and began dive-bombing bits of wreckage that were strewn about, leaping high in the air, and coming down hard with all four feet together. Throwing things up in the air and catching them.

Why didn't the mines go off? That dog was as heavy as a grown man . . . Then Brian looked at the sand under the wire. There were all sizes of dog-tracks running through it. The dogs of the town had obviously found out something the humans didn't know.

There were no mines. The army couldn't afford them. All they could afford were notices warning of mines. Then the people who read them would think they could sleep safe in their beds at night, thinking the mines were protecting them from the Germans.

Fakes. Like the fake wooden anti-aircraft guns that Tommy Smeaton had found up the coast towards Blyth, guarded by a single sentry against the English kids who might wreck them.

Fakes, like the airfields full of plywood Spitfires that kids played in round the Firth of Forth . . .

Brian didn't know whether to laugh or cry.

Then he followed the dog through the wire. Ran round in circles with it, teasing it with a long lump of seaweed. Jumped up and down expecting, still, with a strange half-thrill that there would be a bang under his feet at any moment, and he would go sailing through the air . . .

No bangs. He sat down breathless, and all that happened was that the damp sand soaked through the seat of his shorts.

When he got his breath back, he began to explore along the tide-line. Oh, glory, what a haul! A sodden sheepskin boot with a zip down the front, obviously discarded by a pilot who'd had to ditch in the sea. And it was a size seven, and the seven had a strange crossbar on it, which meant it was continental. A German pilot's boot!

Then he found a dull brown tin that clearly said it contained ship's biscuits. Iron rations, floated from the lifeboat of some sunken ship! British, so not poisoned, like people said German things were. He'd take them home to Mam.

A cork life-jacket, good as new. Oh, glory, what a place for war souvenirs, and not a kid in the whole town must know about it! A near-new shaving-brush for Dad . . . German or British, it didn't matter. Dad's old one was prewar, and nearly worn down to a stump.

His shirt-front began to bulge like a lady who was having a baby. Sea-water ran down under his belt, down the front of his shorts, but he didn't care. A brier pipe, an aluminium pan without a dent, a good broom-head, a lovely silver-backed mirror. He had his pockets stuffed, his hands full, things tucked under both armpits so he could hardly walk. In the end he had to make dumps of useful stuff, every few yards above the tide-line. He couldn't carry them all home at once; he must hide some, bury some in the dry sand and come back for it later.

The last find took his breath away. A violin in its case. The strings had gone slack; no sound came when he twanged them, but surely it must be worth a bob or two? Dad would know.

He moved on into sudden shadow. He looked up, and saw that he was nearly at the foot of the far cliff. Where the Mermaid's Cave was.

Nobody called it the Mermaid's Cave but him. He had found it in the last year of peace. There was nothing in it but a long floor of wet, glistening pebbles, full of the smell of the sea. But each pebble glowed wonderfully in the blue-lit gloom. It was a miraculous place; the kind of place you might expect to find a mermaid . . . if anywhere on earth.

Not that, at thirteen, he believed in mermaids any more. Only in soppy poems they taught you at junior school. 'The Forsaken Merman.' Hans Christian Andersen's 'Little Mermaid'. And his cousin George's RAF joke, about what are a mermaid's vital statistics . . . 38–22–1/6*d*. a pound!

But he wished there *were* mermaids. He had a daydream about coming into the cave and surprising one, combing her long blonde hair down to half conceal her rosy breasts, like in fairy-tale books or the photos from the Windmill Theatre. It would be nice to . . . his mind always sheered away from what it would be nice to do with her.

Ah, well. No mermaids now. Just war souvenirs. You couldn't have everything, and already today had been better than Christmas. Still, he'd look inside, like he always had. Might be a lump of Jerry aeroplane or something . . .

There was *something*. Something long and pale, stretched out. Almost like a person lying there . . .

Barmy! Things always changed into something else, when you walked right up to them boldly. But that could almost be a long leg, a long bare leg, as shapely as the girls' at the Windmill.

He shot upright so hard, he banged his head painfully on the rock roof. But when he opened his eyes after the agony, she was still there. The Mermaid. Her hair was gracefully swirled across the pebbles, the way the sea had left her. Her wide grey eyes were looking straight at him, with an air of appeal. Her face was pale, but quite untouched. She'd been wearing a dress, but there wasn't that much left of it. Just enough to pass the censors at the Windmill.

Transfixed, he slowly reached out and touched her. Her face was cold. Not human cold, like when somebody comes in from a winter's day, or has been bathing. No, she was as cold as a vase full of flowers. As cold as a thing that is not alive.

Dead. But death and the sea had been kind to her; and to him. Nothing had touched her except the thing that had killed her. If there had been blood, the sea had washed it away on her voyage ashore. She was dead, but she was entirely beautiful. She was beautiful, but entirely dead. On the beautiful pebbles of the cave, with her hair around her. No smell but the clean smell of the sea. She might have been a lovely ship's figure-head, washed ashore after a shipwreck.

He just stood and stared and stared. She must have come off some ship. What was she? Norwegian, Dutch, Danish? Sometimes their coasters carried the captain's wife and family.

He was there a long time. Somehow he knew that once he moved, nothing would ever be the same again. She would change into something else, like the piece of wood that wasn't a bird; like the minefield that wasn't really a minefield.

He would have liked to take her home.

He would like to have kept her here, and come to see her often.

But he was a realist in the end. He remembered the cods' heads on the rocks. Once he moved, they would put her in a hole in the ground. Once he moved, she would only exist on a written form. And she was so beautiful, here in her cave . . .

He might have stayed . . . how long? But he heard the roar of the waves; the roar of the returning tide. He ran out in a panic. Waves were starting to stream up the beach, and the dog was nowhere to be seen.

He began to run up the beach. There was a khaki-clad

figure on the cliff, striding to and fro on sentry-duty. Brian waved and shouted, and then began to cry as he ran.

He had no idea why he was crying. All the rest of his life, he could never quite work out why he had been crying.

AFTER THE FUNERAL

There's only one British plane flying over Germany at night, and that's a BA 146, the quietest jet in the world. That's why the Federal Republic tolerates it – Bonn is very fussy about its citizens enjoying unbroken sleep; keeps them placid, law-abiding little Germans.

The 146 is an express-parcels plane run for TNT, the Rupert Murdoch crowd who took such a lot of flak at Wapping. Unlike Wapping, the flight's as quiet as the grave. No passengers, no cabin crew, just the captain and first officer and a lot of dark empty air over Germany.

I know all this, because I fly it most nights. It's such a doddle it's hard to keep awake. You have the German air-traffic control nearly all to yourself, and they're good and reliable and clear. You don't have to worry about near-misses in the air, like approaching Prestwick, or over Greece in the holiday season.

A graveyard shift, so it's important to have a nice lively first officer to keep you awake. Like Fairhurst was, when I flew to Majorca for Britannia. Fairhurst used to spend his spare time practising balancing a small light-bulb in the upward stream of warm air from the gasper. He practised so long he could get it to balance perfectly; just hang in the air, motionless. Then he'd summon the senior air-hostess and kid her the damned light-bulb hovering there was a new and infallible lie-detector. She'd fall for it usually. Then he'd start to question her about what she'd been up to, and who with, the previous night. A riot, that would keep us happy right across France. Bright lad, Fairhurst. He'll do well, if he survives to maturity . . .

Unfortunately, I no longer had Fairhurst. Most nights I got Stringer. Now I don't want to knock Stringer. A decent lad, and a thoroughly painstaking first officer. Not the sort to get aboard with a hangover and pull up the flaps in a fit of abstraction while you're still trying to gain height. But his idea of a rave-up is stamp-collecting. When you're in foreign parts for the night, he can never let his hair down – he's like a good little schoolboy who thinks the Head's always watching. It's hard even to get him out of uniform, whereas most of us can't wait to get out of our monkey-suits. A child of older parents . . .

The night I'm talking about, he was especially bad. We'd no sooner taken off and climbed up through Manchester Control to our cruising altitude of 24,000 feet, heading for Pole Hill VOR-beacon, when I realized there was something really wrong with him. Soggy as a drowned hamster. Not one inessential word could I get out of him: not even about stamp-collecting. I looked across to where he was sitting in the right-hand seat. The dim white light from the instruments wasn't exactly penetrating, but I could see pretty dark shadows under his eyes. I thought I'd better get him to talk. In a cabin not much bigger than a toilet-cubicle, bad vibes can get pretty lethal on a long flight.

'Got gut-ache?'

'No . . . no.' He was silent for a long minute, then seemed to think he owed me some sort of explanation.

'It was my father's funeral, yesterday.'

Talk about a conversation-stopper. But you have to say something. 'How old was he?' I don't know why everybody always says that. I suppose they're hoping the deceased was about ninety-seven. As if being ninety-seven makes it any better.

'Sixty-three.'

We flew on in that awful silence.

'Had he been ill long?' Another stupid question, but you *have* to say something.

'He wasn't ill. He went out with a shotgun and blew his head off.'

Even I could think of nothing to say to that. Luckily,

we were just reaching Pole Hill and the fuss of turning for Otringham, the next beacon near Hull. I suppose I hoped in a cowardly way that the interruption would change the subject. But Stringer, having got started, was obviously going on.

'It's my mother I feel sorry for. He led her a hell of a dance all their married life. Brooding for weeks on end; not speaking a word. Then he'd get these sudden black rages. Couldn't hold any sort of job down, for years. My mother had to go out to work, to keep things going. At least it got her out of the house.'

'What did he do – when he was working?'

'He was in the RAF in the war. With BEA after that, flying Yorks. Then he flew a desk. That was the one thing I ever did that pleased him – learning to fly. He liked to talk to me about my flying.'

The silence got really massive after that. I took refuge in looking out of the cabin window. It was a glorious moonlit night, without a cloud in the sky. We were just crossing the coast. The whole Humber Estuary was laid out like a map, as they say in books. The sea shone under the moon like beaten pewter. We were turning a bit now, heading for an imaginary point in the North Sea known as Dogger.

'A pointless bloody life,' said Stringer, 'and a pointless bloody death. Pity he didn't do it years ago, then my mother could've found somebody nicer.'

He was almost talking to himself by this time. Not a happy sensation, being cooped up at 24,000 feet with a guy who was talking to himself. I just hoped he wasn't going to do anything embarrassing, like cry. Let alone something dangerous. I didn't think he would. Got the stiff upper lip, has old Stringer.

More's the pity perhaps. He was damming it all up inside. We flew on in a silence that got denser and denser, full of electricity building up, like inside a bank of cu-nimbus. If you've ever had the misfortune to fly through a bank of cu-nimbus clouds, you'll know what I mean. A big bank of cu-nimbus can tear an aircraft to bits in seconds. You fly in one side, and you don't come out the other.

It was a relief when we reached Dogger, half-way across the North Sea, and it was time to transfer to Maastricht Control in Holland. The controller had a good stolid Dutch voice, which I clung to like a drowning man to a life-raft. Somewhere out there were ordinary Dutch humans. Windmills, daffodils and tulips, pretty girls in fancy dress offering you bits of Gouda cheese, and much more if you got lucky. The Dutchman spoke in English, of course; all air-traffic controllers do, even the Greeks try to. The Dutch are hard to tell from the Germans, but occasionally the Dutch make ponderous, boring little jokes. The Germans never do; it would not be *korrekt*.

It was at that point that the first odd thing happened, though it didn't seem very odd at the time. It was just a strong smell of leather. Real sweaty leather. Much lived-in leather. Like when you stand next to a motorcyclist in a Chinese takeaway.

I knew it wasn't coming from me. I glanced at Stringer. He sat there, as immaculate as ever in his white shirt and tie. He'd never smelt of anything worse than Denim aftershave before. Perhaps under the burden of bereavement, he'd forgotten to change his socks . . .

I don't want to sound carping, but that sort of thing matters when you're in a tiny pressurized space. Little things mean a lot, in the wrong sort of way. I once had a first officer who whistled television jingles under his breath when he was concentrating. He didn't even know he was doing it. By the end of a five-hour flight, I felt like pulling out the control column by the roots and braining him with it.

Still, this wasn't the night to say anything to Stringer. He had enough to put up with.

But the damned smell didn't go away, even after I'd turned the air-conditioning right up. It got stronger, rottener. And there was another acrid smell now; an old-fashioned smell right out of my childhood . . . Carbolic. What they used in school toilets. And, in fact, in other ways the whole cockpit was starting to smell like the worst kind of school toilet.

I was relieved to see, glancing sideways, that Stringer's nostrils were working as well.

'Something wrong with the bog?' he said.

'Go and check.'

The bog in the 146 is just behind the flight deck, and about as big as a large suitcase. I am always amazed at the ingenuity of those who design aircraft bogs. Never was so much crammed into so little for the use of so many. As a place, it didn't take long to check.

'Clean as a whistle,' I heard Stringer say behind my head. 'Smells like a rose. Wherever it's coming from, it's not coming from here.'

'Maybe there's a dead ferret trapped in with the nosewheel,' I said. But neither of us laughed.

When Stringer got back into his seat, he went on sniffing. 'I can smell petrol too.' Which was just plain stupid. The 146 runs on kerosene, like any other jet. The only petrol you get in a jet is in the pilot's cigarette-lighter.

But he was right. The whole cabin was reeking of petrol, like a car with a leaking tank.

I looked at Stringer, and Stringer looked at me. We both had the same thought; the parcels behind us. Maybe some Arab terrorist was giving us an early Christmas present. I got up and checked the parcels myself; they just smelt of cardboard.

'Oil pollution at sea?' suggested Stringer. 'Coming in through the air-intakes?'

It seemed a bit unlikely at 24,000 feet.

Then the smells just went away. We sniffed and sniffed, but there was only Stringer's Denim aftershave, as usual. So we forgot it. Just one of those things.

Then we had something else to worry about. A little burst of vibration through the airframe; then another, then a third.

Stringer started sniffing. 'Smells like Guy Fawkes night . . .'

He was right. It was just as if some fool had let off a firework in the cabin. For a second I had the illusion that the cabin was full of smoke.

But in a second, it was gone again.

We flew on, waiting for the vibration to come again; wondering whether to get the plane down, and fast. But she flew on without a flaw.

'It didn't feel like real trouble,' said Stringer. 'All the dials are reading OK.'

Oddly enough, I agreed with him. You get lots of funny little vibrations when you're flying that you can never explain. But they don't kill you. I decided to fly on. Once you divert from a flight, there's endless admin, hassle. TNT don't like parcels arriving late, and there are bloody awful forms to fill in.

'Coast coming up.'

From our height you could see it all: from the German islands round Borkum in the north, to the many mouths of the Rhine, the Maas and Waal to the south. Like black embroidery on silver lace.

'Hey,' said Stringer, 'the coast looks different.'

It did. There seemed to be a hole in it, where the old Zuyder Zee used to be. The Dutch drained their inland sea after the war – turned it into farmland, the polders, behind high dikes. Where once fishing-boats had sailed, tulips now grew. One of the seven new wonders of the world.

But it looked for all the world as if, tonight, the dykes had burst and the sea flooded back, drowning the farms under the waves.

'There was nothing about it on the ten o'clock news,' said Stringer. 'I think it must be low-lying mist, over the polders.'

'Yeah,' I said. I had enough to think about, without what was going on 24,000 feet beneath me.

Then he said, 'It's odd, that's all. That's how the Zuyder Zee must've looked when my father flew over it.'

'Ah, well, not our problem.' I was just relieved he was talking about his father in a more normal voice.

You're always afraid it might happen; you never stop watching out for it. But when it does happen, it's still like a 20,000-volt electric shock running through your muscles.

A near-miss. One hell of a near-miss. One minute we were sailing along through clear air, and the next there was this black plane only fifty feet in front.

Thank God it was heading away from us; thank God we were only slowly overtaking it.

I went into a dive to the left before I knew it. I shall never forget the way it hung over us, the great black wing, with the semi-circles of four whirling prop-blades beneath it. Then it was gone. I straightened up, near-rigid with shock. 'What the hell *was* it?'

Stringer took out a very white handkerchief and mopped his face. 'Four engines,' he said. 'Prop job. Twin tail. No navigation lights.' Then it seemed to hit him. 'The crazy bastard was flying without navigation lights . . .'

When I got my wits back, I gave the controller at Maastricht what for, in no uncertain terms. If another Anglo-Dutch War ever breaks out, blame me.

He was maddeningly calm and smug, like the Dutch usually are. 'There is no aircraft within fifty miles of you . . .'

'You want to get yourself a new radar, chum!'

'There is nothing wrong with my radar. I see you quite clearly. You are too low. Please climb 500 feet . . .'

'I'm reporting it as a near-miss . . .'

'You must do what you think best. Please climb back to 24,000.'

I vowed inwardly to fix him in the morning, and shut up. There is no point in getting them upset; that way you cut your own throat. We flew on, drinking coffee and trying to get over it, at least so our hands would stop shaking.

'Look at that stuff over at three o'clock,' said Stringer.

I gave a quick glance to starboard. As you can imagine, my mind was strictly on what might be straight ahead, so I didn't pay much attention to what was silhouetting his dark profile. But I remember there were a lot of searchlights waving about, mostly that slightly yellowish-white, but there was one distinctly blue and much thinner than the rest. The spectacular thing, though, was the fireworks. Green clusters hanging motionless in the sky, which must have been attached to parachutes, and a lot of red and yellow stuff, moving in slow arcs.

'Must be a festival,' I said. 'Queen Juliana's birthday or something...'

'It's not Juliana now,' he said. 'She abdicated. It's her daughter. I can't remember her name.'

'Well, somebody's birthday,' I said. 'Somebody important. There's the same sort of thing going on over Arnhem, on my side.'

'But some of that stuff's going up to 20,000 feet. That's downright bloody dangerous to aircraft.'

'Well, it's not at 24,000. That's all I care about.'

'And it's after midnight...'

'Look, just concentrate. Time we switched to Rhein.'

I thanked Maastricht, without any warmth creeping into my voice, and got the sober Teutonic tones of the Rhein controller that promised no messing about. We turned to starboard slightly, now flying towards Dortmund beacon. I wasn't sorry to say goodbye to Holland; all Holland seemed a bit spooky, kinky, off-key that night. It happens sometimes, but you're always glad when it's over. Change your controller, change your luck.

We flew on over that quiet dark bit, between the Dutch border and the Ruhr. It calmed me, but Stringer continued twitchy.

'There aren't any streetlights down there.'

'For Christ's sake, it's after midnight...'

'There's always street-lights. There weren't any streetlights over Holland, either...'

'Must be your bloody ground-mist, drifting off the Zuyder

Zee.' To tell you the truth, I wasn't paying much attention to his babbling on. I was fed up with him; I was fed up with the whole trip. Roll on, Frankfurt!

'Anyway,' I added, 'there's plenty of light over the Ruhr.'

There was too. A great dim mass of light, reaching far into the sky far ahead. It did strike me it wasn't quite the usual colour. It's usually yellow, from the sodium lamps. This was a fiery pink.

'Freak weather conditions.' I got the Frankfurt *Volmet* weather-computer on our second radio.

No ground mist over Frankfurt. None anywhere over the Ruhr. I remember how clear the recorded voice was; no static or interference. So it was a bit of a shock when the other voice broke in, blurred and full of static. A German voice, speaking German. Then another German voice replied, speaking German.

They were talking to each other, and in spite of the static and the foreign language, it was definitely an aircraft talking to its controller. I haven't got much German, but I could make out the word *Libelle* – Dragonfly. Dragonfly control to Dragonfly. The quality of transmission was pathetic, like an old scratched 78 gramophone record. As a pilot, it gave me the heebie-jeebies.

'Who the hell is that on the air?' Stringer nearly yelped, and I didn't blame him. Your controller is your lifeline. Some other silly bastard blocking up the airwaves, you could end up dead. Not at 24,000 over Germany at night, of course. But on the run-in to landing at Frankfurt . . .

The voices came again. Something about a *kurier* flying at 22,000, and steering a course 105 to intercept.

'Sounds like the German Air Force – sounds like some sort of night-fighter exercise, using the wrong frequency.'

We told Rhein. Rhein was positive and reassuring. Rhein had heard none of it. There was no German Air Force exercise scheduled for that night. Which means, to the Teutonic mind, that it can't possibly exist . . .

I tried to console myself that Dragonfly and his control had by now shut up. Maybe they could take a hint. Maybe they knew they'd dropped a clanger and had buggered off quietly, hoping they wouldn't be reported in the morning. It seemed to me I was going to report half of Europe in the morning. Maybe I was getting stroppy in my old age.

'What on earth *is* that ahead?' asked Stringer in an awed voice. And I must admit it was odd. The pink glow ahead had got much bigger. It was still blurred, but it seemed to be filling the horizon now, as if the whole bloody Ruhr was on fire.

That was the last sane thought I had for half an hour. Because suddenly another voice came through our headphones. An English voice; a cockney voice; a voice hoarse with excitement. No, to be frank, a voice shit-scared, babbling.

'Rear-gunner to skipper. Corkscrew. Corkscrew right.'

The plane just seemed to go bananas under my hands. The right wing dropped until it was pointing at the ground. We fell in a sickening dive. There was the sound of something like a dustbin breaking loose in the compartment behind. All the evil smells came back with a rush, and overpowering all, a strong smell of shit. Then both the voices together. Dragonfly yelling he had the *kurier* in his sights, in German. And the cockney voice shouting, 'Corkscrew left, skipper. Corkscrew left,' in a high-pitched scream.

Then little vibrations the same as we'd had before. Then a much heavier vibration; a really nasty vibration, as if the 146 was in some way damaged. The smell of fireworks. The smell of rubber burning. A terrifying roar of engines, old prop-job engines, totally deafening.

Then the cockney yelling, 'I got him skip. I got him. He's burning.' With a kind of savage, screaming exultation that made you feel sick. Or was it the way the 146 was falling around? I knew the 146 couldn't take that kind of bashing. Any minute it would break up . . .

Then, before I could gather my wits even to move the controls and try to get the plane upright . . .

Nothing.

The 146 was flying on over Germany, level and the right way up, as if nothing had ever happened.

No noise, no smell, no vibration. Rhein control broke in calmly, if a little reprovingly. Telling me to maintain my correct flying altitude by climbing 300 feet.

I obeyed, automatically, and got his approval, as if I was a small but beloved pupil.

I glanced over at Stringer, who hadn't said a word. He didn't turn towards me, like he normally does. He just said, in a dreamy voice that didn't sound like him at all.

'That was close, skipper.'

'What the hell do you mean?' I shouted. His voice scared me; it sounded like he was an actor, taking a part in a different play.

He didn't reply. At least he didn't reply to my question. He just said,

'Big fires ahead. The PFs must have got their markers down right for once.'

I became convinced I was going mad. Or I was in some horrible dream, and really safe back in England, in my bed at the Birmingham Holiday Inn.

Because, where Frankfurt airfield should have been, and Rhein control, there was just fire. Fire that spread out mile after mile. Fire that shot in towering pillars fifteen thousand feet into the air. A fire that seemed to breathe like a giant obscene living animal, crouching over a Germany that was its prey.

Another voice; another voice like a cracked 78 gramophone record came through my headphones.

'Five minutes to ETA, skip. Commence bomb-run.'

And another strange voice, slightly Scottish this time. 'Left a bit, skip. Left a bit more . . . right a bit.'

But my hands didn't move on the control-column. I was paralysed with sheer fright, because just ahead of us, outlined against the flames, the black four-engined plane was back.

And between its twin-fins was a bulbous, shiny, glass object with four black sticks jutting out that could only be a gun-turret.

I knew from my time in the Air Training Corps what kind of plane it was. I had seen it doing a fly-past on Battle of Britain Sunday.

A Lancaster bomber of World War II.

And not just one Lancaster. There were dozens of them, flying almost wing-tip to wing-tip, jostling each other like kids queuing up for ice-cream at the cinema, rising and falling as the updraughts of air from the fires below hit and lifted them.

And far below us, crucifixes against the roaring, breathing beast of flame that was the Ruhr, flew other four-engined bombers with long bodies and short stubby wings. As I watched one of them suddenly gave a bright flash, and lost a whole two-engined wing, and fell twisting away into the inferno.

'Poor bloody Stirlings are copping it tonight,' said Stringer in his ghastly dreamy voice. Like a living puppet.

And I was like a puppet myself, hands rigid on the control-column. Because I knew I must not move it. To move it would be to go for ever into that nightmare that Stringer was already caught up in. Move it, and we would end up in some inferno of our own. For the world outside and the world inside didn't fit. My dials said I was flying at 400 knots, whereas the Lancasters outside my windscreen couldn't possibly be doing more than 280 on full boost. I was literally flying blind. In that heat and that stink, and with that inferno outside, only my own instruments were real.

I seemed to fly on forever.

And then, breaking through like a cool clear stream of water, the voice of the Rhein controller, asking slightly querulously when I would be starting my descent, and what was my intended vector? His voice sort of broke up the whole scene, and I was back in the cool dark at 24,000 feet over Germany.

Frankly, I don't know how I got locked on to the ILS beam and got my glide-slope. My body felt like soggy elastic; my hands shook like I'd developed Parkinson's. I was sitting in a puddle of my own sweat. And Stringer was still locked in his dream, babbling to a non-existent radio-operator about checking possible damage to the main spar . . .

But I did it. It wasn't the best landing I've ever made, but I didn't bend anything. And I managed to taxi in the right direction once I was on the ground. I don't think anybody noticed anything . . .

Then I only had the simple job of coping with a totally lunatic first officer before the German ground-crew got to us. But Stringer wasn't mad any more, at least he wasn't babbling. He just sat there in his seat, tears streaming down his face, saying over and over again,

'Sorry, Dad. Sorry, sorry, sorry. I just didn't understand.'

I told the Germans he'd been taken ill, just as we were about to land. Severe headache and abdominal cramps. Some German medics took him away on a stretcher.

They sent him home after a whole week, saying they couldn't find a thing wrong with him. Thorough types, the Hun. I kept my mouth shut, and he didn't lose his licence. He took a short-haul job after that, flying Islanders to the Hebrides. By daylight. As far as I know, he's still doing it without any evil result. Still, I worry about him; and the Islanders.

I checked up on the quiet with RAF records. Wing Commander Stringer, DSO, DFC and bar, flew eighty-nine operations in Lancasters and was demobbed from the RAF in October 1945.

I'm just glad I never had a father like that.

CATHEDRAL

I should never have played the Virgin Mary.

I'm not even a Christian; nothing, really.

But when your father's Dean of the cathedral, Christianity is sort of the family business. You have obligations, unless you're a little bitch who likes making her father's life hell, and I hope I'm not *that* sort. Men like to think that clergy daughters are either frozen virgins or nymphos; but I just like a good time.

Pat Snow should've played the Virgin. I know she prayed for it beforehand, and cried when she didn't get it. She had a sweet little choirgirl-of-the-year sort of voice, and a figure like a sack (which would've suited the part). But she looks a bit like a frog, whereas everyone thinks I've got a spiritual look.

Now let's get this straight. I do *not* have a spiritual look. I do not *wish* to look spiritual. It's just that my father has a high forehead and wide-apart eyes and I take after him.

Which brings us to the Nativity Play, or rather the Cathedral Nativity Rock Opera. For we are a very with-it cathedral. My father wears collar and tie and sports coat most of the time, and Tony the Bishop's Chaplain goes in for jeans whenever he can get away with it, even though he has a fat bottom. Tony also reckons he is a poet, because he's had a few bits published in little poetry magazines. And his best mate is Nev, the assistant organist, who runs rock groups on the side, to eke out his pitiable salary.

Which is where the Nativity Rock Opera came from. Scheduled for early on Christmas Eve, in the cathedral itself. A big do, involving the cathedral choir; three rock groups; numerous junior-school choirs, sickeningly clean and combed and sat-on by their teachers; Tony, Nev and yours truly.

Why did I do it?

Well, I've got a big strong voice, and when you've got a strong voice, the cathedral becomes one great big echo chamber, a marvellous plaything. And they'd written a wonderful song just for me. Called 'Why Me?'

And there was no doubt it was going to be a big success, a sell-out, because they'd written other great numbers, like the Wise Men's 'Africa, Asia or Anywhere'. And the rock groups had set a lot of old favourite carols to a heavy rock beat, for the congregation to join in with. (In the manner of a Bach Oratorio, thus reviving an ancient tradition, as my father was quick to point out.)

I suppose I wanted to be a star. You don't often get the chance to be a star, in a little cathedral town like Sencaster.

And I was a star. The place was packed for the only performance (mainly with the parents of the junior-school choirs, I suspect). And the congregation really dug that heavy rock beat (when it was hallowed by carols) because they sang their heads off, and even clapped themselves afterwards. (Clapping in cathedrals is on, now, since the Pope's visit.)

And I really made that old cathedral ring, to its very furthest corners, with my echoes. That old cathedral and I really made sweet music together, like Stephane Grapelli and his violin.

Maybe that was the trouble; for cathedrals are strange beasts.

Or maybe it was Nev's wife's Christmas punch, at the party that they gave the grown-up (and semi-grown-up) members of the cast afterwards. We had to have it in the large clergy vestry, because it was late, and the restaurant in the cloisters was already locked up.

I remember that punch well; I shall remember it for the rest of my life. There can't have been much alcohol in it, the party being on sacred premises. But she'd put in everything from mint leaves to oregano, to try to give it some semblance of a kick.

Of course we were going on to a *real* party afterwards. With real booze. An all-night party, actually. My father didn't dig that much, on Christmas Eve. He'd rather have had me at Midnight Mass. But he owed me a favour, because I'd played the Virgin, so we both left any arguments unsaid.

Three different blokes had offered me lifts to the all-night party, and I hadn't quite made up my mind who to go with. The punch party in the vestry was just starting to wind up, and wind its scarves round its throats when, perhaps as a result of the aforesaid punch, I felt a sudden greasy queasy dagger strike me deep in my interior. I fled to the clergy loo, and spent a long time seated therein, staring at the odd cassock and surplice someone had left hanging on the back of the door.

You see, it was bad. Seriously incommoding. Not a gastric blizzard so much as a series of gastric squalls. Every time I thought it was over, it would start again.

I heard them, faintly, asking where I was. I heard them, faint and far off, calling my name. But I didn't worry. Someone would wait for me . . .

The last squall subsided. I wiped my bum, and, rather weak on my pins, staggered to the small clergy mirror, and decided I looked pale but interesting, and stayed to comb my hair and put on more lipstick.

Then I walked out; into pitch darkness. I grabbed backwards to put the toilet light on, and that switch clicked on total darkness too. Somebody, somewhere, had just switched the cathedral's mains power supply off. Even cathedrals are hard-up these days. Or maybe it had something to do with the fire insurance . . .

Somebody had *just* done it.

I screeched my head off trying to make them hear. And in reply I heard a door bang shut with that thud and clink that all church doors make. Nobody had waited for me. Everybody had thought I'd gone to the all-night party with somebody else.

I was alone with the cathedral.

I told myself to stay calm. To stand still and let my eyes get used to the inky dark. No point in falling over something and adding a sprained ankle to my troubles.

It's amazing how your eyes slowly get used to the dark. First the big lancet windows of the vestry swam down at me, dark blue against black. Then the glimmer from the white formica table tops. Then a dark spiky huddle of stacked chairs.

But your eyes don't just get used to the dark; your ears get used to the silence, too . . .

I heard something approaching my hand along the nearest table top, which I was hanging on to for grim death. Something tiny and metallic; tiny footsteps, click, click, click. Dear God, what? A giant armoured spider? A rat on crutches? I gave a little yelp and pulled my hand away and hugged it with the other hand.

The clicking went on, but seemed to get no nearer. After a while, I grew bold, and felt out towards it. And my hand touched the warm smooth surface of a cooling electric kettle . . .

Idiot, I told myself. And groped through the door into the nave.

All the nave glimmered faintly in the dim orange glow of the street lamps outside the great windows. I could see right to the rose window at the far end. But it was the worst of lights. It lit up the backs of the rows of chairs, but it left all sorts of nasty black shadows in corners. And it made the stained glass windows, with their familiar pictures of saints look . . . unfamiliar. I suppose it was the reddy-orange of the street lamps. It turned the calm blues of heaven, the reassuring green of fields and trees into the reds and oranges and purples of . . .

I had really believed in hell when I was little. God was real to me then, and when God is real, so is the Devil.

I passed the window of St Peter raising Dorcas from the

dead. St Peter had always been my favourite; with his curly white beard he reminded me of the retired sea captain who always spoke to my father after Matins, and gave me a sweet, when I was little.

St Peter was still watching me tonight; but I couldn't see the expression on his face.

But if the windows were bad, the carved statues were worse. They lurked all round the walls of the aisles, deep in their own shadows. The early bishops, lying flat, carved as flat and grim as stony kippers, on the boxes of their tombs . . . The later bishops that seemed to float upwards in a billow of marble clouds, cherubs and draperies. Those were the ones that used to make me giggle, they were so fat and pompous in their piety. But tonight I couldn't see their expressions; or their expressions were subtly different. As if they said, 'You have laughed at us all your life, my dear, but tonight is *our* time.'

I told myself it was just the strange way the light fell . . . Look how clearly it picked out that piece of lettering. Why, I could *read* it!

NEERE THIS PLACE IS INTERRED YE BODDY OF . . .

That was the worst moment. Of course I'd always known the dead were there; that the cathedral was as riddled with dark holes as a piece of Gorgonzola cheese, and that in every hole was a body in a lead coffin. My father had shown me some, once; when repairs were being done because the altar steps had begun to sag.

The strangest thing was that lead is not rigid, like a sheet of steel. Over the centuries, lead flows, droops. The lead of these coffins had drooped down on the skeletons beneath, as if they were no more than linen sheets. Every edge of every bone was visible; though my father said that probably the bones were crumbled to dust by this time, and the lead would flatten and flatten till in the end it covered . . . nothing.

Oh, yes, the dead were there all right. Nobody knew how many. Row upon row in the crypts beneath my feet. Stacked like forgotten books in some forgotten library, beneath the very stone slabs I was walking on. Were they listening to my footsteps pass?

They had always been there. But who remembers them while the cathedral's busy, and the organist is practising his voluntary, the vergers stacking hymn books, and the tourists flashing with their cameras?

I told myself not to be a morbid fool, and hurried towards the south transept door, which had a little door set in it; this was how we always got in and out when the cathedral was closed. It only had a Yale lock; one twist of the worn brass knob and I'd be out in the friendly bustle of Christmas Eve.

I reached the south transept door; reached up in the dark, with easy familiarity, for the worn knob.

My hand found a cold short lever instead, that would not move no matter how hard I twisted it. God, the new anti-burglar security. The cathedral contained many treasures, and a month ago there'd been a break-in and a sixteenth-century triptych and two Tudor chairs had been stolen from the Lady Chapel. This was a five-lever mortice lock, that would only turn, even from the inside, with a key.

There was no way out, till the head verger came to unlock the doors for Midnight Mass at half past eleven . . . Desperately I held my watch up, so the strange light from the windows caught it. Twenty past nine. It had been gone nine when I dashed for the loo. Had time *stopped*!?

Then I remembered the phones. We have phones all over the place; for we are a *very* with-it cathedral. The nearest was in the head verger's office. I took a short cut across the chancel, trying not to look at the tiny point of red flame that hung above the high altar. This meant the Host was reserved there; the incarnate body of a God I no longer believed in . . . and yet the point of red light made me uneasy. If somebody had offered me a million pounds to blow that flame out, I could not have done it.

I did not want to look at it, there in the dark. But I looked, and saw it. Something made me. I just *had* to. Then I looked away again, where I was going. I wanted a sprained ankle now even less than I had in the vestry. With two good legs I could keep on the move, dodge dangers. But to lie helpless in the dark . . .

What dangers?

It was then that I saw it again; the red light from above the altar. Only now it had moved. Now it was floating in front of the pillar I was just approaching. Only ten yards away . . .

I didn't even stop to think; I blundered backwards in the darkness, terror rising like bile in my throat. When I looked again the red light was no longer there; it was floating in front of the next pillar instead.

A tiny click made me whirl. Now it was floating in front of the pillar behind me. And . . . click . . . there was another. There were three now, all round me.

I think it was only the tiny clicks that saved my sanity. How could anything Holy and Dreadful give tiny metallic clicks like . . . ?

Our new infra-red burglar alarms, just fitted. I'd seen them often, in friends' houses. They clicked off and on when you moved, even in daylight, without setting the alarm off. But in the daylight, with friends, they were just a joke. We'd played games with them, waved our hands above our heads to make them click off and on.

I moved about now, making them switch off and on, listening to the clicks. They were not Holy and Dreadful; merely my obedient servants. I gave a rather wild giggle. They would be switched on tonight. An alarm bell would be ringing in the police station, in my own house. I would be rescued at any moment by my own father, followed by a mob of excited policemen. What a giggle!

But I still wanted a telephone. I wanted to hear my own mother's voice chiding me for my foolishness, while I waited.

When I got to the door of the verger's office, it was locked. More damned security . . . Oh well, there was another phone in the cathedral shop, by the main door. That was just behind wooden screens. They couldn't lock that one away. I trailed down the centre aisle of the nave.

Until I heard the voice. It was so low, so continuous, that I doubted at first whether it was a voice at all; or merely some other piece of machinery left running.

But I had to know one way or the other. In the dark, you have to know, one way or the other. Or you'd go potty. My heart in my mouth, on feet I tried to keep silent, I crept towards it. The noise was coming from the north aisle, and when I reached the north aisle, it seemed to be coming from the tiny Mountfield Chapel at the far end. And by this time, I could tell it was human noise. A kind of babble.

The Mountfield Chapel is set aside for private prayer and meditation.

Had I a fellow prisoner in the dark? How had he evaded the vergers at closing time? Swallowing, I crept nearer. It came to me that the babble was a babble of grief. There was a sobbing in it. Who could be sobbing on Christmas Eve? I'd always rather avoided the Mountfield Chapel. I didn't approve of people praying in public, except during services. I thought them holy nuts at best, and attention-seekers at worst. Mostly women.

But this was definitely a man. The weeping was very dreadful and yet very human. I could hear the ragged intakes of breath, blurred individual words. I was sure it was a living man. And I determined I would not let him weep like that, alone. Not on Christmas Eve. Christmas was the time of good cheer. I would show him sympathy, that there was always a bright side, if you looked hard enough for it. I would do him good. Then we would wait together for rescue to come.

The door to the Mountfield Chapel is extremely narrow. I put a hand to each side of it, and leaned my head through.

The strange orange light flooded in. There was a street lamp just outside the window. It seemed as light as day . . .

And the Mountfield Chapel was quite empty. It only

held six chairs and a tiny altar and cross against the far wall. Nowhere for anyone to hide. And yet grief filled the place; echoed off the stone walls, assaulted my ears.

Oddly, I had no impulse to run away. I suppose I just knew there was nowhere to run to. I was here, alone, with everlasting grief. Instead, I felt a far-off anger; had the Church reduced some poor dead soul to such a state, with the burden of guilt it put on people? Madly, I even began to wish to comfort a ghost, to have mercy where God had none . . .

The voice, when it became clear, made me nearly jump out of my skin.

'Aah've been a bad bugger, a wicked bad bugger. Aah'll gan to hell an' burn . . .' It seemed right next to my ear. And yet I think I sensed there was something not quite ghostly, even before I heard the sound of vomiting. Even before I heard the sound of two sets of approaching footsteps outside, and saw two shadows of men cast on the window.

'Here he is! Jack? Jack? What ye doin' man? My Gawd, he's spewing up against the cathedral wall. Ye can go to hell for that kind of thing, Jack! Didn't ye know that? You drunken old sot. Here, give us a hand wi' him, Stan. Let's get him home, the miserable old beggar. All that money poured away in drink, and he doesn't even enjoy himself . . .' The two shadows hauled another to its feet, and only then did I notice the open ventilator in the chapel window, low down.

My legs felt so weak, I sat down right there in the Mountfield Chapel, though I've always avoided the place. I tried a short scornful laugh, just to see if I could manage it. Nothing but a maudlin drunk!

Then I stopped laughing suddenly. A soul in torment was a dreadful thing; alive or dead; drunk or sober.

Meanwhile, there was the matter of the cathedral shop telephone.

But when I reached it, it too was dead. Cut off at the cathedral exchange, no doubt. Which was locked away in the head verger's office.

A numbness seemed to be coming over me. The cathedral, never warm in winter, now seemed icy as the last hot air effects of the congregation's singing at the Rock Opera wore off. I sat down in a pew, with my legs curled up under me, and under my coat, and my hands thrust up my opposite sleeves for warmth. My watch said ten more minutes had crept past on leaden feet. My father and our gallant police force were taking a hell of a long time getting here . . . Maybe the wonderful burglar alarm wasn't working yet. I tried blowing on my hands to warm them; it only made them damp.

I closed my eyes, thinking I might doze till the head verger ushered in Midnight Mass. Suddenly I had an overwhelming sense of someone tall standing over me, only inches away. I jerked open my eyelids and there was, gulpingly, no one there. And yet somehow I knew that if I let myself doze off again, my dreams would not be pleasant.

I must keep on the move. I must talk to old friends. For you cannot dwell all your childhood among tombs, without having your favourites.

Sir Rafe de Easenby; the great arch-tomb that blocked off a whole window of the south aisle.

Sir Rafe, according to cathedral records, had been a great and wealthy landowner of the thirteenth century. We still had the village of Easenby, five miles away.

Sir Rafe's wife had died in childbirth; along with his newborn only son. He had sold all the family estates and spent the lot on the great tomb. Then gone off and 'dyed in foreyne warres'. I was sure, as a child, that the 'foreyne warres' must have been a crusade. And it was so romantic; he must have loved his wife so much; not even thought of remarrying.

There they lay, in the glimmering orange light, amongst a great host of carved angels. Sir Rafe in full armour, with his crossed legs, and his mailed arm reaching across his body to draw his great sword. And his lady long and stiff with her many-buttoned bodice and wimple headdress. And the child, carved beneath them in his cross-banded swaddling clothes . . .

But they did not seem romantic tonight. They seemed a great scream of despair in stone. It was not a sane act, to spend all your living on one great tomb, before you died. It had shouted at God, at all Creation, 'They *will not* be forgotten, wiped out as if they'd never been.'

It shouted still, after seven hundred years. And I knew Sir Rafe had gone off to get himself killed. Suicide by holy war; a permissible suicide when any other would send your soul straight to hell . . .

As I stood staring, there came more noise from outside. I could spot when noises came from outside now. Besides, this could only be a sound of the present. Drunken young voices, laughing. Screeching music from a ghetto blaster, a cheap cocky confident girl's voice, singing over and over:

'It's got to be-heeee-heee *per-fect*,
It's got to beee-heee *per-fect*.'

You could tell from her falsely amorous tones that she was singing about sex.

Such brainless braying; such silly arrogance. What was ever perfect in this world? Sir Rafe knew the truth; and so did I. Then it seemed to me that these people laughing outside were as insubstantial, as easily blown away, as a wisp of steam, as a used Kleenex blowing along the gutter. If there were ghosts, tonight, it was those people laughing outside. They would be annihilated for ever, once they passed out of earshot round the corner of the nave.

Whereas Sir Rafe was getting more real all the time . . .

In the end, his realness got too much for me. He began to make me feel like a ghost too. I drifted away, towards Bishop Vavasour's pulpit.

Bishop Vavasour's pulpit was no longer used. It lingered dustily, behind a pillar, in the south aisle. It was carved with intricate medieval foliage. But, in the foliage, three dreadful flower-shaped scars. And in the middle of each scar, buried deep in the soft limestone so you had to wipe away the dust to see them, a round dark-grey mark.

Bullets. Round lead bullets that had once sat ready in the pistols of Oliver Cromwell's staff officers.

In 1647, one Sunday morning, General Cromwell, passing by, had called in to hear the sermon. Bishop Vavasour had been preaching a godly High Church sermon, a forbidden sermon, a Royalist sermon. Even after he had seen the General frown, Bishop Vavasour had continued his godly sermon. Cromwell, provoked beyond measure, had called on him to desist, in a bull-like voice that carried the length of the cathedral.

Bishop Vavasour had frowned at the unseemly interruption, and carried on. Cromwell had ordered his officers to draw and cock their pistols, then called on Bishop Vavasour to cease his blasphemy if he valued his life . . .

'What value is my life without my God, Master Cromwell? The cock shall not crow thrice for me . . .'

All three officers fired. All three missed. Perhaps the officers had tender consciences, and all aimed low, expecting another to kill the troublesome priest . . .

The Bishop continued to preach, dusting the stone-chips from his surplice. 'God has judged between us, Master Cromwell. See the three new marks of the Trinity . . .'

'Throw him out,' shouted Cromwell. 'He shall not preach again.' But the Bishop continued to preach, as they bore him struggling down the aisle. A year later, he died, some say of starvation . . .

Another ghetto blaster came by. Rap, this time, echoing through the thin glass of the windows.

'Gotta get me a girl, gotta get me a drink,
If you think I'm evil, I'm what you think . . .'

Rap. Made up today; forgotten tomorrow.

Vavasour's pulpit, seven hundred years of stone.

Who are the ghosts, girl? Who are the ghosts?

It seemed to me that I was entirely absorbed into the cathedral now. As cold as its stones; as dried-out as the dust in the crypt. I no longer had any will of my own. I somehow knew I was walking to the base of the north-east tower. I just didn't know why. The whole place seemed as light as day, now, in the orange light from the windows. The saints watched from the stained glass as I passed, the floating bishops from their marble tombs. Far up in the root I could see the carved winged angels watching. And I knew that every one of the dead had an ear cocked to listen to my progress.

There is not much at the base of the north-east tower. They say it is the oldest part of the cathedral; and hardly anybody ever goes there. The walls are black greasy stone, mainly Norman work, and the windows are tiny.

The one thing there is, is an iron cart, a black thing with huge spoked wheels like a Victorian pram. They used to lay the dead on it, in Victorian times, when they spent the night before burial laid out in the cathedral. I was afraid that *something* would make me lie on it . . .

But that wasn't what I was being led to. My attention was being drawn instead to the base of the wall. Where, more by memory than by sight tonight, I knew there was a herring-bone pattern of small narrow bricks, in a layer before the massive stones started.

The Saxons, long before the Normans, had used the herring-bone pattern. And they made it in Roman bricks, filched from the ruins of Roman villas long abandoned and ruined. They weren't good at quarrying stone, the Saxons; that's why they used anything that came to hand to build the first tiny church on our cathedral site. And in one brick is the pawmark left by a Roman cat. My father had showed it to me, when I was little. He said it was from the first century AD. And of course I believed him . . .

Like I believed in Bishop Vavasour and Sir Rafe de Easenby. Like I believed in the Saxons and the Romans. Like, for that matter, I believed in Julius Caesar, whose works I was struggling over in Latin in the sixth form at the grammar school . . .

But now I stood baffled. What did the cathedral want with me? I seemed to have come to a total halt. But all around the dead seemed to listen. Everything around me was the work of dead hands; even that little 1920s rush chair . . .

Out of the corner of my eye, I saw the little red point of light above the high altar that seemed to me then the very eye of the cathedral.

Why had I accepted all the rest of history and yet rejected that red light? Why had I torn the red light out of the fabric of history?

Why are you rejecting me? asked the cathedral.

I don't know if I screamed at it out loud, or only in my mind. Because you're a *bully*, I shouted. Because you were built on the torn muscles and bloody bones of your builders; because your stone was bought with the money of the poor, so that their children starved. And you didn't *care*. And if I believed in you, you would start to eat *me*. Well, you're finished, finished, finished! People only come to *stare* at you now, because you're in the guidebooks. Soon, no one will believe in you. I don't believe in you; but I still hate you. I'm not a cringeing wet like Pat Snow, snivelling at her prayers. I'm going to be *free*!

It seemed to do the trick. The whole place became . . . just an empty box. Like a disused warehouse. The stone was just stone and the glass was just glass, and the red light at the altar was no more to me than the flicking red eyes of the burglar alarm system. That was all. Empty nothing. One and a half hours of empty nothing, except the noise of the drunks reeling home outside, and the stupid songs they were singing and blasting on their ghetto blasters. An hour and a half during which I realized that nothing is the most frightening thing of all.

And then there was the creak and bang of the head verger coming in, his crisp footsteps in the aisle, the lights going on one after another, driving the darkness away with pools of pure gold. I hid from him behind the pillars; I had no intention of embarrassing either of us. And then as people began coming in for Midnight Mass, I slipped out unnoticed. Realizing I'd lost all taste for the all-night party, too.

But as I loitered, my father came hurrying up to the lighted door, his vestments over his arm. He looked a little tired, and a little worried, as usual. But his face lit up when he saw me, and he grinned and put his arm round my shoulders and said, just jokingly, and referring to my recent performance:

'Behold the handmaid of the Lord, be it unto me according to Thy word.'

I mean, being a Dean, he's always turning quotations from the Bible into little pleasant jokes. All our clergy do it all the time.

But this time, it went home like a spear. Be what you are. Say what you mean. Never pretend to be what you're not.

I'll never play at being the Virgin Mary again.

Not in that cathedral.

'Come to Midnight Mass,' my father said, 'since you seem to have abandoned your all-night party. Come to please *me*.'

And with a good heart, and his arm around me, I went.

To please him.

ZAKKY

Dad's Army?

I'll bet it made you laugh. But none of it was true, not round where I lived.

That rubbish about drilling with pitchforks and broom handles. Every lad in our village had his own shotgun by sixteen; been using one since he was ten. They could drop a half-grown rabbit at a hundred yards. What else d'you think they lived on? Farm-labourers' wages? All the government had to do was issue shotgun cartridges containing one big solid shot, which would have blown a hole in Jerry big enough to put your hand through.

We had five gamekeepers in our lot; knew every spinney and gap in the hedge for miles. And twice as many poachers, fly enough to swipe the Lady Amherst pheasants off the terrace of Birleigh Manor, while his lordship sat there drinking afternoon tea. Brutal men, all of them. I've known some stagger home needing sixteen stitches in their head after some little encounter in the dark. They made peace while they were on Home Guard duty, and went back to their private war afterwards.

Yes, we did have a poet. Laurie Tomlinson. Professor somewhere now. But then he'd just got back from the Spanish Civil War. Showed us how to garrotte a man with a piece of piano wire so he died without a sigh. Showed the village blacksmith how to make a two-inch mortar from a yard of steel gas-piping. The army took those off us later, saying they were too dangerous to use. But they fired mortar-bombs all right; the ones Pincher Morton pinched from the Polish camp down the road.

And we never drilled in pinstripe suits or cricket shirts.

We never wasted time drilling at all. We went on patrol in the washed-out browns and greys that poachers wore, which blend with the woodland at five paces. Laurie taught us how to put boot-polish on our faces so that it didn't crack and drop off like mud. Our village poachers still use boot-polish . . .

And, poachers or not, they were all old *soldiers*. From the Last Lot. Hard-bodied farmhands of forty, who'd been snipers in the mud of the Somme, or bomb-throwers in the Ypres Salient. When we finally got our old Canadian rifles, dating from 1912, they nursed them like grim mothers. Very anxious to get their hands on the bayonets. First they sharpened them on their own whetstones, then they blackened them so no glint would give away their position.

All the young lads were mad to join. The veterans wouldn't have 'em. War wasn't for kids, they said. Forgetting they'd been little more than kids themselves in the Last Lot. We only ever had two young 'uns in our platoon. I was one.

I'd tried for a commission in our county regiment. Then for the RAF as anything. Even the navy, though I was seasick crossing to the Isle of Wight. But I had flat feet. When I put any weight on my feet, my toes pointed up in the air like ac-ac guns. Didn't count that I played rugger, and ran cross-country. I was *out*.

Went to see Major Newsam; asked if he'd pull a few strings for me with his old mates. He shook his head and told me the best thing I could do was to farm the land my father had left me as well as I damned well could. Damned U-boats would try to starve the country out, just like the Last Lot.

As a sop, he let me join his Home Guard. As second-in-command, with a pip on my shoulder.

'Old soldiers need someone to look up to,' he said. 'Someone to look after. Leave all the organizing to your platoon-sergeant. Never ask a man to do what you can't do yourself.'

It was a rule he kept himself, even though he'd lost half an arm in Iraq in 1924.

When they asked for Draggett's Mill as their HQ, I couldn't refuse. Right in the middle of my land; on the highest hill for miles, to make the best of the wind. But Draggett had been gone a long time, and the mill was just an empty stone shell, like a squat, blackened milk-bottle. They fitted it out with new floors and ladders, and with a parapet of sandbags and a corrugated iron roof, it made an ideal look-out for German paratroopers dropping in.

It was there, as we stood-to one lovely soft summer evening in 1940, that they dragged Zakky in. They'd caught him following them, and they thought he was a German spy. He'd put up a hell of a fight; three of them were bleeding. They'd had to knock him senseless with a rifle-butt. They poured water over him from our brew-up milk-churn, and he opened one swollen eye a green slit and said,

'*English!* If you had been Germans, I would have killed you all.'

'Nasty little sod, sir,' said Curly Millbank. 'He had this hidden under his shirt, at the back of his neck.' He passed me a simple flat knife, honed to a needle point.

'Give me my knife!' The thin wet figure on the floor came at me so fast he knocked me clean across the trestle table that served as our office. All knees and elbows he was, and they felt as sharp as needles too. It took four of them to drag him off me, and somebody else got bitten.

'Who are you?' I asked, when I'd got my breath back.

'I am *soldier.*' He drew himself up to his full five foot three. 'Zbigniew Zakrewski, Polish Army.' He gabbled some long number. 'They give me a number. They had no rifles.'

'I think I've seen him hanging round the Polish camp, sir,' said Pincher Morton. 'The soldiers feed him. But he's not one of them.'

Zakky pulled a horrible face. 'I go to them. Tell them how to kill Nazis. They make me peel spuds.' He spat on our highly polished floor. 'That is why I follow your men. I will show *you* how to kill Nazis.'

He drew his hand across his throat.

Major Newsam came in then, and took over. I was still feeling a bit shaken.

'Checked up on him with the Poles,' Newsam told me at stand-to next evening. 'He's Polish all right. Thirteen years old. Joined the Polish Army in their retreat last September. Never had a rifle, never had a uniform. Marched five days, then met the Russkis coming the other way. Got away when the rest surrendered. Seems to have sneaked out through the Balkans and stowed away on a ship from Piraeus. Lot of Poles came that way. The Polish Government in exile tried putting him in a children's home, but he just kept running away. Apparently he eats at the Polish camp and sleeps in the woods. Keeps trying to nick weapons from their armoury. They're terrified he'll end up doing somebody an injury. I mean, all the Poles are fighting-mad, but he's got even them scared *silly*. They asked if I could get somebody to adopt him . . .' He looked at me queryingly. 'Think your mother could take him on?'

Old Newsam was a bit sweet on my mother; thought she was wonder-woman.

I looked him straight in the eye. 'You'll have to bribe him. Let him join the Home Guard . . .'

He grinned and said, 'Pity about your flat feet, Keith. You wouldn't have made a bad officer, given time.'

So I drove him home in my old farm van, the scruffy little tick. He ponged out the van to high heaven. When we got home, I heard my mother playing the piano. Chopin. She used to work like hell all day: the farm, evacuees, WVS, the lot. But when she was finally done for the day, she still liked to get dressed up a bit, and have a drink, and light the tall thin brass candles that stood on the piano, and play Chopin. Said it convinced her there'd be a better world again, some day.

I was going to march straight in and interrupt her, because

I wanted to get back to the mill in case anything had happened while I'd been gone. But, in the half-open doorway, a small, steely hand caught my wrist. And Zakky just stood there till she had finished, the tears running down his cheek in the candle-light. It was the Chopin, I suppose.

When she had finished, and turned and smiled at us, he went straight up to her, clicked his heels together, and gave a funny little bow of his head. He was such an odd little scruff, I wondered how even a woman as wise as my mother would take it. But she took it all in her stride, shook him by the hand, and asked him if he'd care for a bath?

So I left her to get on with it. The next morning he came down to breakfast in one of my old grey school suits, white shirt and tie, long dark hair slicked down with tap water. Apparently she'd laid out the suit and shirt next to his pathetic rags on his bed, while he had a bath, and he'd chosen freely to wear them. Only he'd asked her to wash the rags for him, because they were Polish and precious. (And she spent hours mending them, as well.) And he'd showed her a solid gold locket, with a photo of a fierce, moustached military man on one side, and a rather lovely dark-haired woman on the other.

'My father. My mother.' He had clicked his heels again.

'Where are they now, Zakky?'

'Dead,' he said and took the locket back, and he never showed it to anybody else, ever. She said it was the only thing he had, except for the throwing knife that he still wore at the back of his neck, under the grey English suit.

I studied him over the bacon and eggs. I think his family must have been pretty well off, back in Poland, because he had exquisite table manners, only a little strange and foreign. And though he had the body of a half-starved kid, his face was . . . ageless. Beaky nose, strong Polish cheekbones and a strong Polish jawbone, the sort you never see in an Englishman. His eyes were deep-sunken. They were either blazing with excitement, or too sad to look at direct.

They only blazed when he talked about Poland; or killing Nazis. Or when he was talking direct to my mother. In his eyes, my mother could do no wrong. He always called her Madam Bosworth, whether she was there or not. I think he would have done anything for her, even died.

I think she could even have got him to go to our village school, when it reopened in September. But she hadn't the heart. She soon found he spoke excellent French, and they would prattle away for hours, faster than I could follow. She found he knew quite a lot of German too, but he would never speak it, even for her.

'German is language for pigs.' He also said 'Russian is language for pigs', so I suppose he had Russian as well. Neither of us could imagine him sitting at a desk among the village children.

Anyway, all his heart was set on killing Nazis. He was at the mill every spare hour. When he wasn't cleaning rifles (which he learnt quickly and did with incredible thoroughness), he was our look-out, following every vapour-trail in the sky, like a cat following the flight of birds. We found him some Home Guard overalls, nearly small enough. My mother took three inches off the leg. And we ordered him to stay at his post of duty on top of the mill, whatever happened. I think old Newsam was afraid of something nasty happening. It was the height of the Battle of Britain, and there were a lot of parachutes coming down during the daytime air-battles, and, thank God, the majority were Jerries. The farmhands of our platoon worked in the fields with their rifles at the ready. But any Jerries they rounded up, they always took straight down to the police-station in the next village. By tacit agreement, nobody ever brought a Jerry to the mill.

But Zakky certainly earned his keep. As he learnt to trust us, he would bring in the weapons from his hidden caches in the woods. Two Bren guns we returned to the Poles; Newsam gave their CO a right rocket about the security of their armoury. But the rifles we kept, and the Mills bombs and mortar-bombs. With Jerry waiting just across the Channel, we weren't inclined to be over-generous.

And at stand-to and stand-down, we would gather in amazement to hear his impromptu lectures on how to kill Nazis. He had some incredible idea about electrocuting tank-crews with the fallen electric cables from tram-cars, but as the nearest trams were fifty miles away, in Piccadilly Circus, that wasn't much good. But we liked his idea about stretching a steel cable between two tree-trunks, to decapitate Nazi despatch riders. And he showed us how to make a Molotov cocktail that really worked. And explained how to feed petrol-soaked blankets into the tracks of tanks, and how to leap on tanks from behind and block up their periscopes with a handful of mud. From the way he explained it, I thought he'd really done that. So did old Newsam.

Zakky was good for us. Half our men saw war as charging with fixed bayonets across the sea of mud and shell-holes that was no man's land. The other half saw it as slinking through the bushes, taking pot-shots at Jerries as if they were pheasants.

Zakky had seen tanks. In action.

But the men never loved him; he never belonged. He accepted being called 'Old Zakky' with good grace. But he would never laugh, never take part in their jokes and horseplay. Jokes were a serious waste of time. And he could never bear to be touched. Once Curly Millbank grabbed him from behind in fun and ended up on his back with a sprained wrist, which put him off work for a week.

Then came 'Cromwell'. The codeword for 'Invasion Imminent'. We shouldn't have been told, but Newsam had mates at Southern Command.

At stand-to, the men took it silently, very silently. Only Pincher Morton said, 'So it's come, then.' Some asked permission to go and say goodbye to their wives, but Newsam said no. He didn't want a panic like in France, with refugees blocking the roads. There was no argument; they were old soldiers. They got on with it.

We half blocked the London road, rolling out the great cylinders of concrete. Then all we had to do was wait, and inspect the passes of any car or lorry that passed. And watch from the top of the mill, for Jerry paratroopers landing.

I was up there with Newsam and Zakky. Below, the men who weren't manning the road-block were huddled round our transport: two private cars and a farmer's motorized haycart. The men were smoking, but cupping their hands round the glowing ends. The night was moonlit through wispy cloud. A good night for spotting parachutes. Behind our backs, London was burning again, a pulsating pink glow in the sky.

'Think we can hold them, sir?' I only said it for something to say. It felt like the start of a rugger-match against a big rugger school: not much hope of winning, but wanting to put up a good show.

'If the army can hold them on the beaches, I think we can mop up any paratroops.'

'If?' I squeaked. 'Montgomery's Third Division's down there.'

'They've got no heavy stuff; they had to leave all their heavy stuff behind at Dunkirk. Hardly an anti-tank gun to bless themselves with, poor bastards. Hardly a heavy machine-gun . . .'

'So what are *we* supposed to do?'

'I expect we'd last about five minutes against tanks. But some of the men should get away into the woods. After that, it's up to them. Might as well go back to their wives; sniping won't stop an armoured column . . .'

'Oh,' I said again. Was 'oh' all I could find to say? I nodded down towards the hands cupped round cigarettes. 'Do *they* know that?'

'They know. Sorry to be a pessimist, Keith, on your first show. But I don't want you having any illusions.'

'We will kill Nazis!' said Zakky harshly, from across the observation platform. 'We will kill *many* Nazis!'

We both jumped; I think we had forgotten he was there. He came across and glared at us. I could see, in the moonlight, that he was trembling. Not with fear, I think. More like a whippet just before you unleash it against a rabbit.

'Many, many Nazis,' he said again, then went back on watch, turning his back on us. As if in disgust.

'That boy worries me,' muttered Newsam. 'Keep a tight rein on him. He's going to kill somebody before the night's out, if we're not careful. I wish we could send him home. But he'll just bugger off into the woods. Best here, where we can keep an eye on him.'

The waiting was appalling. The night was so still, except for the odd rumble or series of sharp cracks, ghosting down the warm night wind from London. The countryside I loved lay on peacefully, under the dim moon. The black bulk of the church tower. Silver light gleaming on the huddled thatch of the village. The stooks of corn in my own top field, standing neat as guards on parade. We were too far west to be in the direct path of the Jerry bombers heading for London.

Then the phone rang. A man seen climbing through the window of Elm Cottage . . . Newsam shot off in his old Morris, four riflemen jammed in with him.

They were back in ten minutes. Newsam settled again, elbows on the sandbags of the parapet.

'Well?' I asked, after a long silence. I saw his shoulders heave, and thought for a wild second that he was crying. Then he said with a snort,

'Bobby Finlayson in bed with Len Taylor's missis. We dragged them both out mother-naked. There'll be hell to pay in the morning.' He couldn't stop laughing.

We were busy after that. Impounded a lorry of black market meat on its way up to London. Caught a vicar with six rover-scouts, all looking for a place to die for their country.

Two courting couples in lay-bys, tanks full of black-market petrol. One enterprising burglar, with a mixed bag of silver from Mottersdon Court.

'Had no idea there was so much night-life in the country!' snorted Newsam.

'English!' muttered Zakky darkly to himself. But all this dashing about did everyone a bit of good. It was better than hanging around. Every time they came back they were laughing over something.

And then, just before dawn, we had three phone-calls in rapid succession, and I was left alone on top of the mill with Zakky.

Why was it then that we heard the sound of planes above the hazy moonlit clouds? And saw two parachutes sloping gently down, towards the wooded crest of Burrow's Hill, across our little valley.

While I was still dithering with shock, Zakky said 'Nazis' and was gone down the top ladder.

I suppose I should've done something intelligent, like phone for help. But I couldn't think of who to phone. Perhaps I should have run to the men manning the roadblock, but they were a hundred yards away. So I stupidly left my post of duty and ran after him.

As I said before, I'd been a cross-country runner. But pound along in my hobnailed boots as I might, I couldn't catch up with Zakky. I had him in sight as far as the village, but in the cornfields beyond I lost him. I knew where the parachutes had fallen, roughly. I knew the short-cuts through the wood. But Zakky knew them even better than me . . .

Yet it seemed as though I had got to a parachute first. No sign of Zakky. The chute was caught up in a tree, like a great white rustling ghost. A dark figure dangled below, about four feet off the ground, helpless, silent. I ran up to it, pulling out my dad's old Webley revolver from its First World War leather holster. I didn't know what to expect. They told us that in Holland and Belgium the German paratroops came down disguised as policemen, vicars and nuns. But this one . . . as the body swung and turned in the breeze, I saw the round top of a flying helmet and the glint on goggles. The bulk of a sheepskin flying-jacket.

'Christ,' said the body suddenly, 'cut me down, for God's sake. This crotch-strap's nearly got me cut in half.' He did sound like he was in agony. And he had a very Welsh accent.

I got out my clasp-knife and climbed the tree and cut him down somehow. I suppose it never occurred to me that a Nazi might have a Welsh accent. Anyway, once he was free, he just fell in a heap on the ground.

The next thing he said was, 'You'd better go and find Stan – Stanislav – my gunner. His English isn't much cop – he's a Pole. I don't want some yokel lynching him for a Nazi.'

'Where'd he come down?'

'Over there, somewhere.' He pointed vaguely towards the edge of the wood.

I've never run so fast in all my life. But I was too late: I found Zakky crouching over a body.

'Is dead,' said Zakky, with a lot of satisfaction.

'He's one of ours,' I said numbly, staring down at the dim white face beneath the flying-helmet. 'He was called Stanislav. He was a Pole.'

There was a long and terrifying silence. It just went on and on and on. When I couldn't stand it any longer I said,

'There's another one down the hill. He's Welsh. I think they bailed out of their night-fighter. You'd better give me a hand getting him back to the mill.'

It helped, getting the pilot down off the hill. He was quite badly hurt, and we had to carry him between us, making a chair of our hands. It gave me something to do, instead of thinking about Zakky and the dead gunner. Then I had to get the ambulance out to us.

The Welshman asked about his gunner, and I told him the gunner was dead. He just closed his eyes and nodded: I suppose they were used to losing their mates. He was a Defiant pilot, and Defiants didn't have much luck in the Battle of Britain.

Then some daft bugger over Malbury way rang the church bells, meaning the Invasion had really started, and all hell broke loose, with civilians taking to the roads, trying to get away from the coast. And then suddenly it was dawn, and word slowly trickled through that bugger-all had happened anywhere, except an extra-big raid on London.

'Ah, well,' said Newsam, 'we live to fight again.'

'Nearly time to get the cows milked,' said Pincher Morton. 'No point goin' to bed now. Just makes you feel dopey.'

I drove Zakky home. Neither of us said a word. I didn't ask him how the gunner died; I couldn't bear to know. Maybe he just found him dead. I preferred to think that. Nothing I could do would bring the gunner back to life.

They came with a hearse and took the gunner's body away, later that morning. We never heard any more about it.

Then came October, with the equinoctial gales lashing up the Channel, and news that Hitler was dispersing his flat-bottomed barges at Boulogne. We were safe for the winter.

Newsam still drove us hard. He talked endlessly about *when* Hitler came in the spring. We trained more men; we were a full company now, four platoons and I was a platoon-commander. They built us pill-boxes of foot-thick concrete, and we trained with something called a Blacker Bombard that threw thermite-bombs at fake tanks made of corrugated iron which ran down a little railway outside Eastbourne. But somehow we couldn't *quite* believe in it; there was a feeling that Hitler had missed the boat.

All except Zakky, who grew grimmer than ever. He made this huge plywood cut-out of a Nazi storm-trooper, advancing with a hideous grimace and a sub-machine-gun. Spent hours throwing his knife at it. I'd never believed in throwing-knives, couldn't see how they could even go through the cloth of a uniform. They were something you saw in the movies.

But Zakky could throw from all angles and never missed, and I once tried levering his knife out of the thick plywood. It was embedded two inches, and I had a hell of a time getting it out. One or two of the platoon had narrow squeaks, coming across Zakky without warning when he was practising. It didn't make him any more loved. But he was something to talk about in the dull times, when we were out all night in the rain, and had nothing to show for it but the crew of some Jerry night-bomber, well soaked and ready to surrender for a mug of tea.

But we had to find him something to do, besides endlessly oiling rifles and throwing his knife at plywood. My mother got more and more worried about him. And the rabbits he brought back from the woods, always killed by his knife, did nothing to lessen her worries, though they helped out the rations.

Then came the blessed day that my new Fordson tractor broke down, only a week out of the factory. Furious, I rang Tom Hands the blacksmith, who fiddled with cars as a side-line.

That evening, when I got back from ploughing with our two old horses, the tractor was mended, and Tom and Zakky were in the kitchen with my mother, drinking tea from white enamel mugs, smirched with oily fingerprints. They were all as thick as thieves. Tom announced that Zakky had a gift with engines. My mother announced that Tom was taking on Zakky as an apprentice. As spring broadened into summer, Tom and Zakky became inseparable. Worn-out farm machinery kept breaking down all over the place; they never had an idle moment.

And then Hitler invaded Russia, and we knew the threat from across the Channel was gone. To celebrate, Pincher Morton bought himself a plot in the village churchyard. Said he felt happier, knowing where he was going to end up.

We all felt happier; except Zakky. The further away the threat of invasion got, the blacker he became. You could feel the pressure building up in him. He was always wanting to *wrestle* with me. I took him on once or twice, in fun. Going gently, not wanting to hurt him, for I was a big lad by then, nearly fourteen stone.

He had me on my face in about ten seconds; somebody had taught him unarmed combat along the way. He never hurt me, but it was bloody humiliating. In the end I refused to do it any more, so he began jumping out on me from dark corners. Said I had to learn, for when the Nazis came.

But it wasn't the Nazis who came; it was the Canadians, whole divisions of them, armed to the teeth with American tanks and guns and lorries.

We had to pretend to defend the villages, while the Canadians pretended to attack them. Quite realistic, it was. Blank ammunition, thunderflashes, wired explosions, smoke grenades. The trouble was, we were pretty good by then, and we knew the countryside. And they were so *green*; lousy soldiers who bunched up too close together, and stuck to the metalled roads. We ambushed and slaughtered them over and over again. Then they gave us fags and chewing-gum, grinning sheepishly. The battle-umpires kept running up and telling us *we* were dead, without giving any reasons. I don't think they wanted the Canadians to get too discouraged. Our old hands weren't too surprised when the Canadians finally got a bloody nose from real Germans, in the Dieppe Raid.

It was from one of these exercises that Zakky didn't come home. My mother and I were just setting out to look for him, in the van, when word came that Zakky was being held by the military. It seemed he had gone berserk and seriously injured a Canadian . . .

Major Newsam drove up to London, with my mother and the vicar. They must have talked bloody hard, because they brought Zakky back with them, paler and more silent, and blacker in his moods than ever.

Some weeks later, as we were getting ready for Christmas,

the japs attacked Pearl Harbor. In the New Year, we settled down to teaching the first American troops a thing or two.

All except Zakky.

The Americans were even more generous and clumsy than the Canadians had been. But, as Major Newsam said sadly, when we got our first issue of American tommy-guns, us Home Guard were all dressed up with nowhere to go. We were just actors now; the invasion threat had gone for ever. Still, we enjoyed the Camels and Hershey Bars.

Zakky was sixteen by then; as tall as he ever got, five feet seven. He shaved earlier than me, had a fine black moustache, whereas I could still get away with shaving twice a week. I suppose he was handsome in a thin, peaky, tragic sort of way. A lot of the local girls eyed him, even with the Americans about. Rosemary Thomas, whose dad ran the White Lion, especially, though she was older than he was. I suppose the girls sensed the darkness in him; wanted to rescue him from it. But he had little time for them . . .

He was well in with the local farmers too. A natural mechanic, which was quite something in those days when we had to hold tractors together with tin cans and wire. I know he brought my mother's car back from the grave more than once, though he always insisted afterwards that she crawl underneath it, to be shown exactly what he'd done. He'd still do anything for her.

He even talked German now. Because she'd hit on a way of holding him steady. Soon, she told him, a great army would be invading Europe to fight the Nazis. They would need people who could speak French and German fluently . . . I think Major Newsam had something to do with that. He and my mother were as thick as thieves by that time. But I wasn't jealous. It was just nice to see two people I liked being happy.

They got married after harvest. October 1943. The whole village nearly went mad over it. We'd had a lot of wartime weddings, with blokes going off to the war, and people thinking they wouldn't come back. Desperate weddings, a kind of laughter on the edge of the grave. But my mother's wedding was different. It was, in a way, the first of our post-war weddings. People knew *they* were going to stay around and be married for the rest of their natural lives. There was no desperation in the laughter. We held the reception in the village hall, and the whole neighbourhood made a festival of it. They were both pretty popular with the locals and everyone chipped in with the eats, so we had a good spread in spite of the rationing. I gave my mother away in church and made a speech afterwards, which got a lot of laughs. Major Newsam being older than me, and my commanding officer in the Home Guard, which gave me plenty of openings for funny cracks.

I still have a photo of Zakky taken at the reception. My mother had asked him to be a groomsman, and he looked very dashing in hired morning-dress, holding his glass and laughing. He was willing to be happy for my mother, when he would never be happy for himself. And behind him in the photo is Rosemary Thomas, looking at him as if she wanted to eat him. Even now, when I look at it, it makes me shudder.

That Christmas Zakky got his chance. Major Newsam took him up for an interview at the War Office, and apparently he chattered French and English and German and Polish like a bird, and they grabbed him like he was the best thing since sliced bread.

He came back for a fortnight's leave in May 1944, in the uniform of the Intelligence Corps. He was truly happy, I think, for that fortnight. Southern England was, by that time, as packed with allied soldiers as an egg is full of meat, and he knew at last he was going to have his feast of death. He wasn't even eighteen, but he'd have passed for twenty-five with his hair cropped.

We went for a last walk before he left. My bottom field was full of Shermans under camouflage, and the Yank tank-crews bivouacked. He was quickly among them, shaking hands and laughing and talking about killing Nazis. It was pretty crazy and pretty painful, because the Yanks kept looking at each other and tapping their heads with their fingers, once he'd passed. I was bloody terrified he'd see them, because the little bulge at the back of his battle-dress collar told me the deadly knife was still there.

Walking home, we met Rosemary Thomas in the lane outside our house. I think she'd come looking for him. They went off together, his arm around her waist, natural as any young couple, laughing.

But I shuddered. He could afford to laugh, because he was going to kill. He could afford to love, because he was going to die. He was like a dragonfly that only lives a few days of summer; a dragonfly that is a gaudy killer.

I thought of him on D-Day. D-Day was a strange time for us Home Guard. Endless streams of allied planes flying east, where once there had been endless streams of Germans flying west. Endless streams of American armour pouring through our village, where once we'd stood expecting streams of German panzers.

In one day we became pointless. No one left to fight; no one even left to train. Our hands full of the very latest, useless guns. Newsam told me an order was coming out, to disband us, with thanks. We'd never fired a shot in anger; only blanks at friends.

Still, there was the harvest to get in. The hay was early that year. And that night I first met Shirley Harris, as we gathered round the radio in the pub to listen to the news from Normandy.

He never wrote.

There was one snippet about him in the local paper.

BIRSBY MAN WINS MILITARY MEDAL.

Major Newsam tried to find out more from his mates at the War Office. He got very little, except that Zakky had been promoted to sergeant. And a hint of cloak-and-dagger. Raids behind enemy lines, co-operation with the French Maquis, throats cut and no questions asked. A very dirty war indeed.

'Not my kind of war,' said Newsam. 'Not my kind of war at all.'

And then, nothing. VE day passed with great rejoicing, our village green packed with trestle tables, hung with red, white and blue bunting left over from the Coronation, the Silver jubilee. Queen Victoria's birthday, for all I knew. We choked with the dust as we hung it up. A little band played for dancing, and women danced with women and children. Then VJ day, and the men began coming home, and still nothing. Six weeks later I married Shirley Harris. There was nothing to stop us. My mother had gone to live with the Major, in a country club he was trying to haul back to life further along the south coast.

And then, towards the back-end of 1945, I got home from a cattle auction, and Shirley met me in the yard and said,

'You've got a visitor.'

She looked scared to death, and she's not the nervous sort. So I went in feeling very proprietorial, and rather angry.

He was sitting at the kitchen table. Shirley had given him a cup of tea and a piece of home-made cake, as she did with everybody who called. He'd let the tea go cold, and rolled her good cake into tiny dark balls on the plate. Our kitchen was full of . . . the smell of him? The vibes of him? The only thing I can compare it to was the atmosphere at the funeral of a friend who had committed suicide. It was that black.

I made myself shake hands. His hand was very bony and cold. His hair was cropped like a convict's; you could see the white scalp showing through the black stubble. His flamboyant moustache was gone. So was any glint of life in his eyes; they were like two holes burnt in a grey blanket.

I said I was glad to see him, but I wasn't. I asked him whether he'd been demobbed. He said,

'They have stopped killing Nazis. Germany is full of Nazis but they are making them into burgomasters now. Because they are the only ones left who can run that country.' I noticed he was wearing one of those awful demob suits; it hung on him as it might have hung on a rail.

I tried to tell him about this and that; country gossip. But he cut me short, he didn't want to know.

I told myself he was still only a kid, not yet nineteen. But he wasn't. I even began to wish he had died, like the dragonfly, that gaudy killer. So that he didn't have to come back here and plague us. I began to worry he might ask after my mother . . .

In the end I said, straight out,

'What can I do for you, Zakky?'

'I wish to rent the mill. I will pay you fair rent.'

Should I have said no? So he might have drifted off and plagued somebody else? But all I wanted was him out of my kitchen, and the mill seemed a cheap price to pay. It still had its floors and roof, as the Home Guard had left it. I had no use for it.

We agreed a rent. I wasn't such a fool as to offer it to him for nothing, but I threw in some old furniture. Anything to get him out of my kitchen. He was death, walking. They had glutted him with killing, then turned him loose on a world at peace.

And yet, it might still have worked for him. Lost in the world as he was, the mill became his fortress, the one place where his life had meaning. He kept it spotless, I was told. He even filled the little walled enclosure full of flowers. Only all the colours were those of the old Polish flag. A Polish flag now flew from the little flagpole we'd left on the roof. Inside, there was another Polish flag, draped round a photograph of the late General Sikorski. And there was a large radio, permanently tuned to Radio Warsaw.

But Poland was Communist now; full of Russians talking the language of pigs. We all knew he could never go home.

He scratched a living, mending machinery. Tom Hands offered him a partnership, but he refused. You never saw him talking to anybody round the village. But when he met any member of the old Home Guard, he would give a curt, abrupt nod of the head.

Only Rosemary Thomas did not despair. She beat against the walls of that mill, like a moth beating against a lamp. But, it seemed, in vain.

Yet she found fresh-killed rabbits on the pub doorstep some mornings. Killed by a knife-throw.

And then PC Morris from the next village came to see me. He'd heard rumours that Zakky had guns hung on the wall. Not shotguns, either. Guns from the war, people said . . .

I told him it was rubbish. They *must* be shotguns. I said I would be responsible for Zakky; see he didn't cause any trouble. Frankly, I told him anything I could think of, to get him to go away.

To tell the truth, I feared for his life, if he tried to interfere.

And then, God help us, came the start of the post-war housing boom. Homes fit for heroes. Town vied with town. And our blessed district council decided to double the size of our village. On my land. By compulsory purchase order.

Mind you, they offered a fair price, and I had my eye on a bigger farm. I had no cause to grumble.

Till I heard the mill had to go, too.

I *pleaded* with the clerk to the council. I spent four hours trying to explain about Zakky. Didn't make a ha'p'orth of difference. Even ex-servicemen with valiant war-records must learn to make way for progress. Why, this whole scheme was *designed* for ex-servicemen. Mr Zakrewski might apply for one of the houses, if he was a married man with at least two children. But if he insisted on being awkward, that was surely a matter for the police . . .

Truly, I felt the ground open up beneath me.

I was still moving in that dark nightmare the following morning when I drove my tractor on to a too-steep bit of hillside, and it turned over on me. I was in a coma for six weeks, and my life was despaired of.

The morning Shirley finally drove me home from hospital, we came in on the road past Draggett's Mill.

It was gone; flat. All around, workmen were digging foundations for houses.

'Zakky . . .' I said. Full of dread, loss, a terrible feeling of letting people down.

'Gone,' said Shirley. 'Safe gone.'

'HOW?'

'Birsby Home Guard's last and best manoeuvre . . .'

'What *sort* of manoeuvre?'

'Old Comrades' Reunion. At Rosemary's pub. Zakky was formally requested to attend, or his old comrades would be *deeply* insulted. Given that Polish sense of honour, could Zakky refuse? Just for half an hour of course . . .'

'And then . . . ?'

'Well, people began to drink toasts, with vodka bought off a Polish ship in Southampton. Oh, so *many* toasts. The late General Sikorski, and every member of his late government. Major Newsam had all their names off by heart, and nearly cracked his jaw pronouncing them. Zakky kept correcting him. Then Mr Churchill, President Roosevelt, President Truman, Chang Kai-shek, General de Gaulle, the RAF, the Home Guard, the Royal Navy. You name it, we had it. And Zakky couldn't refuse to drink to a single one, could he? On his Polish honour. And he was drinking neat vodka, and the rest were drinking vodka and water. Half the pub's glasses ended up smashed at the back of the pub fireplace. And every time a vodka glass was smashed, the flames would leap up nearly to the pub ceiling. A right little fire risk. Zakky loved every moment of it. Till he passed out cold.'

'Then?'

'Well, they had to carry him home to the mill, didn't they? And they took the rest of the vodka with them. And he'd left a fire burning at the mill. And . . . or so they said . . . they started drinking again, and smashing more glasses in the fireplace in true Polish fashion, and a full bottle of vodka somehow got broken in the fireplace, and . . . well, the whole mill went up in flames, and they only just got Zakky out in time. The mill was alight from top to bottom by the time the fire brigade got there. Weapons, bullets, hand-grenades, the lot went up. Quite a little fireworks display. There wasn't a lot left of the mill by the time they were finished. Even the stone walls fell in.'

'How did Zakky take it?'

'Well, they'd carried him back to the pub, overnight. And Rosemary was fluttering about him, tending to his hangover. And they all looked very sheepish, and told him what they'd done, and how sorry they were. And that they felt honour-bound to make amends for his loss.

And he could hardly blame them for going on in such a Polish way could he? Nor refuse their honourable desire to make amends. He went off with five hundred quid in his pocket. I think Major Newsam gave half . . .'

'What good is *money* to him?' I asked desperately.

'Oh, I wouldn't worry too much about him. Rosemary went with him.'

'Where, for God's sake?'

'Marbury, in Cheshire, according to Rosemary's letters. Hundreds of ex-Polish army up there. Starting to marry local girls, thinking of building their own church. She still has hopes he'll do the honourable thing, and marry her. Of course, she had a hand in the whole thing from the start . . .'

'*Women,*' I said.

'Women,' she agreed, smiling. 'What would you all do without us? Welcome home, Keith.'

THE MAKING OF ME

You see the state I'm in now, as I sit here.

Do not blame me. My grandfather made me what I am.

With one blow. In one minute.

I had a happy childhood, except for one thing. I hated being 'left with' people, when my parents went off somewhere. You could never tell what people would *do* with you, once your parents had gone.

Like my holy aunt, for instance. No sooner had my parents waved goodbye than one of her holy friends would turn up, hold my head between her hands, look deep into my eyes and ask if I said my prayers and hoped to go to heaven? I mean, what do you *say?*

Other times my aunt, who was Sally Army, would take me off round the streets, marching with the band. I quite liked the band, though I hated the way people stared at us. Especially when we stopped on some wet and windy corner and the Major began shouting wildly about Jesus Christ and Salvation, to the two men and a dog who'd stopped to listen.

He lisped. He kept asking people if they were 'thaved' or were still wallowing in their 'thins'. Some of my mates from school saw me standing next to him once, and I was regularly asked in the playground if I'd been 'thaved' from my 'thins'. For a whole three years, till I went to grammar school.

My unholy aunt wasn't so bad. She might condemn God non-stop, for letting little children die of diphtheria or for sinking ships in storms, but at least she stayed home to do it, with nobody to hear but me. And she kept very good chocolate biscuits.

The person I really dreaded being left with, though, was my grandfather. He was not a *person*, like my mum and dad, or my little round laughing nana. He towered above me, six feet tall. I would sometimes glance up at him, as one might peer up in awe at a mountainous crag. The huge nose, the drooping moustache, the drooping mass of wrinkles. Then his eyes would peer down at me, too small, too close together, pale blue, wild and empty of everything but an everlasting, baffled rage. And my own eyes would scurry for cover, like a scared rabbit. He never spoke to me, and I never spoke to him, and thank God my parents never forced me to, as they would force me sometimes to kiss hairy-chinned old ladies.

There were old tales of his violence. How when his second child was born dead, he ripped the gas-cooker from the wall and threw it downstairs (and gas-cookers were solid cast-iron then, and weighed a ton). How when he came home drunk on a Saturday night, Nana and my eleven-year-old father would hear his step and run to hide in the outside wash-house, till he fell into a drunken sleep before the fire. And then Nana would stealthily rifle his pockets for the remains of his week's wages, and go straight and buy the week's shopping before he woke. And when he woke, he would think he'd lost all his money in his drunken stupor.

But the Great War had done for him. Unlike anybody else I knew, he had a Chest, because he'd been gassed in the trenches. His Chest made a fascinating symphony of noises at the best of times. So I would listen to it, rather than the chat round the meal-table. But when he was upstairs in bed, bad with his Chest, the whole house was silent and doom-laden, and my parents tiptoed about and talked in whispers.

He was also shell-shocked. Nana always had to be careful with the big black kettle she kept simmering on the hob to make a cup of tea. If it was allowed to boil, the lid would begin to rattle, making exactly the same noise as a distant machine-gun. And that would be enough to send him off into one of his 'dos', when he would imagine he was back in the hell of the trenches and would shout despairing orders, and I would be sent out for a walk till one of his powders settled him.

They said he had killed an Austrian soldier in a bayonet fight and taken his cap-badge. I was sometimes allowed to handle the strange square badge, to keep me quiet. It had a picture in brass of charging infantrymen, and strange, eastern, Hungarian writing. When Granda was *really* bad, he thought the dead Austrian had come back for his badge.

And, above all, he still drank. Perhaps to drown the memories he never spoke of. Oh, the silent agony of waiting to eat Sunday lunch, because of him, at our house; my mother fretting and the painful smell of good roast beef being singed to a crisp in the oven. Every ear cocked for his wavering footsteps. The strange bits of French songs or German marches that he would hum while he pushed his food unwanted round his plate.

Afterwards he would fall asleep with his mouth open. There was never any blackness for me like the blackness of the inside of his mouth.

But, while my parents were there, and the Nana I loved, he was just a fascinating monster, a fabulous beast. Safe to watch, like a tiger in a cage.

But being left alone with him . . .

A dreadful silence always fell. Perhaps he thought he had nothing in his mind fit for a child's ears. And my childish prattle, which so made the other grown-ups laugh, just got on his shell-shocked nerves.

Once, without warning, he clouted me across the ear. I think I wasn't so much hurt as *outraged*. Nobody had ever hit me, except my father twice, and that after plenty of warnings. The unfairness of it made the world reel about me. He told my father, afterwards, that I turned to him with tears in my eyes and said,

'Why did you hit me, grandfather?'

It sounds like something out of a Victorian novelette. But it must have cut him to his shell-shocked heart. When my parents returned they found me barricaded safely inside the outside loo, and him rocking with his head in his hands, full of agonized remorse that he had hit that innocent bairn. And vowing never to do it again till the day he died, or might his hand wither and drop off.

The innocent bairn wasn't slow to make the most of such an opening. Next time I was left with him, I found him still silent, but strangely obedient. I soon grasped he would do anything I wanted, just to keep me happy.

To be honest, I don't think I meant to be cruel: I wasn't a cruel child. But I had suffered a kind of personal earthquake at his hands, and I was very keen to prove his present mood would last, and the earthquake wouldn't happen again.

And I had a hopeless yearning to imitate my father, who was the engineer at the gasworks, and to me, a great wizard who dwelt among roaring furnaces and stamping carthorses, among great heaps of smoking slag and clouds of green gas, and who could start great steel dinosaurs of engines with one push of his small shoulder to an eight foot flywheel.

I wanted to make a *machine*. A machine of brass and steel that swung rhythmically and jangled loudly, and flashed with steel and brass.

I asked Granda to get Nana's washing-line.

He did.

I asked that he string it round the room from the hook on the kitchen door where her apron hung, to the rail above the kitchen range where she dried her tea-towels; from the handle of the cupboard to the hooks on the Welsh dresser. When it was firmly secured, we proceeded to hang from it every pot, pan, ladle and spoon in her well-stocked kitchen.

I pulled on the line. Everything swung, danced, jangled with the most satisfying cacophony. It was like entering into a new world.

Two hours later they found me still happily pulling and clanging, with my grandfather cowering in the depths of his chair with his hands pressed over his shell-shocked ears.

He had kept his word; he had not laid a hand on the innocent bairn. I don't know why he didn't strangle me; it must have been a close-run thing. Even I was scared at what I'd done – afterwards. When I saw the look on my father's face.

And then my unholy aunt fell ill, and was rushed to hospital and not expected to live. Suddenly the family were going to see her every night, and my mother thought that hospital was no place to take a child. From now on I was going to be left with my grandfather not once a month, but every night. A terrifying desert of silence and strangeness stretched before me. If I'd had any pity to spare from myself, I might have pitied Granda. But I was just plain terrified. What were we going to *say*? What were we going to *do* in that desert of time? I went, that first evening, thinking the end of the world, so often foretold by my holy aunt, was upon me.

I settled myself in the deepest chair, behind a mass of old comics I'd read ten times already. But the *Wizard* (and the famous Wilson, who had run the three-minute mile at the Berlin Olympics when he was a hundred and twenty years old, because he lived on rare herbs) had no charms that night.

I furtively eyed my strange sighing Beast as his Chest made its odd symphony of noises, and the terrifying sweet smell of sick old man came through the air to my cringing nostrils. I did not want to breathe the air he breathed. As my mother might have said about something I'd picked up in the street, I did not know where that air might have been. It might still have had bits in it from the trenches of the Great War, where dead men hung rotting on the barbed wire. Particles of poison gas; or the dying breath breathed out by the dead Austrian . . .

In the soft glow of the gas-mantle, his face was all wrinkled and shadowed pits, mysterious as craters of the moon. He was fiddling with the tap of the gas-light, fixing a little bit of wire round it. Perhaps it was his way of keeping me at bay, as my comics were my way of keeping him at bay.

He had dragged out of some cupboard a large old stained tea-chest. It was full of strange shapes, trapped in tangled coils of wire. The strange shapes drew me irresistibly; perhaps I had some wild hope of building another jangle-machine. I put a tentative hand inside. There was the most huge rusty hammer I'd ever seen . . . a long weird knife in a scabbard. I tugged at the knife; it resisted. I tugged harder . . . then harder. It leapt out of my hand, dragging behind it, in a web of tangled wire, a queerly shaped, huge brass tap, and a short brass cylinder. They all fell on the floor with a terrible bang. He swung round, ever-jumpy . . .

I gabbled out, before he could hit me,

'What's that funny tap, Granda?'

He picked up the tap, as if he hadn't seen it in a long time.

'By,' he said dreamily, 'that's a spare tap left over from the old *Mauretania*. Finest and fastest ship in the world, she was. Held the Blue Riband of the Atlantic for twenty years. The day she was launched – she had no funnels or nothing, mind – the shipyard workers got up steam in a little donkey-boiler in the bows. The old Morrie was the only liner ever launched wi' steam up. And when she sailed on her maiden voyage, people lined the banks of the Tyne for eight miles to bid her Godspeed. As if the King was passin' . . . and when she came home from her last voyage, to be broken up to make razor blades, the people lined up again to say goodbye to her. Look, here's the pictures.' And there, on the wall, were two photographs of the old Morrie sailing and the old Morrie coming home. And she looked the same in both.

'Why did they break her up? She looks as good as new.'

'Aye, but she was tired *inside*,' he said. 'Things look the same, but they get tired inside.' There was something in his voice I couldn't face. So I held up the short brass cylinder before the silence came back like the frozen Arctic.

'That's the lens of the film-projector that showed the first movie ever shown in North Shields. The show was held in the Temperance Hall, and it cost a penny to get in. Fatty Arbuckle was the star – he got sent to prison in the end. We saw Charlie Chaplin through that. Rudolph Valentino. No talkies of course – just a lady playing the piano for the exciting bits.'

'How did you get it?'

'George Costigan gave it to me in Guthrie's Bar, the night the old King died . . .'

'And what's this?' I held up a worn long block of rubber.

'That's the brake-block off me old bike – the one I used to ride round Holywell Dene, when I was courting your nana. I was taking that brake-block off, the night your dad was born . . .' A new kind of awe swept over me. My mother had often talked about the night *I* was born (and what a hard time I'd given her, and how she'd almost died of me), and that was mysterious enough. But the night my *dad* was born . . . that was as incredibly far off as the Pharaohs building the pyramids.

We were off in style now. Every object told a story. The dead rose up and walked again. Admiral Jellicoe and Earl Kitchener of Khartoum. Kaiser Bill and Marie Lloyd. Lloyd George and Jack the Ripper. They streamed out of my grandfather as they might have streamed out of the first cinema-projector to show a film in North Shields.

Only once was he silent. About the long knife in the scabbard. He took it in his hand and was silent, then he put it back in the box. I knew it was the bayonet that had killed the Austrian, for his face went grey, and his eyes were far away. I knew he hated it. I also knew he would never throw it away. Just like the cap-badge.

'What did you do in the trenches – in between?' I asked.

'I'll tell yer.' He pulled out a steel helmet, thick with rust. 'See that little hole in the top?'

'Is it a bullet-hole?'

He actually laughed. 'No, no. It's a screw-hole. We used to pull the screw out and stick a nail through the hole, and stick a candle on the nail. So we could see to play cards. Look – you can still see a bit o' candle-grease. I was good at cards – three-card brag, a quick game – it didn't matter if you were interrupted, like. I won a lot o' money. Lot o' fellers still owe me money, but they're dead. So I took a little thing from their kit, instead. To remember them by. See . . .' He reached up and took down his shaving-tackle from above the sink.

'That's Gerry Henry's shaving brush, and Mannie Webber's bowl, and Tommy Malbon's mirror . . . Good chums, every one.'

Now we were both silent, and it was all right. For I knew who was in the silence now. The good chums, every one.

It was Granda who broke the silence. 'There was a joke as we used to have, us Shields lads out there:

The boy stood on the burning deck,
His feet were full o' blisters.
His father stood in Guthrie's Bar
Wi' the beer running down his whiskers.

We always said that, when we were down. It always got a laugh.'

He laughed. I laughed. It seemed good to laugh with good chums.

When my parents got back from the hospital, it was over for that night. I was reverently arranging objects in sections and patterns across the clippie rug, and Granda was peacefully snoring in his chair.

But he'd done enough. Taught me that every object tells a story, and every dent in every object tells a story. Within a week I was pressing my nose against the window of every junk-shop in town. Regarding the scruffy little men who stood inside, rubbing their hands together against the cold, as the Lords of Time who knew all mysteries.

After that, museums. Like the museum I sit in now.

Then, it was a dent in a tap made thirty years ago. Now it is a dent in a Pharaoh's head made four thousand years ago. All part of my journey back in time. The world goes forward to drugs and violence and fruit-machine addiction. I go backwards, to where I am truly free.

My grandfather, long gone where old soldiers go, still accompanies me. His photograph is on my desk as I write; his photo before the gas got him, on the Somme. When my nana married him, she said he was the handsomest feller in Shields, with his bonnie blue eyes . . . He is much younger in his photo than I am now.

Each year I look more like him, as I remember him: the incredibly bushy eyebrows: the hairs that persist in growing on the end of my nose. When I laugh, I hear the echo of his laugh. Sometimes I hear myself wheezing in the mornings, though I was never gassed at the Battle of the Somme.

Time moves; in all directions. My grandfather made me.

THE CHRISTMAS CAT

I

A Cold Welcome

Granddaughter, I was once as young as you. My legs were as long and thin and could run as fast. I could climb a wall better than any boy, even when there was broken glass on top. And my glory was my red hair, so long that I could sit on it.

That was the year 1934, my parents were abroad, and I spent Christmas with my Uncle Simon. My Uncle Simon was an Anglican priest. A vicar. Vicars then were not like vicars now. If you know any vicar now, he is probably a young man who dresses in ordinary clothes, and tries to make friends with everyone, even if he has a rather desperate smile and a rather uneasy laugh. Vicars are a threatened species now, and they know it. Soon there may be hardly any vicars left, and some will be young women.

But vicars then . . . they had the *Power*. They dressed all in black, and people were rather afraid of them. I have seen a vicar empty a railroad carriage, just by sitting in it. Just being there, they made people, ordinary people, mums and dads, aware of their Sins. They made them feel feeble and wicked and helpless. So people avoided them if they could.

I did not want to go to the vicarage for Christmas. I would rather have stayed on at school, with the headmistress, who was a good sort. But my father had written: "You must go and stay with Uncle Simon. He has asked for you. Perhaps you will be able to cheer him up.'

I had doubts about cheering myself up. Uncle Simon had

no wife and no children. The family said he had given himself to God. God did not seem to have made a good job of cheering Uncle Simon up. Uncle Simon always sent dark small miserable Christmas cards, with Holy People on them, that wished you a 'Blessed and Peaceful Christmastide.' I much preferred Santa, grinning with a sackful of presents.

Still, off I had to go, with my whole school trunk, and a purseful of silver sixpences, to tip the railroad porters.

All I knew about North Shields, when I arrived that Sunday, was that the people there made their living from fish, and I would have guessed as much as soon as I put my head out of the railroad carriage. There was a mountain of kipper boxes on the platform, and the smell of kippers would have knocked me flat if the smell from a mountain of dried-cod boxes had not pushed me the other way. Outside, the cobbles of the taxi stand were stuck all over with tiny silver scales, and the air was thick with the smell of fresh fish, frying fish, rotting fish, boiling fish, and guano. Sea gulls sat on every rooftop, nearly as big and arrogant as geese, and splattered the slates with their white droppings and filled the air with their raucous cries.

When I gave the taximan the address of the vicarage, he stopped being jolly and friendly, and went all quiet, as if I, too, was dressed all in black and had a huge Bible in my hand. We drove through the town. Every street end gave us a view of the river Tyne with its mass of moored boats. The men and women looked strange to my southern eye; the men in huge caps and mufflers, the women in black shawls. There were shops, but most people seemed to be buying stuff off little flat barrows. There were no cars and lorries, but a lot of horses and carts, and the cobbled streets were thick with flattened masses of horse-dung, looking a bit like big round doormats.

'Here's the vicarage, hinny,' said the taxi-man, pulling up with a squeak and a jerk. I saw a great high, black brick wall, with broken glass set on top in concrete. Tall, shut green gates. And dark trees, massing their dull green heads over the wall, like a curious crowd.

'That's a shilling, hinny,' said the taxi-man, putting my trunk on to the pavement. Then he added, doubtfully, 'I hope you'll be all right,' and drove rapidly away.

I stared at the wall and gate aghast. It looked like the wall and gate of a prison, or at least a home for naughty children. The gate looked as if it was locked; but I managed to wrestle it open, and saw a short weedy drive leading up to a house that might have been pretty, except that the smoke and soot of the town had painted it black, too. I dragged my school trunk inside, and closed the gate and went and knocked on the door of the house. The knocker gave a terrible boom that seemed to echo in every room inside. It seemed to make a noise that was far too important for *me*.

At last the door opened. The woman who opened it didn't see me at first; she was looking over my head. Then she looked down and saw me and said, 'The vicar's out.'

'But—' I said.

'But nothing. The vicar's out. He's down at the church if you want him. Saying Evensong. I've nothing for you here.'

'But . . .' I said again.

She'd closed the door in my face.

By this time I was close to tears, but I'd long since learned that tears don't get you anywhere. So I sniffed them back, and went to look for the church.

There were plenty of people around, but I didn't know who to ask. They were such a strange crew: blacks and Chinese with pigtails, even the men. Groups who looked like East Indians, only they wore rags around their necks and suits of thin blue washed-out cotton, and talked at a great rate in their own language. Men who might have been Spaniards, with gold earrings and thin mustaches and flashing smiles; and men who might have been Germans, with cropped hair, and a stolid unsmiling way of stumping along. Even the women talked in a strange accent, though you could pick out the odd English word.

Then I saw this ordinary man ambling toward me. He

seemed to be slightly ill, for he swayed as he walked, and wobbled across the sidewalk, several times nearly falling into the gutter. But he had a nice face, and was smiling to himself. An unbuttoned sort of man; an unbuttoned overcoat over an unbuttoned coat, over an unbuttoned vest.

'Please could you tell me the way to the church?'

He looked at me like a wise owl, and the smell of his breath was worse than the fish. Whiskey. I always hated the smell of whiskey. My father sometimes drank it, in the evenings, and I would not kiss him then.

'Aye,' he said, 'but which church? Are you a damned Papist, or a damned Nonconformist, or a True Believer?'

'Sir,' I said, looking him straight in the eye, so that I made him sway a good deal more, 'I am a True Believer!'

'God bless you, honey,' he said, tears springing into his watery blue eyes. 'I'm a Sinner, a Terrible Sinner. It's the drink, you see. I drink and then I do terrible wicked things . . .'

'The church,' I said, as firmly as possible.

'I'll show ye.' And the next second he had enclosed my hand in his huge warm dry one, and was leading me a staggering dance along the sidewalk, still telling me of his wicked sins, though not in any detail, which might have been interesting . . .

'There's the True Church,' he said at last, pointing. And I had no doubt it was. For it was as black as coal, and the door was barred by huge rusty iron railings, and a black notice board announced Uncle Simon's name in small gold Gothic letters.

I thanked him; but he would not let go of me; he kept on going on about his sins. At last I had a brainwave.

'Come and see the vicar. He's inside. He's my uncle. He'll help you with your sins.'

'God forbid,' said the man fervently. 'My sins are too black for any vicar to help.' And then he was gone.

The rusty gate was not so fortress-like as it looked. It opened under my hand. So did the great studded door. I was in dimness, with the saints staring down at me, all purple and red and blue, from out of their stained-glass windows. There was a smell of polish and incense and dust and mice.

And the sound of my uncle singing. He had a very beautiful voice; his voice was the only beautiful part of him. He was singing half the service, and a cracked old voice was singing the other half.

'O Lord, open thou our lips.'

'And our mouths shall show forth thy praise.'

'O God, make speed to save us.'

'O Lord, make haste to help us.'

I sat, and listened to the end. I listened to that lovely voice preach about the feeding of the Five Thousand with the loaves and fishes. He preached very well.

The only thing was that apart from me and the old lady at the organ, the huge church was completely empty.

'You walked down here by *yourself?*' said my uncle. 'You must never do that again. I cannot imagine what Mrs Brindley was thinking of, letting you come down here by *yourself.*'

He did not look at me. He looked at his pulpit, at the board that gave the numbers of the hymns, at the saints in the stained-glass windows. Never at me. Not all the time I stayed with him. I got the feeling, in the end, that I was accompanied by an invisible person, two feet to my left, that my uncle talked to all the time.

'Why not?' I asked, greatly daring.

'Child! This town is filled with such wickedness that your poor young mind could not contain it. You cannot breathe the air of these streets without being defiled. Such *sins* . . .'

But he didn't go into any detail, which might have been interesting. Just like the poor whiskey man . . . My mind went over the wickedest things I knew. Which were not very wicked in those days, granddaughter. I have learned a lot since.

'We must rescue your trunk. Before they steal it.' That at least made sense. We'd had thieves at school.

Together we hurried up the road. A way cleared before us, through the milling crowd, as if by magic. A lot of people actually crossed the road to avoid us.

My uncle seemed surprised to find my trunk still lying where I had left it. He picked it up with a grunt that made me worry for him. He was older, much older, than my father. He had silver hair; and an old cracked broad leather belt, around his long black cassock, that strained at the last hole. Tall and portly, my uncle was.

Mrs Brindley opened the door to his knock, undoing both the top and bottom bolts with a rusty squawk.

'Oh, it's you, Vicar! Is this young woman pestering you?'

'Of-course-not,' gasped my uncle, lifting my trunk again. 'She-is-my-niece-my-brother's-daughter-that-I-told-you-of.'

'Oh.' Mrs Brindley looked at me; for the first time, really. There was a certain amount of curiosity mixed with her hostility.

'Well, I only hope she's not too much for you, Vicar. You've got so much to do, and so have I.'

Such was my welcome at the vicarage.

2

A Pinecone in the Ear

I spent three days of sheer misery. It was not that my Uncle Simon was at all a cruel man. He simply forgot I existed, unless I reminded him, and then he did not know what to say to me, and there were long terrible silences, especially at mealtimes.

I certainly wasn't starved. Meals were the one way Mrs Brindley spoiled him, and he ate a lot, and I ate a lot, too. It helped to fill up the silences at mealtimes. Real heavy stodge it was; worse than school.

But I was so *cold*. The vicarage was huge; like a great polished refrigerator of dark wood. My uncle had a fire in his study during the day; but I was forbidden to go there, in case I disturbed his reading. The only other warm room in the house was the kitchen, and that was Mrs Brindley's lair, and she hated me. She thought she owned my uncle, and I think she saw me as a rival.

I couldn't even stay in bed to keep warm; I tried that once, and Mrs Brindley soon rooted me out. Staying in bed during the day was sinful, and she had a terrible nose for sinfulness, like a bloodhound.

No, I must go out and play. Only when I went outside could I wear my coat and beret and scarf and gloves. Wearing them indoors was also sinful for some reason.

So I went out. Not, of course, out of the green gate into the sinful town. I soon learned that Mrs Brindley kept a keen eye on the gate; I was even accused of going too near it, of *thinking* about going through it. No, I was confined to an acre of woodland, inside the high wall.

Woodland? It was ornamental trees of the darkest, most hideous sort. Pines and firs and monkey puzzle trees and holly bushes grown fifteen feet high, with nothing but pine needles in between. And wretched dark rhododendrons. It couldn't even boast a bird, let alone a squirrel.

There were the old stables; they gave me a happy hour, exploring, for they had only just been abandoned. Harness still hung in the harness room; there was still straw and hay in the stalls, and even a pony cart with its spokes loose with damp and its tires red with rust. I thought of lighting a fire in the little grate in the harness room; but I knew Mrs Brindley would soon spot the smoke from the chimney.

Yet it was there that I made my first friend. An old black-and-white cat with long thin legs and a bulging belly. She was terrified of me at first; but I had patience, and all the time in the world. And she was hungry, so hungry, and I got into the habit of smuggling an old cloth pouch into the dining room, in the pocket of my sweater, and popping tidbits from my plate into it. My uncle never noticed; most of the time he was lost in his book at table, though my parents had always said reading at table was very rude. But I had to be careful when Mrs Brindley was about. Still, it was my first defiance, and my first victory.

My second victory started like a defeat. I was wandering aimlessly through the wood, by the high wall at the back, when a pinecone hit me sharply on the nose. It really stung; my eyes filled with tears. When I had wiped them, I stared around, but there was nobody about. I thought perhaps the pinecone had fallen off a tree; but as I was thinking that, another hit me on the ear.

I whirled around; no way had that one fallen off a tree. Again, there was no one to be seen. But I noticed a place where a dense holly tree grew up against the wall. It was the only spot in that dreary place where anyone could hide. I went on as if aimlessly wandering; but now I picked up the odd pinecone as I went, choosing the wettest and heaviest ones and pretending to examine them with interest.

When I had about ten in the pocket of my coat, I heard a third missile land in the pine needles behind me. I spun quick as a flash, and saw the holly tree move, and threw my heaviest cone as hard as I could. Then another, and another. I was no mean shot at throwing a cricket ball, and now I could see a vague shadow through the dense leaves. My fourth pinecone hit the shadow. The shadow said 'Ow' in a loud voice.

My fifth cone hit as well; and my seventh. There was a frantic scraping of feet on the wall top; then a smashing and crashing that carried on all down the tree. Something hunched up landed at the bottom, on the dead dry holly leaves.

It was a boy, about eleven, my own age. He hugged himself and glared up at me.

'You silly tart! You've broke my leg.'

'You started it!'

'I didn't break *your* leg.'

'Let's have a look at it.' I started forward, a bit worried.

'Get off me.' He jumped up so quickly I knew his leg wasn't broken, though he was limping quite badly. He walked up and down, like a soccer player who's been hurt, trying to walk the pain away.

'I can't climb the wall like this,' he stormed.

'Then you can go out of the gate . . .' I was glad he wasn't badly hurt.

A look of terror came across his face. 'The vicar will catch me. He'll fetch the police to me. For trespassin'.'

'I'll say you're with me.'

'You're trespassin' an' all.'

'No, I'm not. I'm the vicar's niece.'

He eyed me with fresh horror, and turned and made a frantic attempt to climb up between the tree and the wall. But three feet up he stopped, grimacing with pain.

'I'll give you a leg up if you like,' I said. And went and pushed up on his bottom until, with a terrible struggle, he made the top of the wall. 'Can you manage now?'

'I can drop down. I can crawl home. You can crawl even with a broken leg,' he said bitterly.

Suddenly I didn't want him to go. So, greatly daring, I said, 'I'm not Frankenstein's monster, you know.'

'No,' he said. 'You just look like him.'

I got one of my last pinecones out of my pocket . . .

'O.K.,' he said, putting his hands in the air, like somebody in a cowboy movie. 'I surrender.' He grinned. He had rather a nice grin. It went with his snub nose. And his blue eyes were suddenly merry. 'You're not Frankenstein's monster. He wouldn't dare push a boy up the bum.'

'I'll come up,' I said. Anything he could do I could do.

'Mind the broken glass,' he said. He had put his overcoat over the glass on top of the wall, and he moved along to make a space for me, and pulled up his long socks that had fallen around his ankles, and wriggled himself inside his short trousers.

'I don't usually talk to girls.'

'Why not?'

'Girls are soft.'

'I'm not.'

'You're not a bad climber. For a girl. And a toff,' he said grudgingly.

'Who're you calling a toff?'

'You. You sit all la-di-da in that big vicarage and eat banquets off silver plates. All toffs do. And ride around in big cars and tread on the faces of the workers.'

I'm afraid I burst out laughing. Though it was a cold little laugh.

'You'll not laugh when the Red Revolution comes,' he said fiercely. 'We'll string your sort up from lampposts.'

'*You'd* do that to me?'

He gave another grin, with a bit of shame in it. 'Well, not you personally. But the vicar . . . Religion is the opium of the masses.'

'Who says so?'

'My Uncle Henry. He's only a workingman, but he's read Karl Marx.'

'If you only knew,' I said, 'how us toffs *really* live.' And I told him about being so cold all the time.

'By heck,' he said, 'you ought to come to live wi' us workers. Me granda's a retired miner. We're not short of coal. Every time I go to me nana's, I break out into a sweat. Specially today. It's her baking day. Hey!' He turned to me. 'Why don't you come? It's only across the road . . .'

I looked down the other side into a back alley with cricket wickets chalked on the brick walls every ten yards or so. It didn't seem too hard a drop. I glanced at the gold-plated watch that my father had given me for my last birthday. It was two whole hours until Mrs Brindley would call me for tea. I looked up and caught him looking at my watch, and thinking I was a toff again.

'S'all right. We won't nick your watch. When the Revolution comes, we'll *nationalize* it. All proper and legal . . .'

'Thanks,' I said. 'That's a relief . . .'

'Us workers is honest. Not like the thieving bosses, grinding the faces of the poor.'

'Shut up,' I said. 'Or I'll grind your face personally.'

'You don't talk like a girl at all.'

I think he meant it as a compliment.

We walked up the back alley, past women who were gossiping by their gates, their arms entangled with their black shawls. They had very lined faces, and gaps in their teeth as they grinned.

'You courting, young Bobbie?'

'Hello, hello, who's your lady friend?'

Bobbie muttered darkly under his breath. I thought for a moment he was going to take to his heels and leave me standing there. But he went up to a back gate and opened it, saying, 'This is me nana's.'

The yard was full of washing, billowing sheets pegged carefully in position so that their snowy white bellies missed touching the sooty brickwork by a fraction of an inch. I edged through them, gingerly; they reached out and enfolded me like clammy ghosts. I was lost in a wilderness of snowy wetness . . .

'Don't touch them,' came Bobbie's muffled voice. 'Your hands'll make them dirty, so she'll have to do them again. Just keep walking.'

I emerged damply from my shroud at last.

'She takes in washing,' said Bobbie, his voice a bit subdued. 'From the toffs. Retired miners don't get much; you have to make ends meet.'

He opened the back door and yelled, 'Yoohoo.'

A yoohoo in reply came from the right, behind a door. When Bobbie opened it, a blast of heat, like a furnace door being opened, hit me.

The room was lit with a red glow, in which a lot of bits of brass glinted like red jewels. Horse brasses hung around the kitchen range; little rows of miniature pots and pans and windmills stood on the mantelpiece.

There were great bowls of dough, set to rise in front of the range. Half the great table was covered with wire racks of cooling bread, of all shapes and sizes. The smell was wonderful.

And on the other half of the table, his nana was kneading dough. Great muscular arms rising and falling, large hands twisting. She had a powerful beak of a nose, and her dark hair pulled back in a tight bun, and little patches of flour on her high forehead. She gave me a quick look, her hands never stopping. Her small dark eyes missed nothing about my clothes, my watch, the way I stood.

She knew I was a gentry child, as I knew from the straight-backed way she stood that she had once been a cook in a big house, with a lot of kitchen maids under her. But she didn't bat an eyelid.

'Won't you sit down, miss,' she said, very stately and dignified, as our cook might have said it. And gave me a wink.

'I'm afraid I'm not one of the workers,' I said. 'I'm just hanging on until the Red Revolution . . .'

She threw back her head and laughed a great laugh. She still had all her own teeth. 'Our Bobbie's got a head full o' rubbish. Our Henry's always filling him wi' daft ideas. Give your guest a plate, Bobbie. One of the best, the rosebud ones out o' the front room. You'll have a hot bun and butter, miss, on a cold afternoon like this?'

I sat on her black horsehair sofa and ate a bun, two buns, three buns, dripping with melting butter.

'Set you up,' she said, thumping dough into loaf shapes, 'for when those Red Revolutionaries come to chop your head off. Are you staying somewhere local?'

'The vicarage,' I said, expecting the Ice Age to descend at any moment.

But she just paused and sighed, and said, 'Oh, that poor man.'

It was the first kind word I'd heard about my uncle. I was so grateful I could have wept. She didn't miss that, either.

'It's that Polly Brindley,' she said, thumping the dough as viciously as she might have pummelled that lady. 'It's that Polly Brindley I blame. He was a decent little feller, your uncle, when he first came. Always gave you a smile. Till Polly Brindley got her claws into him. Like she got her claws into the last vicar. She thinks she runs the parish. Always coming to the vicarage front door and telling folks that the vicar isn't in, when he is. Or the vicar's too busy to bother wi' the likes of us. She's set people against him something cruel. And I reckon she's on the fiddle at the corner shop. She buys far more stuff than one poor man could ever eat . . . Still, that's none o' my business. Another bun, miss?'

She went on talking as she worked, and worked prodigiously. About the old days in the servants' hall, and the hunt gathering in the park for a stirrup cup on New Year's morning. I think she told me things she hadn't thought about for thirty years. The time just flew, and our Bobbie listened open-mouthed. It must have been hard for a young Red Revolutionary to take. Then I looked at my watch. It was five minutes to teatime.

'I must get back,' I said in a panic. 'Thank you for the buns.'

She smiled, a slightly sad smile. 'It's been nice talkin'. Come whenever you like. When you can get. She'll have you cooped up an' all, has she? No going out around the town, mixing wi' the riffraff?'

'How did you know that?'

'I know my Polly Brindley. I was at school wi' her. She thought she was too good to mix wi' the likes of us, even in those days.' Bobbie opened the door, and we went into the icy hall. As we stood on the worn doormat, I heard the sound of a racking cough upstairs. Terrible coughing, as if someone was coughing their very soul out.

'Me granda,' said Bobbie. 'It's the coal dust in his lungs. She has him to see to, an' all.'

Then we were running down the lane, to the high wall of the vicarage. Bobbie showed me where to put my feet, where two missing half bricks made good footholds, and gave me a push on my bum in his turn. I threw down his overcoat, and then we heard the cold, hating voice of Polly Brindley calling me from the kitchen door.

'Miss Caroline. Miss *Caroline*.' It wasn't the first time she'd called. She was brewing up for making a fuss.

'Goodbye,' I whispered. 'Come again.'

'We'll string *her* up from the lamppost,' he said, 'when the Revolution comes.'

I went back into that cold, cold house.

'You were a long time coming,' said Polly Brindley accusingly.

'I had to tie my shoelaces,' I said.

She sniffed her disbelief.

3

Money Matters

Next morning, over breakfast, Uncle Simon looked up from the dark grey book he was reading. 'Only a few days until Christmas,' he said, with a weak attempt at a smile. 'I've been thinking about Christmas. What we should do, now you've come to spend it with us. I thought of having a Christmas tree. But Mrs Brindley has pointed out that they are heathen things, Christmas trees, and she's quite right. Heathen things from Germany, originally used in worshipping the pagan god Wotan. Brought over by the late Prince Consort. Quite wrong in a vicarage. And their pine needles do make a mess.' He shuddered delicately, and I knew then that he was afraid of her. 'Still, we must get you some presents. But I'm leaving that to the good offices of Mrs Brindley. I'm sure I don't know what young ladies like for Christmas.'

And he returned to his book, and Christmas seemed already over, shot on the wing before it got to us, like a poor pheasant.

I felt so sick of Mrs Brindley, who came in at that moment to clear the table, and who I was sure had been eavesdropping at the door, that I grabbed my coat and gloves and went out into the garden, where I could rage in peace.

A pinecone hit me on the ear.

'Don't start *that* again,' I said dangerously.

'Hey,' he said. 'Look what I got for you.' I saw, dangling down the wall, the rustiest old kerosene stove I had ever seen in my life. The tall cylindrical sort, with three legs.

'We're not a *rubbish* dump.'

'It works. My dad got it off the dump and mended it. You can have it in the harness room, to keep you warm. Make a den. Old Brindley will never spot this.'

'Mrs Brindley to you.'

'Us workers call her old Brindlebags.'

I couldn't suppress a snigger. He *was* awful.

'Only,' he said, 'it hasn't got no kerosene in it.'

'Well, what good is it?'

'I thought you might have some money . . .' he said longingly.

'How much do you want?'

'Just twopence. I've got a beer bottle to carry the kerosene in!'

I reached up and gave it to him, and he vanished.

We sat on old wooden chairs, and stretched out our feet to the stove, which burned well, in spite of the cracked glass in its window.

'We could brew tea,' he said, 'if we had some tea. Or roast chestnuts, if we had some chestnuts.' He sounded wistful. I couldn't help noticing how thin his legs were. And his shirt collar, though clean, was ragged.

'What does your father do?' I asked.

He said, proudly, 'He's a fitter, a foreman fitter. He used to build ships. But they don't build ships anymore. He's on the dole. But he can do all kinds of things. He can sole and heel shoes and mend bikes and sometimes a car for one of the toffs. We keep going somehow.'

'That's *awful*,' I said.

'Oh, we're lucky. My mam and dad have only got me; some fellers on the dole have eight or ten kids. They run about in bare feet, even in winter, 'cos they haven't got no shoes. Everybody's on the dole. But they say, if a war comes... there'll be work for everybody again.'

'How awful... I don't want there to be a war.'

'A lot of my dad's mates would rather get killed than rot on street corners. That's why there might be a Revolution...'

'Oh, don't start that again.'

Just at that moment, the cat walked in for her morning scraps. She came as regular as clockwork, now, though Bobbie had never seen her before.

'That's another poor bugger in trouble,' he said gloomily.

'In trouble?'

'Goin' to have kittens. Any minute now. Don't they teach you nothin' at your private school?'

'*We* only have dogs,' I said, a bit snootily.

'For chasing poor bloody foxes with...'

But I didn't rise to his bait. I was too worried about the cat.

'She can't have kittens here. It's too cold.'

'Reckon she hasn't got anywhere else to go. She's flipping starving.'

'But why hasn't she got a home? She's so tame.' The cat finished her bacon rind and came and rubbed against my hand for more.

'People chuck them out, 'cos they can't afford to feed them. Lot of people drown them. Put them in a sack and chuck them in the river. River's full of 'em.'

The cat rubbed against my hand, and looked at me, trusting, confiding.

And suddenly it wasn't a matter of kindness to animals anymore; it was a matter of life and death. She was just as much in need of love as our dogs at home.

'This is *intolerable*,' I stormed.

'Ye'll just have to learn that's the way things are around here. We have to put up wi' it. There's little kids starvin', let alone cats.'

'We must do *something*. Can't *you* take her home?'

'We got a dog already, an' we can hardly feed that. Only the butcher gives me mam free bones, and she boils them for soup, then the dog has them afterward.'

'What about your nana?' I thought of that stout, determined, redoubtable woman.

'She's got two cats already. She couldn't cope with six more.'

'*Six?*'

'The kittens, stupid. Kittens grow up to be cats.'

'I could give her money for them . . .'

He gave a look that was suddenly cold, remote. 'We don't accept charity.'

'Sorry,' I said. 'It's just that I'm scared Mrs Brindley will find out . . . She'd have them destroyed. She can twist my uncle around her little finger.'

'Aye,' he said bitterly. 'Reckon she'd have poor people destroyed if she could. When the Revolution—'

'Shut *up*!'

There was a long silence. After a while he said, 'I could build her a hiding place. To have the kittens in.'

He got up, and rooted around the harness room. Got an old thick cardboard box that said NESTLÉ'S MILK, ONE GROSS. He went out to the stable, and came back with it half-full of clean crumpled hay. Then he folded the lid, leaving only a small hole in the top. Put it back against the wall, under the big table once used for cleaning harness. Laid one or two old planks of wood and an empty paint can on top.

His hands were clever. It was a good hiding place, warm

and dark, and no one would ever think of looking inside it, it looked so normal, boring. He gently picked the cat up and showed the box to her, let her sniff it. Then popped her inside. We listened to her rustling about in the hay, pounding it with her paws. Then she poked her head up through the hole, and sat looking at us with such a comical expression of triumph on her face.

'She's taken to it,' he said, in a voice of low glad glee. 'She'll have her kittens in there now.'

'If only the kittens don't cry out!'

'They'll know enough to keep their mouths shut when the Brindley's prowling around.'

'You make her sound like a tiger or a wolf or something!'

'Aye,' he said grimly.

'There's one more thing worrying me. I'm stealing scraps from the table to feed her. If Mrs Brindley catches me . . .'

'Goodbye, scraps. And goodbye, cat . . .'

'Oh, don't worry,' I said loftily. 'I can tell a lie. I can lie as well as anybody when I want to. She won't find out about the cat. But I won't be able to come here anymore—she'll be watching me like a hawk. Will you go on feeding the cat?'

'What with?' He shrugged, looking down at his feet, ashamed of his poverty and helplessness. 'She can't eat grass, you know.'

'I'll give you money to buy things. I've got plenty of money.' I reached into my purse and pulled out the five-pound note that Daddy had sent me for the Christmas holidays. They were huge plain white things in those days.

'What the hell's that?' he asked. 'Your school report?'

'Five-pound note.'

He took the bill from me and examined it closely; crinkled it between his fingers, smelled it, like a little animal. Then he gave it back quickly. The shine went out of his eyes; they went as dull as ditchwater.

'If the feller at the corner shop saw me wi' a *ten-shilling* note, he'd send for the police.'

'But it's all I've got,' I said, tears of frustration seeping into the corners of my eyes. 'Except two sixpences.'

'Ah can do a lot wi' a sixpence . . .'

'No,' I said. 'I'll go to the bank and change it. What kind of money do you need?'

'Nothing bigger than a two-shilling piece,' he said.

'We'd better go now,' I said. 'Before it gets dark. It's an hour till teatime yet.'

'C'mon, then. I'll show you the sights o' North Shields. Bring on the dancing girls . . .'

You cannot imagine, granddaughter, the sights I saw that day. Groups of unemployed men, squatting at the street corners, passing around the flattened butt of a cigarette from one to the other; smoking it, with the aid of a pin stuck through it, until it was only a quarter-inch long. A man with no legs, just flat worn black leather pads where his legs should be, singing carols in a deep sweet voice from a doorstep, with his little dog nearby and a flat cap into which some passersby put half-pennies.

But in the end we reached the bank, with its tall sandstone columns.

'You're never going in *there,*' whispered Bobbie, awe-struck.

'Why not?' I said. 'It's *my* money.'

And I sailed in, as I often had before, and the man behind the counter not only changed the note exactly as I asked, but called me 'madam,' of course. What was the difference between me and Bobbie, I wondered. I wasn't dressed grandly, I can tell you. Only a sensible country tweed coat and hat. But I suppose my voice was what Bobbie would have called posh. And the man behind the counter was my servant; I expected him to obey, and he did. With a little subservient smirk. I had a brief thought about Bobbie and his Red Revolution . . . Were Red Revolutions infectious? The man behind the counter wouldn't like a Red Revolution at all. The workers would probably string him up from the nearest lamppost. Before helping themselves to his bank . . .

When I got outside, Bobbie caught my arm.

'We'll have to run like hell,' he said.

'Why, for heaven's sake?'

'It's starting to rain . . . Brindley'll be out in the garden looking for you in a minute.'

I have never run so fast in my life.

Bobbie gave me a last heave up onto the wall, and I listened in the growing dusk. The vicarage lights were on, and the rain was now falling steadily.

'You got that money safe?' I whispered down to him.

'Yeah,' he whispered back. 'Best of British luck wi' Brindley.'

Then I was dropping down into the wet garden, and he was gone. I felt very alone. But rather excited. Like a spy. I listened more carefully. No sound of Brindlebags calling for me; that was bad. That meant she'd been calling and given up. Maybe she had even searched the garden for me, and not found me. Still, I walked around to the front door, sauntering along as if I didn't have a care in the world. As luck would have it, I met my uncle as he came through the gates.

'Caroline,' he said, 'what are you doing out in this rain?'

'Oh,' I said gaily, 'I sheltered in the old hayloft. It's quite dry up there.' How easy it is, to lie.

'I hope you looked where you were going,' he said. 'They say the hayloft floor is rotten in places . . .'

Just then Mrs Brindley opened the front door.

'Where have you been, you wicked girl! I've looked everywhere for you. You were nowhere to be found . . .'

I remembered the bank, where the man had been my servant. Mrs Brindley was also a servant, though she had long since forgotten her place.

'Oh,' I said, in a voice of disgust, 'I heard you calling. I'm sick of you calling for me. Like I was a pet dog. Or a cow.'

'Caroline!' said my uncle, in a very shocked voice. Adamsons are *never* rude to their servants. It might have gone hard with me, if Mrs Brindley hadn't forgotten herself again, and been ruder back.

'She's lying. I looked everywhere.'

'Up in the hayloft?' I asked sweetly, looking up and down her massive fat body. 'How many rungs are missing on the ladder?'

She knew she was beaten there; she shot me a look of pure hatred. But she wouldn't give up. She turned to my uncle. 'She's so disobedient. I can't be expected to take responsibility . . .'

'I can be responsible for myself,' I said stoutly. 'I *am* nearly twelve years old . . .'

For the first time, I saw a flicker of fear in her piggy little eyes.

'Come, come now,' said my poor uncle, all atremble, 'let us have peace and harmony. This is a Christian household. I want a word with you in my study, Caroline.'

Mrs Brindley smirked and left, quite sure she had won. I followed my uncle into his cold study, with its poor, smoking fire. How different from Bobbie's grandmother's generous blaze. And the hearth hadn't been swept properly. There was a rim of ash half-hidden behind the fender, half an inch high. Mrs Brindley was a lazy housekeeper as well.

My uncle sat down, his pale podgy hands clasped between his black thighs.

'Caroline,' he said, as severely as he could muster, 'you know what I am going to say to you . . .'

'She called me a liar,' I said coldly. 'She is a *servant*, and she called me a liar. What do you think my father is going to say about *that?*'

Poor weak man, how we tormented him, Mrs Brindley and I between us. He wrung his hands and did not know what to say.

Except: 'Is there no peace in this world?'

I wondered then what God thought of me; for God was

very close and real to me in those days. And then I thought of God's cat, God's creature that Mrs Brindley would destroy if she could.

'She is overfamiliar,' I said. 'She has got above herself.' I thought of all the other things I might have said: the grocer's bill, the filthy fireplace. But I was only a child; he would not have taken it from me.

'She has so much to do,' he said. 'It makes her overhasty. But she means it for the best.' Poor fool. I made up my mind then that I would destroy Mrs Brindley. But I just said, 'Very well, Uncle. I will try to be civil to her,' and got up and went to the door.

'There was one more thing,' he said, with a little shy, timid smile, staring at something over my shoulder. 'Miss Stevenson—my organist—has sent to say she is unwell and unable to play for daily Evensong. I was wondering if you would come and sing it with me?'

'With all my heart,' I said, and meant it. It was a way of saying sorry to God.

4

A Game of Spies

He lifted the heavy latch, and the metallic clink echoed up and down the dark empty church. The stained-glass angels of the windows were pointed islands of dim light in the blackness.

'Wait here,' said my uncle, 'while I put on the lights.' He walked into the darkness ahead, where only a tiny red flame flickered high up in the sanctuary lamp, red as blood. His footsteps were sure and confident, as if he knew the way by heart.

Then the chancel lights came on, dimly golden, and he was taking off his dark overcoat, and slipping on his white surplice.

'You know the service?'

'We sing it every Sunday in school chapel.'

'Good girl. Do you think you can manage without the organ? It's a good church for singing in. Fine echo!'

'I can try!'

'Good girl!' he said again.

And it worked. He was a singer, and I was a singer, and the dark aisles and pillars of the church took us up and echoed us as if they were a whole multitude. We made the stones ring into the very far corners, where the cobwebs hung and the mice ran. There is no feeling like that.

'O Lord, open thou our lips.'

'And our mouths shall show forth thy Praise.'

'O God, make speed to save us.'

'O Lord, make haste to help us.'

I sang like an angel, and plotted like a devil. The downfall of Mrs Brindley. I could not think what God must have thought.

We came to an end and stopped. Uncle Simon buried his face in his hands in prayer, and I pretended to do the same, but watched him through my spread fingers. He seemed to be praying an awfully long time, even for a vicar. And then I noticed that his back was heaving, as it heaves only when somebody is laughing or crying.

I knew my uncle would never laugh in church. I was left with the terrible knowledge that one of my grownups was crying.

And a man at that. I had sometimes seen my mother cry, though not often, and usually about the death of a beloved dog. I had never seen my father cry; though if a favourite dog had died, the muscles of his cheeks twitched very fiercely, and he chewed savagely at the ends of his gray mustache.

I walked over to Uncle Simon, cautiously. I was a little afraid, and yet I felt a power; or the beginnings of a power. I touched him on the shoulder, gently. 'Uncle?'

He raised a face wet with tears, and yet twisted with shame that I should see him thus.

'It was so beautiful,' he said. 'The singing.'

I nodded, not knowing what to say.

'It seemed so *right*.'

I nodded again.

'It always seems right in church. Yet the moment I go outside . . .' He looked around the church, as if desperately seeking an answer. 'They are a hardhearted people. They have hardened their hearts against me . . .'

'There *are* some good people,' I said. Thinking of Bobbie with the cat, and his nana looking after the whole family.

'How can *you* know, child? You haven't been among them!'

Suddenly his eyes were very sharp, even through their tears. I had nearly fallen into a snare. But I said quickly, 'There are good people everywhere.'

'True,' he said. 'Out of the mouth of babes and sucklings . . . Then it is *my* fault . . . Some did smile at me when I first came. There were people who came to church, then . . .'

I took a deep breath and said, 'I don't think it's *your* fault.'

His eyes clung to mine, as a drowning man clings to a straw.

'*She* turns people away. From the vicarage door.'

Again his eyes went sharper. 'How do you know that, child?'

'She turned me away. She didn't know who I was, but she turned me away. She didn't even ask what I wanted. I could have been someone whose mother was dying or *anything*.'

'She apologized for that; she had something in the oven and was afraid it was going to burn. You mustn't make mountains out of molehills, Caroline. But'—he got up—'thank you for bearing with me. I feel better now.' And the vagueness came back over his eyes, and my chance was gone.

For the moment.

I knew she was looking for an opportunity to spy on me; so the next morning I gave it to her. For the cat's sake, the sooner it was over, the better. I laid a trap for her; I went out on a morning when even I might have lurked indoors, a morning with a steel-gray sky and biting wind. It was three days to Christmas.

I had a cold hour of it, crouching in the rhododendron bushes that overlooked the back door. I think I must have turned blue with cold; I almost despaired.

And then I saw the back door cautiously open, and her head come out, and look left and right. Then the whole bulk of her was tiptoeing in among the trees. It was ridiculous, the care she took; and yet she was so clumsy she made more noise than a herd of elephants. At least, in future, I knew what kind of noise to listen for.

What games I had with her; following her, ten yards behind, mimicking her rolling, waddling gait, until I had to stuff my hankie in my mouth to stop myself giggling out loud. (Like any fool, she never looked *behind.*) I picked up pinecones and threw them to left and right, making her jump with the small rustlings and crashes. Oh, such a game. And then, when she was at the far end of the garden from the stable, and bent almost double to peer under a monkey puzzle tree, with her great rump in the air, I crept across the silent pine needles and poked her in the bum and shouted loudly, 'Boo!'

She jumped a foot in the air; whirled with her hand at her throat, as if she was about to have a heart attack.

'Oh, Miss Caroline,' she blustered, when she got her breath back. 'You gave me such a turn.'

'Were you looking for me?' I asked mock-sweetly. 'Was there something you wanted?'

'I just wanted to know if you could do wi' a hot drink. It's such a nasty morning.'

'That's very sweet of you.'

She smirked. Then I added, 'I've been following you for ten minutes. You were trying to *spy* on me.'

All pretence of sweetness fled. She gave me such a look of hatred that I recoiled. I suppose even stupid people hate being caught out in their stupidity.

'You're up to some game, miss,' she said, 'and I'll find you out. I know what you're up to.'

'And I know what you're up to,' I said.

'What *do* you mean?' She drew herself up to a great height, though her little piggy eyes flickered.

'I know what you get up to at the corner shop. Buying too much.' I suppose I meant to *really* frighten her; to frighten her away from me altogether. Blackmail, I suppose.

But it didn't work. If she'd hated me before, she only hated me more now. Some people are so stupid they have no sense of their own good at all.

'You think you're so *clever*,' she spat. 'But I'll settle your hash, missie, you see if I don't.' And then she stalked off back to the house.

I knew she would never spy on me in the garden again. What I didn't grasp was that the garden was my territory, where I had the advantage. The house was hers.

I slid carefully into the harness room. The gentle smell of burning kerosene told me Bobbie was there. There was a second object burning kerosene now: an incredibly battered old hurricane lamp hung from a long nail, casting a soft yellow light.

Bobbie was kneeling on the floor, beside the cardboard box. He looked up, his grin enormous, his blue eyes shining as they had never done before. It might have been Christmas morning.

'They've come,' he said. 'They've come. Three of them.'

'Who?' I asked stupidly, still full of the bitterness of my quarrel.

'The *kittens*. I watched them being born. An hour ago. They came in little shiny sacks, like cellophane, on the end of little strings. She chewed them out of the sacks. I was so scared. I thought she was eatin' them. Then she licked them dry, all over. And now they're feedin' off her. All purrin' their heads off. I *wish* you'd been here. It was marvellous.'

I suppose it should have taught me a lesson. I'd been so busy feeding my hate that I'd missed all the glory. Though of course I had seen puppies born, and I don't suppose kittens are much different . . .

'Come and see.' His voice was low and reverent, as if he was in church. And there they lay, on the hay, between their mother's outstretched legs. Climbing and pummelling with their tiny paws and treading in each other's faces; and sucking and purring at the same time like tiny bees. One all-black one, one nearly all white, with black spots, and one ginger and black.

'I think I know the dad,' said Bobbie. 'Mrs Haggerty's ginger tom. He's a crafty old sod.' He picked one up and showed it to me, cupping it ever so gently in the palm of his hands. It was the little ginger-and-black one. Its ears were crumpled like rose petals, its eyes bulged blindly behind closed slits.

Its ginger paws flailed frantic and blind, clawing the air to find a mother who had inexplicably vanished, and it squeaked piteously.

I had never seen anything so vulnerable; to come into this cruel hard world. My heart was a torrent of love. I vowed I would do murder to save it.

'Put it back,' I cried. 'Give it back to its mother. It'll catch a chill.' It was *unbearable*.

He laughed, not unkindly. 'Don't you worry; it's a tough little sod. See how it kicks!' Then he saw the look on my face, and put it back. Quickly it snuggled back in between its siblings, and all was purring and sucking again.

'Got anything to eat?' he asked. 'The mother's ravenous. I managed to nick some bacon rind from me dad's tea, but it was gone in a flash. Like feeding an elephant strawberries.'

I got out my little bag of scraps and offered them to the mother. She sniffed at them, then stirred uneasily, torn between the food and the kittens. I put the bits on the hay beside her and she got upright, the protesting kittens still trying to cling to her belly, then falling away, and squealing loudly. She ate; she was wolfish, and yet with every bite her ears swivelled to the kittens' protests. She was so frantic, my heart went out to her, too.

When she had finished, and all the uproar was over, and the kittens and cat settled in a purring mass again, I said, 'You'd better start buying her food. I can't smuggle out enough for her.'

'That's O.K. I found out when the cat's-meat man comes around with his pushcart. I'll meet him downtown, where nobody will recognize me.' I grinned at him. He had to act like a spy, too, now. He had nosy grownups to dodge as well. I thought he'd make a good spy.

Then I got up. I was very tense. On the one hand were the helpless kittens; on the other, the prowling, hating Mrs Brindley. She would still be watching for me, out of the house windows . . .

'See you tomorrow,' I said.

'Same time, eh?' He grinned. 'I'll bring a bottle of water, too. She's thirsty.'

'Milk would be better . . .'

'I'll get a quarter-pint o' milk. Me nana's got a little chipped jug she won't miss for a bit . . .'

I think I fell in love with him then. With his toughness and reliability.

Oh, yes, granddaughter. You can fall in love when you're not quite twelve. With the most unsuitable people.

Two days to Christmas.

It was at breakfast that disaster struck. I suppose I was too eager to nick the scraps off the plates. My uncle had left a fine big piece of ham fat on the edge of his, and had pushed the plate idly across the breakfast table toward me, lost in his book. I thought I was safe. I could have pinched the tablecloth itself when he was lost in his book. He would merely have lifted his elbows to let me take it . . .

But I didn't hear Mrs Brindley come in through the door to

clear up. She might have been noisy in the garden, but in the house she could move as silently as a mouse, in her old carpet slippers. Too late, I heard the soft creak of her corset stays, and then she cried loudly.

'What are you doing with that ham fat, miss? Don't we feed you well enough?'

My uncle looked up, bewildered, to see the large lump of ham fat in my hand.

'She was going to slip it into her sweater pocket, sir. Look, the edge of her pocket's all greasy . . . What's this, then?' She plunged her great paw into my pocket, and flourished my bag of scraps in triumph under my poor uncle's nose.

'Caroline?' he said.

'She's a-feeding something, sir. Stealing food to feed something. I know her little ways.'

'*Are* you feeding something, Caroline?' asked my uncle, with mild interest.

God, my mind was in a whirl. Could I pretend I was feeding some poor stray dog that came to the gate? But the gate was always shut. Could I pretend I was indeed half-starved? But I had left a lump of bread and butter on my side plate . . .

'Caroline, *please* give me an answer,' said my uncle, starting to get a little cross, while Mrs Brindley breathed heavily through her mouth in triumphant righteousness.

Then a vision of our garden at home came to my rescue in a nick of time.

'Tits,' I said.

'I *beg* your pardon?' said my uncle, very shocked.

I had a ridiculous desire to giggle at his pious, shocked face. But I controlled myself, and said, with an effort, 'Blue tits, great tits, coal tits. They love fat. And it's the winter, and they're so *hungry* . . .'

My uncle's face cleared. 'There's nothing to be ashamed of in that. St Francis *preached* to the birds, Mrs Brindley. If we can't feed our feathered friends in winter . . . But there was no need to be underhanded, Caroline. If you'd asked,

I'm sure Mrs Brindley would have found you lots of bits for the birds.'

'Ain't no birds in this garden, sir. I've looked many a time. She's feedin' something a lot bigger than a bird . . .'

My uncle looked torn both ways. In a moment, Mrs Brindley was going to win. A vision of the cat and kittens swam up in front of my eyes. Living. Dead. Drowned. Mrs Brindley would certainly know a man prepared to drown them, if she didn't take satisfaction in drowning them herself.

'Come and see,' I said. 'They come for me every morning. Down by the gate.' I said the gate, because the only birds I had ever seen in North Shields were sparrows, pecking their breakfasts in the mats of flattened horse dung on the roads. But a sparrow was better than nothing . . .

We all trooped down. It would have looked ridiculous, if it hadn't been a matter of life and death. I scattered the pieces, the precious pieces, on the weedy drive, and we retired to a distance and waited.

Nothing came. We got very cold. My uncle began to fidget. Mrs Brindley's stertorous breathing got more and more triumphant. While I humbly prayed. Anything with wings, please, God. Pigeons, vultures . . . Anything at all.

'Nothing,' said Mrs Brindley at last. 'I told you, sir. No birds in . . .'

And at that moment a solitary starling, black as soot with the smoke of the town, fluttered down. Then two more, then two more. A whole crowd, as starlings do. *Blessed* starlings; blessed, dirty starlings.

'There,' I said, when they had finished the scraps and flown away again.

'I'm not sure they're t—blue tits,' said my uncle doubtfully. 'But I was never one for nature study. However, if you *ask* Mrs Brindley, Caroline, I'm sure she will lay on plenty of scraps for you in the future.'

He walked off back to his study, leaving us glaring at each other.

I knew I mustn't go to the stables anymore. Our margin of safety was now as thin as paper.

5

Double Visions

All I could do was wander around the other bits of the garden disconsolately. I knew Bobbie would figure something was wrong eventually.

I was right. After two weary hours, a pinecone hit me on the ear. It was very welcome.

We hid deep in the rhododendrons while I told him what had happened. He considered carefully. Then he said, 'She's only watching you. She doesn't know about me, right? So I can keep on feeding the cat. She's all right—I got a huge load off the cat's-meat man for a penny. She ate the lot. She's got milk, too.'

'Bless you. But Brindlebags mustn't see you . . .'

'She won't. I can get over the wall, right next to the stables. Lots of bricks are loose—I can make new footholds.'

As I said, he would have made a good spy.

Then he shuffled uncomfortably. 'Can I ask you a favour? There's a little girl lives next door to us. She's got TB—consumption. She hasn't got no toys, they're that hard up. I go in to play with her sometimes, to cheer her up. She gets that bored . . . Well, I told her about the kittens coming.'

'Oh, how *could* you?' I was furious. 'It was a *secret*.'

'It's still a secret, don't you worry. She knows how to keep her mouth shut. So do her parents. And nobody talks to the vicar or Mrs Brindley—they wouldn't tell her the time o' day. We're quite safe; only . . .'

'Only *what?*'

'She wants to see the kittens.'

'No!'

He was silent, for a long time. Then he said, 'She won't make old bones, little Shirley. Me mam doubts she'll last out the winter. Says she'll be gone by spring, like the birds.'

'But how can she see them, if she's that ill?' I was still angry with him, but I was melting, under his serious gaze.

'Her mam lets her out to play, when it's not raining. If she's well wrapped up. We push her about in an old stroller. She's sort of the mascot of our gang . . .'

'But how will you get her over the wall?'

'Our gang will help. Two at the bottom of the wall, and two at the top, wi' a bit o' rope. They're strong lads. We'll manage easy. We'll wait till it starts getting dark. Nobody will see us, honest. We nick the vicar's apples off his trees in summer, and nobody ever sees us.'

'Thanks very much! I hadn't realized you were a *criminal* gang.'

But I couldn't resist his earnestness. Or the thought of little Shirley. I would still be alive next summer.

'Do as you like,' I said. 'You won't see me for a bit. I'm going to stay indoors and annoy the Brindlebags. That'll take her mind off the stables.'

And I walked away, still in a huff. Why couldn't I belong to a gang like that?

It began to snow that afternoon. Big soft flakes whirling down past the library window, as I shivered and tried to read a boring book about Christianity and the unemployed. It was full of ideas about how Christianity could help the unemployed. Setting up soup kitchens and Christian reading rooms for the men. But that was in London. It didn't seem to be happening in North Shields . . .

I heard the front door open, and Uncle Simon come in. He looked in at the library door. He had a lot of holly and mistletoe in his arms and looked more cheerful than usual.

'The Great Feast of Christmas is about to begin,' he said.

Then Mrs Brindley came bustling into the room, and

began to grumble about what a bother putting up holly and mistletoe was, and had the vicar brought any pushpins, for you couldn't put up holly and mistletoe without them, and there were certainly none in the house . . .

That wiped all the cheerfulness off Uncle Simon's face. We'd probably never even see the holly and mistletoe. It would probably just get pushed around the kitchen table until it withered and died. I did offer to go to the corner shop for some pushpins, saying the corner shop sold everything . . . But Mrs Brindley just asked in a nasty voice how I knew about the corner shop, and I had to shut up. Uncle Simon wouldn't have let me out into the godless town anyway.

The next morning, the snow was lying all about, deep and crisp and even. I almost hated it. It ruled out any chance of going up to see the kittens. Footsteps that led anywhere near the stables would be fatal. I just hoped cat, kittens, and Bobbie were doing all right; and annoyed Mrs Brindley by offering to help put up the holly. I could tell she was a bit baffled at my staying indoors. She kept on hinting that I should go out and make a snowman or something. But I wasn't falling for that one, and just said snow was cold nasty stuff, and I *really* hated it.

There was only one consolation. My uncle insisted that she light a fire for me in the library; whether because he'd finally realized I was cold, or merely because it was Christmas Eve, it was impossible to say. She responded with a smouldering mountain of coal dust in the grate, which never showed a flicker of flame all day, however I poked and coaxed it, and which sent a cloud of choking smoke across the shelves of old books every time the wind blew a fresh flurry of flakes against the windows.

I tried to forget myself in an uplifting book, full of death-bed conversions of wicked sinners. But my eyes were constantly drawn to the windows, with their view of the roof of the distant stables. How was the cat doing? Had her supply of milk dried up with the cold? Had the kittens frozen to death? Had Bobbie managed to get food in to them? Had he brought Shirley to see them yet? Several times Mrs Brindley, coming in quietly, nearly caught me staring at the stables. Even when your father was flying jet fighters, granddaughter, I never knew such maternal worry.

But in the end the weary day passed, and darkness fell, and it was time for my uncle's return, and tea. He bustled into the library, rosy-cheeked with the cold, and unwound his enormously long scarf; but I noticed he was too wise to take his overcoat off, and he grumbled a little about the fire. Then Mrs Brindley came in with the tray; my uncle had laid on muffins to mark the occasion, but she had managed to burn them all around the edges. She went across to draw the curtains against the night. Then she stopped halfway, and said, in a dreadful doom-laden voice, 'There is someone in the stables! I can see a light!'

'Nonsense,' said my uncle, a little grumpily, reaching for a muffin. 'What would anyone want in our old stables?'

'Trespassers! Hooligans! Thieves!' Mrs Brindley screeched. 'They will burn the place down.'

My uncle went to the window grudgingly; I think he only meant to shut her up. And I followed him with a sinking heart.

There was a light in the lower window of the stables, showing through the trunks of the trees. Only a dim light; but as we looked, it winked, as if someone had walked across it. I cursed Bobbie in my heart, for his stupidity.

'We must telephone for the police,' Mrs Brindley said.

'I will see to it myself,' said my uncle, huffily. He wound on his scarf again, with a deep long-suffering sigh, and set out, followed by Mrs Brindley, breathing fire and thunder.

'Be silent, woman,' said my uncle, 'or they will hear you and escape.' It worked; nothing else would have silenced her. I had managed to slip between them.

Our approach was quite noiseless through the snow . . .

You may wonder why I did not cry out a warning. But that

would have betrayed my own position completely, and I still hoped to help somehow . . .

The silence inside the stable was absolute as well. Perhaps Bobbie had gone; perhaps the light was only the light of the stove left burning for the cats . . .

My uncle flung wide the door.

And it was then that God played one of his little jokes. Or it may have been purely an accident. I have never, all my life, been able to separate God's little jokes from accidents, granddaughter.

The scene inside the stable was the scene of the Nativity; by the red glow of the kerosene stove and the dim golden light of the hurricane lamp, it was exactly the scene on all the Christmas cards my uncle sent out. Not just the stable, with the straw on the floor, and the disused manger. But Mary was there kneeling in the straw, with her blue-clad arms around the new baby. And the ragged, tousle-haired shepherds knelt beside her in adoration, and on her left the three kings stood, black Balthasar, crowned and splendid in red and gold, and oriental Melchior, with his calm face and blue garb, and flaxen-haired Caspar. And behind Mary, brooding, protective, stood Joseph. And all eyes were fixed in silent worship . . .

And then Mrs Brindley cried, 'Thieves, hooligans!' and the children looked up startled, and King Balthasar was simply a black boy in a red-and-yellow bobble hat and sweater and scarf, and Mary only Shirley, a pale little girl with huge scared blue eyes and a blue overcoat with its hood up, and St Joseph was only Bobbie, with a sack draped around his back to keep out the cold, and a rough stick in his hand, and the baby was only a startled she-cat at bay, spitting in defence of her helpless mewing kittens, who sprawled in the straw.

'Fetch the police!' cried Mrs Brindley.

But my uncle stood as if transfixed, with the tears running down his pale fat cheeks, and I knew he had seen with my eyes, not Mrs Brindley's.

He cried out, in agony, 'Suffer the little children to come unto me, for of such is the kingdom of heaven!'

'I'll run for the police, Reverend!' shouted Mrs Brindley.

'Shut *up*, you stupid woman!' shouted my uncle.

'I'm not standing here listening to that kind of talk!' shouted Mrs Brindley.

'Then *go!*' shouted my uncle.

And all the children just stood, open-mouthed, wide-eyed, paralyzed with amazement that such things should be.

Then my uncle was among the children, shaking them by the hand one by one, babbling strange and discordant jollities.

'You must come into the house. We shall have mince pies! Ginger ale! Pudding!' He must have been lost in some distant dream of his own happy childhood. 'Come down to the house. You are all welcome, most welcome.'

The children were torn between acceptance and flight, at such an unlikely jovial madman.

They all looked at Bobbie. He was the leader. He thought hard, narrowing his shrewd young eyes, weighing up the situation. Then he nodded; and they all trailed after the vicar. For in that town of cold and hunger and unemployment, the promise of *anything* to eat was the kingdom of heaven.

The she-cat was busy carrying her offspring back into their box, wise and prudent mother that she was. I saw her safe in, and doused the lights for fear of fire, and then ran to join the rest.

I found them huddled in the hall. My uncle was shouting at Mrs Brindley again. 'Bring ginger ale, Mrs Brindley! Warm the mince pies!'

'We haven't got none. You didn't ask me to get any in . . . You can't expect a hardworking housekeeper to—'

'Surely we have *something*? Christmas cake, seedcake, anything!'

'Only your dinner tomorrow . . .'

'We *must* have something . . .'

'Don't talk to me like that, Vicar. I think you've taken leave of your senses . . . I will not stay one minute longer and be shouted at like that. I'm giving in my notice, as of now.'

And good as her word, she took her coat off the hook on the back of the kitchen door, and swept away without another word, slamming the front door behind her.

I never heard a sweeter sound. But there was a sudden horrible silence, in which hope faded from the children's faces as the real world returned, and visions of Christmas plenty died. And my poor uncle flapped his hands helplessly, saying over and over again, 'What shall I do? What *shall* I do? What shall I do now?'

Mrs Brindley might still have won then. But Bobbie seized his chance. He stepped forward, and stood to attention before my uncle, like a soldier.

'I can get them for you, sir! The corner shop has plenty of soda, mince pies.'

'Splendid chap,' my uncle said, clapping him on the shoulder. 'Off you go, then . . .'

Bobbie hesitated beautifully; I have never seen the late Laurence Olivier do it better.

'Oh, yes, money, money, you need money,' said my uncle, fumbling up under the long skirt of his cassock and revealing a perfectly ordinary pair of dark trousers, much to the children's amazement.

He produced a very crumpled pound note. 'Here you are!' The children's eyes widened, as at all the treasures of the Spanish Main.

'Here, better have two,' said my uncle, adding another note to the first. The children looked as if paradise was assured. Bobbie and his black friend sped off like the wind.

6

Merry Christmas

It was a marvelous party, all the better for being straight out of bottles, packages, and cans. There should have been crumbs all over the library carpet; but these were children who pursued crumbs and picked them up with the ends of their fingers, and ate them. Afterward, the vicar thumped away on the old piano like one possessed and we sang carols till our throats were sore. For they knew all the carols by heart, from school, even the Chinese boy, whose name, I learned, was, amazingly, Ted Mulligan.

At last, when we could eat no more and sing no more, the vicar led them down to the front gate, pressing on them whatever had not already been eaten, for their parents and brothers and sisters. There were about thirty children by that time, for word had spread quickly from Joe's Corner Shop that the vicar was holding a children's Christmas party, and disbelief had been overcome by hunger, and many had knocked on the door and been let in afterward.

'Good night, good night,' called Uncle Simon, delirious with glee. 'Merry Christmas to you all, and to your parents.'

Now it just happened that a lot of grown-ups were passing the gate at the time, having been out to do what little Christmas shopping they could afford. I heard them muttering to each other, at the strange sight of the vicarage gate open, and happy children streaming out.

'My God, the vicar's been holding a Christmas party!'

'Wonders will never cease! They'll be doubling the dole next!'

Then an adult voice called, back over its shoulder, 'Merry Christmas, Vicar!'

And all the rough adult voices were calling.

'Merry Christmas, Reverend!'

God's little joke, or the accident, was continuing.

We went back indoors, to the litter of bags and boxes and bottles on every chair and table.

'Oh, dear,' said my uncle, his face suddenly falling. 'Whatever shall we do now? However can we *cope?*' He had the petulant baby look of a helpless male suddenly left to manage alone.

I knew he'd *never* manage alone. Over the days, once I was gone, the need for Mrs Brindley would come drifting back. The need to have his meals cooked, his socks darned, his shirts washed . . . inexorable. Mrs Brindley could win yet; and extract a terrible vengeance.

So I took a deep breath, and cut Mrs Brindley's throat for good and all. I was never sure whether that was part of God's little joke or not.

'I know a good woman who could do for you,' I said.

'A *respectable* woman?' A look of fright crossed his face.

'A respectable woman,' I said, 'and a very respectable cook. She used to work in a big house as cook, when she was younger . . .'

His eyes lit up; he was always a bit of a glutton. And I ran to Bobbie's nana's, before he could stop me. God knows how I found the right gate in the dark. But she came, all flustered, with her hair hastily screwed up in a new bun, and a spotless white apron under her best hat and coat.

He never looked back after that. At Midnight Mass that Christmas Eve, where I had expected a dreary congregation of three, we had nearly twenty. More than for years . . . word got around fast in that town. The parents of the children from the party, mainly.

And after that, with Bobbie's nana to take him in hand, and answer his front door, and guide him with her sound common sense, his congregation grew. The next Christmas Eve, the church was nearly full; even if some of them were more than a little drunk, including my old unbuttoned friend, still grieving for his black sins.

As for Bobbie, I didn't see him again for years, after that second Christmas Eve. But I heard about his progress from my uncle. How his father got new work, as the Second World War drew nearer: building destroyers to sink U-boats. So that they could afford to send Bobbie to high school after all. How he was top of his class, and got all his exams. How he joined the air force.

But it was not until 1945, April 1945, that he came walking up our drive one fine evening, when I happened to be on leave from the navy. He was wearing the wings of a navigator, and his left arm was in a black silk sling, and I'm afraid I didn't recognize him at first. He had grown into a very attractive young man. Not good-looking, but snub-nosed still, with warm blue eyes, and a wicked grin.

'Why didn't you look us up earlier?' I cried.

'Not till I'd done something worthwhile.' He smiled.

'Like getting yourself nearly killed?'

'And I'm still only a flight sergeant, and you're a flipping officer . . .'

It was as if I had just left him yesterday.

'Are you going to take me out to dinner?' I asked. I was always very forward, granddaughter.

'I haven't been to the university yet,' he said grimly, almost to himself.

'Oh, I can't wait till you get your degree,' I said.

And we took it on from there.

Look at him now, weeding that rockery. You've guessed, haven't you, the famous Bobbie. Gray as a badger now, though it suits him. And he's still got his snub nose and wicked grin . . .

You wouldn't be here if I hadn't been hit on the ear by a pinecone, in that horrible dark vicarage garden, all those years ago.

The cats? That vicarage was always famous for its cats. That's one of their descendants, asleep in that chair.

Beware of pinecones, granddaughter.

THE HAUNTING OF CHAS McGILL

The day war broke out, Chas McGill went up in the world.

What a Sunday morning! Clustering round the radio at eleven o'clock, all hollow-bellied like the end of an England-Australia test. Only this was the England-Germany test. He had his scorecards all ready, pinned on his bedroom wall: number of German tanks destroyed; number of German planes shot down; number of German ships sunk.

The prime minister's voice, finally crackling over the air, seemed to Chas a total disaster. Mr Chamberlain *regretted* that a state of war now existed between England and Germany. Worse, he bleated like a sheep; or the sort of kid who, challenged in the playground, backs into a corner with his hands in front of his face and threatens to tell his dad on you. Why didn't he threaten to kick Hitler's teeth in? Chas hoped Hitler wasn't listening, or there'd soon be trouble . . .

Immediately, the air-raid sirens went.

German bombers. Chas closed his eyes and remembered the cinema newsreels from Spain. Skies thick with black crosses, from which endless streams of tiny bombs fell. Endless as the streams of refugee women scurrying through the shattered houses, all wearing headscarves and ankle socks. Rows of dead kids laid out on the shattered brickwork like broken-stick dolls with glass eyes. (He always shut his eyes at that point, but *had* to peep.) And the German bomber-pilots, hardly human in tight black leather flying helmets, laughing and slapping each other on the back and busting open bottles of champagne and spraying each other . . .

He opened his eyes again. Through his bedroom window the grass of the square still dreamed in sunlight. Happy, ignorant sparrows, excused from the war, were busy pecking their breakfast from the steaming pile of manure left by the co-op milk horse. The sky remained clear and blue; not a Spitfire in sight.

Chas wondered what he ought to *do?* Turn off the gas and electric? With Mam in the middle of Sunday dinner, that'd be more dangerous than any air raid. His eye fell on his teddy bear, sitting on top of a pile of toys in the corner. He hadn't given Ted a glance in years. Now, Ted stared at him appealingly. There'd been teddy bears in the Spanish newsreels, too; the newsreels were particularly keen on teddy bears split from chin to crotch, with all their stuffing spilling out. Headless teddy bears, legless teddy bears . . . Making sure no one was watching, he grabbed Ted and shoved him under the bed to safety.

Not a moment too soon. Mam came in, drying her sudsy hands.

'Anything happening out front? Nothing happening out the back.' She made it sound like they were waiting for a carnival with a brass band, or something. She peered intently out of the window.

'There's an air-raid warden.'

'It's only old Jimmy Green.'

'Mr Green to you. Well, he wrote to the Air Raid Precautions yesterday offering his services, so I expect he thinks he's got to do his bit.'

Jimmy was wearing his best blue suit; though whether in honour of the war, or only because it was Sunday, Chas couldn't tell. But he was wearing all his medals from the Great War, and his gas mask in a cardboard box, hanging on a piece of string across his chest. His chest was pushed well out, and he was marching round the square, swinging his arms like the Coldstream guardsman he'd once been.

'I'll bet he's got Hitler scared stiff.'

'If he sounds his rattle,' said Mam, 'put your gas mask on.'

'He hasn't *got* a rattle.'

'Well, that's what it says in the papers. An' if he blows his whistle, we have to go down the air-raid shelter.'

Chas bleakly surveyed the Anderson shelter, lying in pieces all over the front lawn, where it had been dumped by council workmen yesterday. It might do the worms a bit of good . . .

'Who's that?'

Jimmy had been joined by a more important air-raid warden. So important he actually had a black steel helmet with a white 'W' on the front. Jimmy pointed to a mad-happy dog who, finding the empty world much to his liking, was chasing its tail all over the square. The important warden consulted a little brown book and obviously decided the dog was a threat to national security. They made a prolonged and hopeless attempt to catch the dog, who loved it.

'The Germans are dropping them Alsatians by parachute,' said Chas. 'To annoy the wardens.'

That earned a clout. 'Stop spreading rumours and causing despondency. They can put you in prison for that!'

Chas wondered about prison; prisons had thick walls and concrete ceilings, at least in the movies. Definitely bomb-proof . . .

But a third figure had emerged into the square. An immensely stocky lady in a flowered hat. A cigarette thrust from her mouth and two laden shopping bags hung from each hand. She was moving fast and panting through her cigarette; the effect was of a small but powerful steam locomotive. The very sight of her convinced Chas that the newsreels from Spain were no more real than Marlene Dietrich in *Destry Rides Again*. Bloody ridiculous.

She made the wardens look pretty ridiculous, too, as they ran one each side of her, gesticulating fiercely.

'Get out of me way, Arthur Dunhill, an' tek that bloody silly hat off. Ye look like something out of a fancy-dress ball. Aah divvent care if they hev made ye chief warden. Aah remember ye as a snotty-nosed kid being dragged up twelve-in-two rooms in Back Brannen Street. If ye think that snivelling gyet Hilter can stop me performin' me natural functions on a Sunday morning ye're very much mistaken . . .'

'It's your nana,' said Mam, superfluously but with much relief. Next minute, Nana was sitting in the kitchen, sweating cobs and securely entrenched among her many shopping bags.

'Let me get me breath. Well, she's done it now. Tempy. She's *really* done it.'

'It wasn't Tempy,' said Chas. 'It was Hitler.'

'Aah'll cross his bridge when aah come to it. You know what Tempy's done? Evaccyated all her school to Keswick, and we've all got to go and live at The Elms as caretakers.'

Chas gave an inward screech of agony. Tempy gone to Keswick meant the loss of ten shillings a term. Thirty bob a year. How many Dinky Toys would that buy?

War might be hell, but thirty shillings was serious.

The siren suddenly sounded the all clear.

Mam let Chas go out and watch for the taxi in the blackout. The blackout was a flop. It just wasn't black. True, the street lamps weren't lit and every house window carefully curtained. But the longer he stood there, the brighter the sky grew, until it seemed as bright as day.

He'd hauled the two big suitcases out of the house, with a lot of sweat. He stood between them, ready to duck in case a low-flying Messerschmitt 109 took advantage of the lack of blackout to strafe the square. Machine-gun bullets throwing up mounds of earth, like in *Hell's Angels* starring Ben Lyon. He wondered if the suitcase would stop a bullet. They seemed full of insurance books and all fifteen pairs of Mam's apricot-coloured knickers. Still, in war, one had to take risks . . .

The taxi jerked into the square at ten miles an hour and pulled up some distance away.

'Number eighteen?' shouted the driver querulously. 'Can't see a bloody thing.' No wonder. He had covered his windscreen with crosses of sticky-tape to protect it against bomb blast and peered through like a spider out of its web.

'Get on, ye daft bugger,' shouted Nana from the back. 'Ah cud drive better wi' me backside.' Granda, totally buried beside her in a mound of blankets, travelling rugs, overcoats, and mufflers for his chest, coughed prolonged agreement.

It was a strange journey to The Elms. Chas had to sit on the suitcases, with what felt like Nana's washday mangle sticking in his ribs.

'I shouldn't have left the house empty like that,' wailed Mam. 'There'll be burglars an' who's going to water the tomatoes?'

'You coulda left a note asking the burglars to do it,' said Chas. It was too dark and jam-packed in the taxi for any danger of a clout.

'Ye'll be safer at The Elms, hinny,' said Nana. 'Now ye haven't got a man to put a steadyin' hand to you.'[1]

'She's got *me*,' said Chas.

'God love yer—a real grown man. 'Spect ye'll be j'ining up in the army soon as ye're twelve.'

'Aah j'ined up at fourteen,' said Granda. 'To fight the Boers. Fourteen years, seven months, six days. Aah gave a false birthday.'

'Much good it's done you since,' said Nana, 'wi' that gassing they gave you at Wipers.'

'That wasn't the Boers,' said Chas helpfully. 'That was the Germans.'

Granda embarked on a bout of coughing, longer and more complicated than 'God Save the King,' that silenced all opposition for two miles.

'It'll be safer for the bairn,' added Nana finally. 'Good as evaccyating him. Hilter won't bomb Preston nor The Elms. He's got more respec' for his betters . . . besides, ye had to

1 Mr McGill joined the RAF in 1938, during the Munich Crisis, but was discharged with flat feet in the winter of 1939, and was at home during the night blitz of 1940-41, as readers *of The Machine Gunners* will know.

come, hinny. I can't manage that great spooky place on my own—not wi' yer granda an' his chest.'

'Spooky?' asked Chas.

'Don't mind me,' said Nana hastily. 'That's just me manner of speakin'.'

Just then, the taxi turned a corner too sharply; outside there was a thump and the crunch of breaking glass. 'Ah, well,' said Nana philosophically, 'we won't be needing them street lamps for the Duration. Reckon it'll be all over by Christmas, once the navy's cut off Hilter's vitals . . .'

'Painful,' said Chas.

'Aah owe it to Tempy,' concluded Nana. 'Many a job she's pushed my way, ower the years, when yer granda's had his chest . . .'

Chas pushed his nose against the steamed-up window of the taxi, feeling as caged as a budgie. He watched the outskirts of Garmouth fall away; a few fields, then the taxi turned wildly into the private road where the roofs of great houses peeped secretly over shrubbery and hedge and tree, and, at the end, was The Elms, Miss Temple's ancestral home and late private school and the biggest of them all.

So by bedtime, on the third of September 1939, Chas had risen very high in the world indeed. A third-floor attic, with the wind humming in the wireless aerial that stretched between the great chimneys, and ivy leaves tapping on his window, so it sounded as if it was raining. Granda's old army greatcoat had been hung over the window for lack of curtains.

Chas didn't like it at all, even if he did have candle and matches, a rather dim torch, a book called *Deeds That Have Won the* VC, and six toy pistols under his pillow. You couldn't shoot spooks with a toy pistol, he didn't feel like winning the VC, and he wanted the lav, bad.

There was a great, cold-white chamber pot under the narrow servant's bed, but he'd no intention of using it. Mam would be sure to inspect the contents in the morning and tell everyone at breakfast how his kidneys were functioning. Mam feared malfunctioning kidneys more than Stuka dive bombers.

Finally, he gathered his courage, a pistol, his torch, and his too-short dressing gown around him, and set out to seek relief.

The dark was a trackless desert, beyond his dim torch. The wind, finding its way up through the floorboards, ballooned up the worn passage carpet like shifting sand dunes. The only oases were the light switches, and most of them didn't work, so they were, strictly speaking, mirages. Down one narrow stair . . .

The servants' lav was tall and gaunt, like a gallows; its rusting chain hung like a hangman's noose, swaying in the draft. The seat was icy and unfriendly.

Afterward, reluctant to go back upstairs, Chas pressed on. A slightly open door, a shaft of golden light, the sweet smell of old age and illness. Granda's cough was like a blessing in the strangeness.

But he didn't go in. He didn't dislike Granda, but he didn't like him either. Granda's chest made him as strange as the pyramids of Egypt. Granda's chest was the centre of the family, around which everything else revolved. As constant as the moon. He had his good spells and his bad. His good spells, when he turned over a bit of his garden or hung a picture on the wall, grew no better. His bad spells grew no worse.

Chas passed on noiselessly, down another flight of stairs.

He knew where he was now. A great oak hall, with a landing running round three sides, and a broad open staircase leading down into a dim red light. Miss Temple's study was on the right.

Miss Temple, headmistress, magistrate, city councillor of Newcastle. He knew her highly polished shoes well; her legs, solid as table legs in their pale silk stockings, her black headmistress's gown or her dark fur coat. He had never seen her face. It was always too high above him, too awesome. God must look like Miss Temple.

At the end of every term, ever since he had started school, Nana had taken him to see Miss Temple at The Elms. With his school report clutched in his hand. They were shown in by a housemaid called Claire, neat in black frock, white lace hat, and apron. Up to Miss Temple's study. There, the polished black shoes would be waiting, standing foursquare on the Turkey carpet, the fat, pale solid legs above them.

A sallow, plump soft hand, with dark hairs on the back, would descend into his line of vision. He would put the school report into it. Hand and report would ascend out of sight. There would be a long silence, like the Last Judgment. Then Miss Temple's voice would come floating down, deep as an angel's trumpet.

'Excellent, Charles . . . excellent.' Then she would ask him what he was going to be when he grew up; but he could never answer. The plump hand would descend again, with the report and something brown that crackled enticingly.

A ten-bob note. He would mumble thanks that didn't make sense even to himself. Then the tiny silver watch that slightly pinched the dark plump wrist would be consulted, and a gardener-chauffeur called Holmes would be summoned, to drive Miss Temple in state to Newcastle, for dinner or a meeting of the full council, or some other godlike occasion.

It never varied. He never really breathed until he was outside again, and the air smelled of trees and grass and not of polish and Miss Temple. Sometimes, hesitating, he would ask Nana why Miss Temple was not like anybody else. Nana always said it was because she had never married; because of something that had happened in the Great War.

And now there was another war, and Miss Temple fled to Keswick with all her pupils, and her study door locked, and outside Hitler and a great wind were loose in the world.

He crept on, past the grandfather clock on the landing that ticked on, as indifferent to him as Holmes the chauffeur in his shiny leather gaiters. Prowled out to the back wing, where the girls' classrooms were. Searched their empty desks by torchlight, exulting spitefully over the spelling mistakes in an abandoned exercise book. There was a knicker-blue shoe bag hanging on the back of one classroom door. He put his hand inside with a guilty thrill, but it only contained one worn white sneaker.

Downstairs, he got into a panic before he found the light-proof, baize-covered kitchen door; thought he was cut off in the whole empty, windy house, with only Granda above, immobilized and coughing.

He pushed the baize door open an inch. Cosy warmth streamed out. A roaring fire in the kitchen range. Nana, in flowered pinny, pouring tea. Mam, still worrying on about burglars, peeling potatoes. Claire the housemaid, raffish without her lace hat, legs crossed, arms crossed, fag in her mouth, eyes squinting up against the smoke.

'Shan't be here to bother you much longer. Off to South Wales next week, working on munitions. They pay twice as much as *she* does. Holmes? Just waiting for his call-up papers for the army. Reckons he'll spend a cushy war, driving Lord Gort about.'

Chas was tempted to go in; he loved tea and gossip. Hated the idea of the long climb back to the moaning wireless aerial and ivy-tapping windows. But Mam would only be angry . . .

He climbed. At the turn of the last stair, a landing window gave him a view of the roof and the chimneys and the row of attic windows. Six attic windows. His was the fourth . . . no, the fifth, it must be, because the fifth was dimly candlelit. Oh, God, he'd left his candle burning, and Granda's greatcoat was useless as blackout, and soon there'd be an air-raid warden shouting, 'Put that bloody light out.'

He ran, suddenly panting. Burst into his room.

It was in darkness, of course. He'd never lit his candle. And his *was* the fourth room in the corridor, the fourth shabby white door.

He ran back to the landing window. There was candlelight

in the fifth window, the room next to his own. It moved, as if someone were moving about, inside the room.

Who?

Holmes, of course. Snooty Holmes. Well, Holmes's flipping blackout was Holmes's flipping business... Chas got back into his ice-cold bed, keeping his dressing-gown on for warmth. Put his ear to the wall. He could hear Holmes moving about, restlessly; big leather boots on uncarpeted floorboards, and a kind of continuous, mournful, low whistling. *Miserable, stuck-up bugger...*

On that thought, he fell asleep.

Next morning, before going to the lav, he peered round his door in the direction of Holmes's. He dreaded the sneer that would cross Holmes's face, if he saw a tousle-haired kid running about in pajamas. Nana said Holmes had once been a gentleman's gentleman, and it showed.

But there was no sign of Holmes. In fact, the whole width of the corridor, just beyond Chas's room, was blocked off by a dirty white door, unnoticed in the blackout last night. It looked like a cupboard door, too, with a keyhole high up.

Chas investigated. It *was* a cupboard; contained nothing but a worn-out broom and a battered blue tin dustpan. Then Chas forgot all about Holmes; because the whole inside of the cupboard was papered over with old newspapers. Adverts for ladies' corsets, stiffened with the finest whalebone and fitted with the latest all-rubber suspenders. All for three shillings and elevenpence three farthings! Better, photographs of soldiers, mud, and great howitzers. And headlines:

NEW OFFENSIVE, MOUNTED AT CAMBRAI
MILE OF GERMAN FIRST-LINE TRENCH TAKEN
NEW 'TANKS' IN ACTION?

Chas read on, enthralled and shivering, until Nana shouted up the stairs to ask if they were all dead up there?

As he was hurling himself into his clothes, a new thought struck him. All those old newspapers seemed to be from 1917 . . . if the cupboard had been there since then, how on earth did Holmes get into his room? He went back and rapped violently all over the inside of the cupboard. The sides were solid plaster, the plaster of corridor walls. The back boomed hollowly, as if the corridor went on beyond it. But there was no secret door at the back; the pasted-on newspapers were intact; not a torn place anywhere.

'Are ye doing an impersonation o' a deathwatch beetle? 'Cause they only eat wood, an' in that case aah'm going to throw your breakfast away.'

Even though he knew it was Nana's voice, he still nearly jumped a yard in the air.

'There's newspapers here, with pictures of the Great War.'

'Ye've got war on the bleddy brain,' said Nana. 'Isn't one war enough for ye? Ye'll have a war on yer hands in the kitchen, too, if you don't come down for breakfast. Yer mam's just heard on the radio that school's been abolished for the Duration, an' it's raining. Aah don't know what we're going to do wi' you. Wi' all the bairns driving their mams mad, getting under their feet, Hilter's goin' to have a walkover.'

But Chas was surprisingly good all day. He did demand his mac and wellies, and walked round the house no less than fourteen times, staring up at the windows and counting compulsively, and getting himself soaked.

'He'll catch his death out there,' wailed Mam.

'He'll catch my hand on his lug he comes bothering us in here. Let him bide while we're busy,' said Nana, her mouth full of pins from the blackout curtains she was sewing.

Then he came in and had his hair rubbed with a towel by Nana, until he thought his ears were being screwed off. Then he scrounged a baking board and four drawing pins, a sheet of shelf-lining paper, and Mam's tape measure, and did a carefully measured plan of the whole kitchen, which everyone agreed was very fine.

'What's that great, fat, round thing by the kitchen sink?' asked Nana.

'You, doing the washing up,' said Chas, already ducking so her hand missed his head by inches; she'd a heavy hand, Nana.

Then, sitting up, he announced, 'I'm going to do something to help the War Effort.'

'Aye,' said Nana. 'Ye're running down to the shop for another packet of pins for me.'

'No, besides that. I'm going to make a plan of the whole house, to help the Fire Brigade in case we get hit by an incendiary bomb . . .'

'Ye're a proper little ray o' sunshine . . .'

'Can I go into all the rooms and measure them?'

'No,' said Mam. 'Miss Temple wouldn't like it.'

'Can I, Nana?' said Chas, blatantly.

'What Tempy's eyes doesn't see, her heart won't grieve. Let the bairn be, while he's good,' said Nana, reaching for her bunch of keys from her pocket.

So, in between running down to the shop for pins, and running back to the kitchen every time there was a news broadcast, Chas roamed the veriest depths of the house.

Looking for the back stair leading up to Holmes's room.

Looking for the hidden stair leading up to Holmes's room.

Looking for the secret stair leading up to Holmes's room . . .

He searched and measured until he was blue in the face. Went outside and counted windows over and over and got himself soaked again.

No way was there a secret stair up to Holmes's room. He was pretty hungry when he came back in for tea.

Nana switched off the radio with a sniff. 'The Archbishop of Canterberry has called for a National Day of Prayer for Poland. God help the bleddy Poles, if it's come to *that*.'

'Nana,' said Chas, 'where does Holmes live?'

'Mr Holmes, to you,' said Mam in a desperate voice. At which Holmes himself, the sneaky sod, rose in all the glory of his chauffeur's uniform and shiny leggings from the depths of the wing chair by the fire, where he'd been downing a pint mug of tea.

'And why do you want to know that, my little man?' he said, with a know-all smirk on his face. Chas blushed from head to foot.

'Because you're in the room next to mine, an' I can't see how you get up there.' He wouldn't have blurted it out, if he hadn't been so startled.

'Well, that's where you're wrong, my little man,' said Holmes. 'I have a spacious home above the stables, with my good wife and Nancy Jane, aged nine. You must come and have tea with Nancy Jane, before I go off to serve my king and country. She'd like that. But why on earth did you think I had a room up in the attics?'

'Because someone was moving last night, an' whistling'

Holmes looked merely baffled, as did young Claire. Mam was blushing for his manners, like a beetroot. But Chas thought Nana turned as white as a sheet.

'It's only the wind in that bleddy wireless aerial. Get on wi' yer tea and stop annoying your elders an' betters . . .'

Next evening Chas pushed open the door of Granda's room, cautiously. The old man lay still, propped up on pillows, arms lying parallel, on top of the bedclothes. He looked as if he was staring out of the window, but he might be asleep. That was one of the strange things about Granda—the amount of staring out of windows he did, when he was having one of his bad spells; and the way you could never tell if he was staring or asleep. Also the fact that his hair didn't look like hair, and his whiskers didn't look like whiskers. They looked like strange gray plants, growing out of his purply gray skin. Or the thin roots that grow out of a turnip . . .

'Granda?'

The head turned; the eyes came back from somewhere. They tried to summon up a smile, but Chas's eyes ducked down before they managed it.

'Granda—can I borrow your brace and bit?'

'Aye, lad, if ye tek care of it . . . it's in the bottom drawer there, wi' the rest o' my gear . . .' The old head turned away again, eyes on a red sunset. Chas pulled out the drawer, and there was Granda's gear. Granda's gear was the only thing Chas really loved about Granda; the old man could never bear to throw anything away. Everything might come in useful . . . the drawer was full of odd brass taps, bundles of wire neatly tied up, tin toffee boxes full of rusty screws and nails, a huge bayonet in its scabbard that Granda only used for cutting his endless supplies of hairy white string. There was the brace and bit, huge and lightly oiled, sweet smelling. He pulled it out, and a hank of wire came with it, and leaping from the wire onto the floor, a small silver badge he hadn't seen before.

'What's that, Granda?'

'That's me honorable-discharge medal, that aah got after aah was gassed. Ye had to hev one o' those, or you got no peace in Blighty, if you weren't in uniform. Women giving ye the white feather, making out ye were a coward, not being at the Front. The military after ye, for being a deserter. Ye had to wear that an' carry yer discharge papers, or ye didn't get a moment's peace, worse nor being at the Front, fightin' Jerry . . . Put it back safe, there's a good lad . . .' Granda's voice, vivid with a memory for a moment, faded somewhere else again. Chas took the brace and bit and fled.

Up to the corridor-cupboard by his bedroom. Soon the brace and bit was turning in his hands, tearing the pasted newspapers (in a boring bit, advocating Senna Pods for Constipation). Then came the curling shavings of yellow pine, smelling sweetly. After a long while, he felt the tip of the bit crunch through the last of the pine and out into the open air behind the cupboard. He withdrew it, twisting the bit in reverse as Dad had once shown him, and put his eye to the hole.

He saw more corridor, just like the corridor he was standing in. Ending in a blank wall, ten yards away. A green, blistered door on the left, but no secret stair. No possible place the top of a secret stair could be. The green door was slightly ajar, inwards, but he could see nothing. The only window, in the right-hand wall, was thick with cobwebs; years of cobwebs. There was a little mat on the floor of the corridor, kicked up as if somebody had rushed past heedlessly and not bothered to replace it. Many, many years ago. The air in that corridor, the kicked mat, were the air and the mat of 1917. It was like opening a box full of 1917 . . .

Then a bedspring creaked; footsteps moved on boards, more footsteps returning, a sigh, and then the bedspring creaked again. Then came the sound of tuneless, doleful whistling, and a squeaking, like cloth polishing metal . . .

Chas slammed the cupboard door and ran through the gathering gloom for the kitchen. He didn't realize he still had Granda's brace and bit in his hands until he burst in on the family, gathered round the tea table.

There were toasted teacakes for tea, dripping melted butter. And on the news, the announcer said the navy had boarded and captured ten more German merchant ships; they were being brought under escort into Allied ports. Slowly, Chas shook off the memory of the noises in the attic. Bedtime was far off yet. He dug into another teacake to console himself, and Nana loudly admired his appetite.

'Got a job for you after tea, our Chas. We've finished all the blackout curtains. When it's *really* dark, ye can go all round the outside o' the house, an' if ye spot a chink of light, ye can shout "Put that light out" just like a real air-raid warden.'

'That was no chink you saw in my bedroom last night,' said Holmes in a girlish, simpering voice, 'that was an officer of the Imperial Japanese Navy . . .'

Mam didn't half give him a look, for talking smut in front

of a child. Which was a laugh, because Chas had told Holmes that joke just an hour ago; he was working hard, softening Holmes up. Know your enemy!

Chas was really enjoying himself, out there in the dark garden. He was again half soaked, through walking into dripping bushes; he had trodden in something left behind by Miss Temple's dog, but such were the fortunes of war.

A little light glowed in the drawing-room window, where the blackout had sagged away from its frame. He banged on the window sharply, indicating where the light leak was, and inside, invisible, Nana's hand pressed the curtain into place. The little glow vanished.

'Okay,' shouted Chas, 'that's all the ground floor.'

'Let me draw breath and climb upstairs,' Nana's voice came back faintly.

Chas paced back across the wet lawn; the grass squeaked under his shoes, and he practiced making the squeaking louder. Then he glanced up at the towering bulk of The Elms. The blackouts on the first floor looked pretty good, though he wasn't going to let Nana get away with *anything*; it was a matter of national security . . .

Reluctantly, his eyes flicked upward . . . Granda's room was okay. There was no point in looking at the attics. There was only his own room, and there was no electric light in there, and his candle wasn't lit . . .

He looked up at the attics and moaned.

The fifth window from the right was gently lit with candlelight. And there was the distinct outline of a man's head and shoulders, looking out of that window. He could only see the close-cropped hair and the ears sticking out. But he knew the man was looking at him; he *felt* him looking, felt the caressing of his eyes. Then the man raised a hand and waved it in shy greeting. It was not the way Holmes would have waved a hand . . . or was Holmes taking the mickey out of him?

Suddenly, beside himself with rage, Chas shouted at the

almost invisible face, 'Put that bloody light out! Put that bloody light out!'

He was still shouting hysterically when Nana came out and fetched him in.

'There's a face in that window next to mine!' shouted Chas. 'There *is*. Look!' He pointed a trembling finger.

But when he dared to look again himself, there was nothing but the faint reflection of drifting clouds, moving across the dim shine of the glass.

Nevertheless, when Nana picked him up bodily and carried him inside, as she often had when he was a little boy (she was a strong woman), Chas thought that she was trembling, too.

He was given an extra drink and set by the fire. 'Drink your tea as hot as you can,' said Nana. It was her remedy for all ills, from lumbago to Monday misery. Nana and Mam went on with the washing up. They kept their voices low, but Chas still caught phrases: 'highly strung' and 'overactive brain.' Then Nana said, 'We'll move him down next to his granda afore tomorrow night.' When Mam objected, Nana said sharply, 'Don't you *remember*? It was in all the papers. 'Course you'd only be a young lass at the time . . .' The whispering went on, but now they had lowered their voices so much, Chas couldn't hear a thing.

He wakened again in the dark. The luminous hands on his Mickey Mouse clock only said two o'clock. That meant he'd wakened up four times in four hours. It had never happened to him in his life before. He listened. Horrible, bloody total silence; not even the wind sighing in the wireless aerial. Then, glad as a beacon on a headland to a lost ship, came the racking sound of Granda's cough downstairs.

It gave Chas courage; enough courage to put his ear to the wall of the room next door. And again he heard it; the creak of bedsprings, the endless, tuneless whistling. Did he never bloody stop? Granda's cough again. Then bloody whistle, whistle, whistle. Fury seized Chas. He hammered on the wall with his fist, like Dad at home when the neighbours played the wireless too loud.

Then he wished he hadn't. Because the wall did not sound solid brick like most walls. It trembled like cardboard under his fist and gave off a hollow sound. And at the same time, there was a noise of little things falling under his bed; little things like stones. He bent under the bed with his torch, without getting outside the bedclothes. A lump of the wall had cracked and fallen out. Plaster lay all over the bare floorboards, leaving exposed what looked like thin wooden slats. Perhaps there was a hole he could peep through . . . He put on his dressing gown and crawled under the bed, and squinted at the place where the plaster had fallen off.

There seemed to be a thin glim of golden candlelight . . . Suddenly Chas knew there was no more sleep for him. He had a choice. The indignity of running down to Mam's room, like a baby with toothache. Or finding out just what the hell was going on behind that wall.

Downstairs, Granda coughed again.

Chas took hold of the first slat and pulled it toward him. There was a sharp crack of dry wood, and the stick came out, pulling more plaster with it.

After that, he made a big hole, quite quickly. But the wall had *two* thin skins of slats and plaster. And the far one was still intact except for a long, thin crack of golden light he couldn't see through. He'd just make a peephole, no bigger than a mousehole . . .

He waited again, for the support of Granda's cough, then he pushed the far slats.

Horror of horrors, they resisted stoutly for a moment, then gave way with a rush. The hole on the far side was as big as the hole this side. He could put his head and shoulders through it, if he dared. He just lay paralyzed, listening. The man next door *must* have heard him; couldn't *not* have heard him.

Silence.

Then a voice said, 'Come on in, if you're coming.' A

Geordie voice, with a hint of a laugh in it. Not a voice to be afraid of.

He wriggled through, only embarrassed now, like Granda had caught him playing with his watch.

It was a soldier, sitting on a bed very like his own. A sergeant, for his tunic with three white stripes hung on a nail by his head. He was at ease, with his boots off and his braces dangling, polishing the badge of his peaked cap with a yellow duster. A tin of Brasso stood open on a wooden chair beside him; the sharp smell came clearly to Chas's nostrils. He was a ginger man with close-cropped ginger hair, the ends of which glinted in the candlelight. And a long, sad ginger mustache. Chas thought he looked a bit old to be a soldier . . . or old-fashioned, somehow. Maybe that was because he was a sergeant.

'What you doing here?' he asked, then felt terribly rude.

But the sergeant went on gently polishing his cap badge.

'Aah'm on leave. From the Front.'

'Oh,' said Chas. 'I mean, what you doing *here?*'

'Aah knaa the girl downstairs. She knew aah needed a billet, so she fetched me up here.'

'Oh, Claire?'

The man didn't answer, merely went on polishing, whistling gently that same old tune.

'Do you stay up here all the time? Must be a bit boring, when you're on leave.'

The man sighed and held his badge up to the candle, to see if it were polished enough. Then, still with his head on one side, he said mildly, 'You can do wi' a bit o' boredom, after what we've been through.'

'At the Front?'

'Aye, at the Front.'

'With the British Expeditionary Force?'

'Aye, wi' the British Expeditionary Force.'

'But the BEF's not done anything yet. The war's just started.'

'They'll tell you people on the home front anything.

Aah've just started to realize that. Wey, we've marched up to Mons, and we fought the Germans at Mons and beat 'em. Then we had to retreat from Mons, shelled all the way, and didn't even have time to bury our mates . . .'

'What's the worst thing? The German tanks?'

'Aah hevvn't seen no German tanks, though aah've seen a few of ours lately. No, the worst things is mud and rats and trench foot.'

'What's trench foot?'

The man beckoned him over and took off his gray woollen sock. Up between his toes grew a blue mould like the mould on cheese. The stink was appalling. Chas wrinkled his nose.

'It comes from standing all day in muddy water. First your boots gan rotten, then your feet. Aah'm lucky—they caught mine in time. Aah've know fellers lose a whole foot, wi' gangrene.' He put back his sock, and the smell stopped.

'Is that why you're up here all day—'cause you got trench foot? You ought to be going out with girls—enjoying yourself. After all, you are home on leave . . . aren't you?'

The man turned and looked straight at him. His eyes . . . his eyes were sunk right back in his head. There were terrible, unmentionable things in those eyes. Then he said, 'Can yer keep a secret, Sunny Jim? Aah came home on leave, all right. That was my big mistake. Aah knew aah shuddn't. Aah didn't for three whole years . . . got a medal for my devotion to duty. Got made sergeant. Then they offered me a fortnight in Blighty, an' aah was tempted. The moment aah got home an' saw the bonny-faced lasses an' the green fields an' trees an' the rabbits playing, aah knew aah cud never gan back. So when me leave was up, the girl here, she's a bit sweet on me . . . she hid me up here. She feeds me what scraps she can . . .' He kicked an enamel plate on the floor, with a few crusts on it. 'Ye can get used to being in hell, when you've forgotten there's owt else in the world, but when ye come home, an' realize that heaven's still there . . . well, ye cannot bring yerself to go back to hell.'

'You've got no guts,' said Chas angrily. 'You're a *deserter.*'

'Aye, aah'm a deserter all right. They'll probably shoot me if they catch me . . . but aah tell ye, aah had plenty of guts at the start. We used to be gamekeepers afore the war, Manny Craggs an' me. They found us very useful at the Front. We could creep out into no-man's-land wi'out making a sound and bring back a brace of young Jerries, alive an' kicking an' ready for interrogation afore breakfast. It was good fun, at first. Till Manny copped it, on the Marne. It wes a bad time that, wi' the mud, an' Jerry so close we could hear him whispering in his own trench, and their big guns shelling our communication trench. We couldn't get Manny's body clear, so in the end we buried him respectful as we could, in the front wall o' our trench. Only the rain beat us. We got awake next morning, an' the trench wall had part-collapsed, and there was his hand sticking out, only his hand. An' no way could we get the earth to cover it again. Can ye think what that was like, passing that hand twenty times a day? But every time the lads came past, they would shake hands wi' old Manny an' wish him good morning like a gentleman. It kept you sane. Till the rats got to the hand; it was bare bone by the next morning, and gone the morning after. Aah didn't have much *guts* left after that . . . but aah cudda hung on, till aah made the mistake o' coming on leave . . . now aah'm stuck here, and there's neither forward nor backward for me . . . just polishin' me brasses to look forward to. You won't shop me, mate? Promise?'

'Oh, it's nothing to do with me,' said Chas haughtily. The man was a coward, and nothing to be afraid of. He must have run away the moment he got to France; if he'd ever been to France at all . . . the war had only been on three days. *Making up these stupid stories to fool me 'cause he thinks I'm just an ignorant kid* . . . 'I won't give you away.'

And with that, he wriggled back through the hole. He pushed his trunkful of toys against the hole in the wall and went to bed and fast asleep. To show how much he despised a common deserter.

The following morning, when he wakened up, he was quite sure he'd dreamed the whole thing. Until he peeped under his bed and saw the trunk pushed against the wall and plaster all over the floor. He pulled the trunk back and shouted 'Hello' through the hole. There was no reply, or any other sound. Puzzled, he shoved his head through the hole. The room next door was empty. Except for the bed with its mattress, and the wooden chair lying on its side in a corner. Something made him look up to the ceiling above where the chair lay; there was a big rusty hook up there, driven into the main roofbeam. The hook fascinated him; he couldn't seem to take his eyes off it. You could hang big things from that, like sides of bacon. He didn't stay long, though; the room felt so very *sad*. Maybe it was just the dimness of the light from the cobwebbed windows. He wriggled back through the hole, pushed back the trunk to cover it, and cleaned up the fallen plaster into the chamber pot and took it outside before Mam could spot it.

Anyway, the whole business was over; either the man had scarpered, or he'd dreamed the whole thing. People could walk in their sleep; why couldn't they knock holes in walls in their sleep, too? He giggled at the thought. Just then, Mam came in, looking very brisk for business. He was to be moved downstairs immediately, next to Granda.

Suddenly, perversely, he didn't *want* to be moved. But Mam was adamant, almost hit him.

'What's the matter? What's got into you?'

But Mam, tight-lipped and pale-faced, just said, 'The very idea of putting you up here . . . get that map off the wall, quick!'

It was his war map of Europe, with all the fronts marked with little Union Jacks and swastikas and hammer and sickles. He began pulling the Union Jack pins out of the Belgian border with France. Then he paused. There, right in the middle of neutral Belgium, where no British soldier could possibly be, was the town of Mons. And there was a river called the Marne . . .

'Granda?'

The old, faded gray eyes turned from the window, from the scenes he would never talk about.

'Aye, son?'

'In the last war, was there a Battle of Mons?'

'Aye, and a retreat from Mons, an' that was a bleddy sight worse. Shelled all the way, and no time to stop an' bury your mates . . .'

'And there was a Battle of the Marne . . . very rainy and muddy?'

'Aye. Never seen such mud till the Somme.'

Then Chas knew he'd been talking to a ghost. Oddly enough, he wasn't at all scared; instead, he was both excited and indignant. With hardly a moment's hesitation, he said, 'Thanks, Granda,' and turned and left the room and walked up the stairs. Though he began to go faster and faster, in case his courage should run out before he got there. He wasn't sure about this courage he suddenly had; it wasn't the kind of courage you needed for a fight in the playground. It might leave him as suddenly as it had come. He pulled aside the trunk of toys and went through the hole like a minor avalanche of plaster.

The sergeant was there, looking up from where he sat on the bed, still cleaning his cap badge, like he'd been last night. The pair of them looked at each other.

'You're a ghost,' said Chas abruptly.

'Aah am *not*,' said the sergeant. 'Aah'm living flesh and blood. Though for how much longer, aah don't know, if aah have to go on sitting in this place, with nothing to do but polish this bloody cap badge.'

His eyes strayed upward, to the big rusty hook in the ceiling. Then flinched away, with a sour grimace of the mouth. 'Aah am flesh and blood, and that's a fact. Feel me.' And he held out a large hand, with little ginger hairs and freckles all over the back. His expression was so harmless and friendly that, after a long hesitation, Chas shook hands with him. The freckled hand indeed was warm, solid, and human.

'I don't understand this,' said Chas, outraged. 'I don't understand this at *all*.'

'No more do aah,' said the sergeant. 'Aah'd ha' thought aah imagined you, if it hadn't been for that bloody great hole in the wall. Wi' your funny cap an' funny short trousers an' socks an' shoes. An' your not giving me away to the folks down below. Where are you from?'

'I think it's rather a case of *when* am I from,' said Chas, wrinkling his brow. 'My date is the sixth of September 1939.'

'Aah *am* dreamin',' said the sergeant. 'Today's the sixth of September 1917. Unless aah'm out in me reckoning...' He nodded at the wall, where marks had been scrawled on the plaster with a stub of pencil. Six upright marks, each time, then a diagonal mark across them, making the whole group look like a gate or a fence. 'Eight weeks aah been in this hole...'

'Why don't you get out of it?'

'Aye,' said the sergeant. 'That'd be nice. Down into Shropshire, somewhere, where me old da sent me to be a good gamekeeper. They'll be wantin' help wi' the harvest, now, wi' all the lads bein' away. Then lose meself into the green woods. Hole up in some cave in Wenlock Edge for winter, an' watch the rabbits an' foxes, and start to forget...' He screwed his eyes up tightly, as if shutting something out. 'That is, if God gave a man the power to forget. Aah don't need me sins forgiven; aah needs me memories forgiven.' He opened his blue eyes again. 'A nice dream, Sunny Jim, but it wouldn't work. Wi'out civvy clothes an' discharge papers, I wouldn't get as far as Newcastle...' Again, that glance up at the hook in the ceiling...

'I'll try and help,' said Chas.

'How?' The sergeant looked at him, nearly as trusting as a little kid.

'Well, look,' said Chas. He took off his school cap and gave it to the man. 'Put it on!'

The sergeant put it on with a laugh, and made himself go cross-eyed and put out his tongue. 'Thanks for the offer, but aah'd not get far in a bairn's cap . . .'

Chas snatched it back, satisfied. 'Wait and see.'

He had to wait a long time before Nana was busy hanging out the washing, and Mam holding the peg-basket, and Granda was asleep. Then he moved in quick, to the drawer where Granda kept his treasures. The honorable-discharge badge and the discharge papers were easy enough to find. Though he made a noise shutting the drawer, Granda didn't waken. The wardrobe door creaked, too, but his luck held. He dug deep into the smelly dark, full of the scents of Granda, tobacco, Nana, fox furs, dust, and old age. He took Granda's oldest overcoat, the tweed one he'd used when he last worked as a stevedore, with the long oil stains and two buttons missing. And an oily old cap. They would have to do. He pushed the wardrobe door to, getting a glimpse of sleeping Granda in the mirror. Then he was off, upstairs. He had a job getting the overcoat through the hole. When he finally managed it, he found the room was bare, cold, and empty. The chair was back in the corner, kicked away from under the rusty iron hook. The sight filled him with despair; the whole room filled him with despair. But he laid the overcoat neatly on the bare mattress, and the cap on top, and the badge, and the discharge papers. Then, with a last look round, and a shudder at the cold despair of the place, he wriggled out. At least he had kept his word . . .

He haunted that room for a fortnight, more faithfully than any ghost. *Perhaps* I *have become the ghost*, he thought, with a shudder. The coat and cap remained exactly where they were. He tried to imagine that the papers had moved a little, but he knew he was kidding himself.

Then came the night of the raid. The siren went at ten, while they were still eating their supper. Rather disbelievingly, they took cover in the cellars. Perhaps it was as well they did.

The lone German bomber, faced with more searchlights and guns on the river than took its fancy, jettisoned its bombs on Preston. Three of the great houses fell in bitter ruin. A stick of incendiaries fell into the conservatory at The Elms, turning it into a stinking ruin of magnesium smoke and frying green things.

Nan surveyed it in the dawn and pronounced, 'That won't suit Tempy. And it's back home for you, my lad. This place is more dangerous than the bleddy docks, and yer mam's still worrying about those bleddy tomato plants . . .'

Chas packed, slowly, and tiredly. Folded up his war map of Europe. Thought he might as well get back Granda's badge and coat from upstairs.

But when he wriggled through, they weren't on the bed . . .

Who'd moved them—Nana or Mam? Why hadn't they *said* anything?

And the chair was upright by the empty bed, not kicked away in the corner. And on it, shining bright, something winked at Chas.

A soldier's cap badge, as bright as if polished that very day. And on the plaster by the chair was scrawled a message, with a stub of pencil:

> THANKS, LAD. THEY FIT A TREAT. SHAN'T WANT BADGE NO MORE—FAIR EXCHANGE NO ROBBERY. YOUR GRANDFATHER'S A BRAVE MAN—KEPT RIGHT ON TO THE END OF THE ROAD—MORE THAN I WILL DO, NOW. RESPECTFULLY YOURS, 1001923 MELBOURNE, W.J., SGT.

Chas stood hugging himself and the cap badge, with glee. He had played a trick on time itself . . .

But time, once interfered with, had a few tricks up its sleeve, too. The next few minutes were the weirdest he'd ever known.

Brisk footsteps banged along the corridor. Stopped outside his room next door, looked in, saw he wasn't there, swept on . . .

Swept on straight through where the corridor-cupboard was . . . or should be. The door of the soldier's room began to open. Chas could have screamed. The door had no right to open. It was fastened away, inaccessible behind the corridor-cupboard.

But there was no point in screaming, because it was only Nana standing there, large as life. 'There you are, you little monkey. Aah knew ye'd be here, when aah saw that bleddy great hole in the wall . . . ye shouldn't be in this room.'

'Why not?'

'Because a poor feller hanged himself in this room—a soldier who couldn't face the trenches. Hanged himself from that very hook in the ceiling, standing on this very chair . . .' She looked up; Chas looked up.

There was no longer any hook in the beam. There had been one, but it had been neatly sawed off with a hacksaw. Years ago, because the sawed edge was red with rust.

Nana passed a hand over her pale, weary face. 'At least . . . aah *think* aah heard that poor feller hanged himself . . . they blocked off this room wi' a broom-cupboard.'

She peered round the door, puzzled. So did Chas. There was no broom-cupboard now. Nor any mark where a broom-cupboard might have been. The corridor ran sheer and uninterrupted, from one end to the other.

'Eeh,' said Nana, 'your memory plays you some funny tricks when you get to my age. Aah could ha sworn . . . Anyway, what's Melly going to say when aah tell her ye made a bleddy great hole in her wall? Aah expect you want me to blame it on Hilter and the Jarmans?'

'Who's Melly? You mean Tempy?' said Chas, grasping at straws in his enormous confusion.

'What d'you mean, who's Melly? Only Mrs Melbourne who owns this house and runs the school and has given ye more ten-bob notes than aah care to remember.'

Chas wrinkled up his face. Was it Miss Temple, shoes, legs,

and gown, who gave him ten-bob notes . . . or was it Mrs Melbourne, who sat kindly in a chair and smiled at him? Who, when he was smaller, had sometimes taken him down to the kitchen for a dish of ice cream from her wonderful newfangled refrigerator? He had a funny idea they were one and the same person, only different. Then time itself, with a last whisk of its tail, whipped all memory of Miss Temple from his mind; and his mind was the last place on earth in which Miss Temple had ever existed.

'Aah don't know what the hell you made that hole in the wall for,' said Nana. 'You could just as easily have walked in through the door; it's never been locked.'

Chas could no longer remember himself, as he tucked the shining cap badge in his pocket and gave Nana a hand to take his belongings down to the taxi.

'Why did aah think a feller hanged himself in that room?' muttered Nana. 'Must be getting morbid in me old age . . .'

'Yeah,' said Chas, squinting at the cap badge surreptitiously.

EAST DODDINGHAM DINAH

East Doddingham Dinah was never a ghost; at least till the end.

She was a living cat; yet as near a ghost as a living cat can be. Long white fur and pale blue eyes. When she let you pick her up (which wasn't often) you'd realise half of her was fur. Only deep inside that luxurious fur you'd feel thin bones and thinner muscles, frail as wire. She hardly weighed a thing. All soul, she was; a loving soul looking out of huge dark unfathomable eyes, set in a head like a beautiful white skull. I never saw a cat that could jump like her; she could almost fly, like the frail thin aeroplanes she loved.

East Doddingham? East Doddingham was a World War II bomber airfield, set in the bleak wastes of Lincolnshire. The evening Dinah arrived, it was under a shroud of snow and thin fog, so it's no puzzle why the ground-crews never saw her.

She was looking for warmth, like the rest of us. But she didn't, like any ordinary cat, make for the glowing stoves of the Nissen huts, or the greasy delights of the cookhouse. She must have climbed up the ladder into B-Baker, on the dispersal pad.

She must have made herself snug in the best place; the rest bed that's halfway down the tail, towards the rear gun turret. Rest bed they called it; that was a laugh. Who can rest on a bombing mission? The rest bed is where we put the dying and the dead; the snug-looking red blankets don't show the blood.

Anyway, the neatly folded piles of blankets were good enough for Dinah. She must have buried herself in them; nobody noticed her till after take-off.

If we'd obeyed orders, she'd have soon been dead. We were

supposed to fly at 26,000 feet where the Jerry night fighters couldn't get at us so easily. At 26,000 feet there's so little air her lungs would have burst. But I followed the gospel according to Mickey Martin. 7,000 feet, where the light anti-aircraft guns are out of range, and the big ones can't draw a bead on you quick enough. I'd followed the gospel according to Mickey Martin for a year; Mickey was still alive, and so was I.

But it's still bitterly cold at 7,000, and it must have been the cold that drove her out. She made for the nearest human she could smell, who was Luke Goodman, our rear gunner. Luke had left his armoured doors a touch open, and she slipped through and on to his lap as if he was sitting by his own fire-side. How can she have known that, of all of us, Luke was the one who was mad about cats?

Anyway, Luke had a lot to offer her, besides his lap. He'd shoved the nozzle of the hot-air hose down his right flying boot, so the air would flow up nicely round his crotch. So Dinah got the full benefit. And of course he was starting to nibble nervously at his huge greasy pack of corned beef sand-wiches . . . And in return she rubbed her white head against his face, and kept him nicely insulated where it mattered most. The pair of them must have been in Heaven. Until Luke hit his first problem.

We were over the North Sea by that time; time to test his guns. He put it off as long as he could; scared the din would frighten her away. But in the end, those twin Brownings are all that stands between a tail-end-Charlie and a nasty end splat-tered all over the inside of his turret. So he fired them.

She didn't flinch an inch; only watched the lines of red tracer flying away behind with an interested lift of her head. It was then he realised that, being white with blue eyes, she was stone deaf, of course. How else could she have borne the endless deafening roar of the engines without going mad?

Anyway, quite oblivious of all this, I made landfall on the enemy coast; picked up the island of Texel, and headed in over the Zuyder Zee. Not much flak that way in, except for a few useless flak ships. But Jerry put up quite a pretty display as we passed between Arnhem and Nijmegen. Luke told me afterwards that Dinah was fascinated, her head darting this way and that, following every flash and line of tracer. She didn't shiver; she sort of quivered with excitement, sometimes dabbing out a paw as if to catch the red and yellow slow-floating balls.

Frankly, when he told me afterwards, I broke out in a cold sweat . . . If he was so busy playing with that damned cat, how could he possibly have his eyes skinned for night fighters? On the other hand, she was at least keeping him awake. For the danger is not the flak, not at our height. But the quiet bits between, when you seem to be flying alone through an empty moonlit sky, and the war might be on another planet. That's when rear gunners actually fall asleep through cold and loneliness and boredom, and the weariness after terror. As skipper, I had to keep on yakking at them, down the intercom, nagging them like a wife, asking if their nose is running or their feet are freezing. Anything to keep them awake. For it's in the peace and moonlit quiet that the night fighters come. Creeping in beneath your belly till they're only fifteen metres away, and they can't possibly miss with their fixed upward-pointing cannons.

Anyway, in the quiet bit before we hit the Ruhr, or Happy Valley as we called it, Luke said he was wide awake, and so was Dinah, just purring like a little engine. He couldn't hear her, of course, but he could feel her throat vibrating against his knee.

Then suddenly, she seemed to see something he couldn't. She tensed, flicked her head from side to side, as if to get a better view, then dabbed out swift as lightning with her right paw, against the perspex of the turret window.

Luke looked where she'd dabbed; but he couldn't see a bloody thing.

She tensed and dabbed out again. And still he couldn't see anything. He began to wonder if it wasn't one of those tiny black flies you get in Lincolnshire, the ones cats chase when you think they're chasing nothing.

And then she dabbed again; and he saw it. Even smaller than a fly on the perspex. A grey shape against the clouds below that could only be a Jerry. Out of range, but hoping to creep up beneath us. Luke was the first to admit that, without Dinah, he'd never have seen it. But now he had seen it, he had the edge; he felt like God, with Dinah on his knee. Invincible.

So he didn't warn me, like he should have done. He just eased his turret round ever so slowly, so that Jerry wouldn't spot that he'd been lumbered. Got Jerry in his ring-sight and watched him grow.

Luke said the Jerry was one of the best, a real craftsman. Took advantage of every bit of cloud to climb, get a bit nearer. Soon Luke could see he was an ME 110, with more radar antennae bristling on its nose than a cat's got whiskers. No front guns to worry about, then: only the fixed upward-pointing cannons behind the cockpit that Jerry couldn't use until he was directly under our belly . . .

Luke waited; waited until he could see the black mottle on its grey wings; waited until he could almost read its serial number, till he could see the white face of the pilot looking upwards. Then he gave it a five-second burst, right into the cockpit. He said the cockpit flew apart in a shower of silver rain; but the thing went on flying steadily beneath us. Perhaps the pilot was already dead. But he gave it another five-second burst into the right engine, and the fire grew . . .

I nearly had a heart attack. Luke screaming, 'I've got him, skipper. I've *got* him.' And suddenly this Jerry in flames appeared directly underneath my nose, so I had to throw the crate upwards and to port, to avoid going with it, when it blew up . . .

I can tell you, the bomb run over Dusseldorf was an anti-climax after that. And the run home was like a party. Because it's not often that a rear gunner gets a night fighter in our lot. I mean, imagine standing on a railway-station platform at night, with kids throwing burning fireworks at you, and a train comes through at a hundred miles an hour and you've got to hit the fat man sitting in the third compartment of the fourth carriage, with your air pistol . . . that's what it's like being a rear gunner. We only got a Jerry once before; in the early days of 1940, a bemused waist gunner in a Wimpey, in the hell over Berlin, saw a Messerschmidt 109, without radar, without a clue, poor sod, sail past his gun at less than a hundred yards range, overtaking a bomber he never even saw. The gunner was so amazed he almost missed the shot. But not quite. The Jerry went down without ever knowing what hit him. But that was the only other time we got one.

But now, my lot thought we were the greatest; thought we were invincible. I was in a cold sweat all the way home, trying to get them to go on keeping a close lookout.

But it wasn't till we crossed the Dutch coast that Luke said he had a cat sitting on his knee.

'Poor sod,' said Hoppy the wireless op, over the intercom. 'Greatness hath made him mad.' Hoppy did a year at Oxford, before he volunteered to be a coconut shy at 26,000 feet over the Ruhr. He hoped to return to complete a degree in English Literature. He may yet make it, if he can find a way to write, with no hands to speak of . . .

There were lots of other witty cracks, catcalls and jeers. But Luke insisted he had a white cat sitting on his knee. And at 7,000 feet, no way could he be goofy through lack of oxygen. So I sent Mike the flight engineer to go and see. Anything goes wrong, I send the flight engineer to go and see; if he's still alive.

Mike poked his head through Luke's armoured doors.

'Gotta cat all right,' he reported back.

'What's it doing?'

'Eating sandwiches . . .'

There never was a cat like Dinah for eating. When she finished Luke's she walked forward and scrounged off Hoppy and Bob the navigator, who sat together in the middle of the plane. And when she'd finished off theirs, she'd come walking calmly through the awful stink of the plane's interior, the smell of sweat and puke and the spilt Elsan, and sit on my knee and wash herself clean, while the sun came up behind us, and the flat coast of Lincolnshire and the big tower of Wainfleet All Saints came pinkly out of the morning mist like the kingdom of Heaven.

She clung round Luke's neck all during debriefing, digging her claws into his old leather jacket. We were the last home, and the other crews usually hang around the debriefing hall, drinking their breakfast, which is supposed to be coffee but is usually stronger. Everybody gathered round open-mouthed. The little WAAF Intelligence officer just didn't know what to write down; she thought Luke was having her on about Dinah and the ME 110. So she summoned her Senior Man, and he summoned Groupie.

Groupie, or Group Captain Leonard Roy to you, ran our lot. Grey as a badger and too fat to get into a Wimpey, but no fool. He knew that cats shooting down ME 110s was against King's Regulations. But he also weighed up the sea of grinning faces. There hadn't been many grins round East Doddingham that winter. We'd lost a lot of planes, we were permanently frozen day and night, on the ground and in the air, the local pubs were hovels, and the most attractive local females were the horses. But above all, we were the forgotten men.

You see, Wimpeys, or Wellington bombers to you, were good old crates that took a lot of knocking out of the air. But they were old, and slow. Not as slow as Stirlings, thank God, that lumbered round the air like pregnant cows, and were Jerry's favourite food. Everybody cheered when they heard the Stirlings were going on an op, because it gave the rest of us a better chance of getting home. But a Wimpey only carries a tiny bomb load. One Lancaster carries as many bombs as five Wimpeys. Why put thirty Wimpey blokes up for the chop, when seven guys in a Lanc can do the same damage (or lack of it)?

But the great British public had to have its thousand-bomber raids on Happy Valley, so we were always sent in to make up the thousand . . .

Anyway, Groupie looks around all the happy faces and says, 'Put the cat on the crew roster. Shilling a day for aircrew rations. These damn Wimpeys are always full of mice . . .'

It got a laugh; though everybody knew no mouse that valued its life would go near a Wimpey, corned beef crumbs or no corned beef crumbs.

She slept with Luke; she ate with Luke. Though in the mess hall, during an ops breakfast, she'd jump from table to table and get spoiled rotten with bacon rind and even whole bloody lumps of bacon. Because every other crew wanted her, especially after she helped Luke get his second Jerry. Aircrews were mascot-mad, you see. I mean, our last Wingco wouldn't *fly* without his old golf umbrella stuck behind his seat. He made a joke of it, of course, saying he could use it if his parachute failed to open. But the night his groundcrew mislaid it, just before a raid, he went as white as a sheet, and threw up right there on the tarmac. He still went on the raid; but he didn't come back. I saw him buy it with a direct flak hit, over the marshalling yards at Hamm. None of his crew got out.

We all had something. Hoppy had a rabbit's foot. Mike had a very battered golliwog. Bob had a penknife, with all the paint worn off, where he turned it over and over in his pocket during a raid.

But all the attempts to get Dinah away from Luke failed. Even the kidnap attempt by G-George. Dinah had been missing all day, before that night. We'd had to practically carry Luke out to the plane, because he was quite certain that without her, we were for the chop. Then, as we were waiting our turn in the queue for take-off, we saw G-George taxiing past, trying to jump the queue. That was their undoing. We saw it all quite clearly, because it was bright moonlight. Wimpeys have these little triangular windows all along their sides. Dinah's little white face appeared at one of them. And those windows are just celluloid. We saw her white paws scrabbling, then the window was out, and she leapt down and ran to us like a Derby winner. Luke, warned over the intercom, swung his turret hard left, exposing the armoured doors behind him. He opened the doors and she jumped in, and he closed the doors and swung the turret back, and we were off to Essen.

She got her third Jerry that night. After that, the Ministry of Information let in the reporters and photographers, and the legend of East Doddingham Dinah was born, with photographs of her clinging to Luke for grim life, and daft headlines like: DODDINGHAM DINAH HUNTS THE HUN.

You'd think, the way they went on, that she and Luke had shot down half the Jerry air force. But they only got four, all told. Still, I suppose it was good for the Home Front and the War Effort. Until some nut began to write to the papers, suggesting that all rear gunners carried a cat. The Air Ministry stamped on the whole stunt after that.

But she did much more marvellous things than just helping Luke shoot down night fighters. She *knew* things. Like the night she walked aboard, and then walked off again. I was just revving up, when she went to the exit hatch and began to claw at it, and give little silent miaows through the roar of the engines, *pleading* to be out.

God, the crew went *crazy* over the intercom. Should we let her out or shouldn't we? The row got so bad they even noticed in the control tower.

We all knew what it meant. She was our luck. If she went, we were for the chop, full stop . . .

Oddly enough, it was Luke who settled it. I heard his shaking voice through my headphones, he was very Yorkshire in his agony.

'She volunteered for aircrew duties, and she can bloody volunteer out, an' all. Aah'm not tekkin' her against her will.'

And nobody stopped him, when he undid the door clips and she dropped to the ground and shot off towards the warmth of the groundcrew hut.

We took off in a silence like a funeral, we went up to seven thousand in a silence like a funeral. Then Mike, the flight engineer, glancing over my shoulder at the dials said, quietly, 'Port engine's acting up, skipper!'

Well, it was. A fraction. Temperature a degree or so too hot, losing a few revs, then gaining a few, without either of us touching the throttles. But B-Baker was old, like I said. And it was the kind of acting-up that usually stopped, if you flew on for a bit. We'd been to Berlin and back on worse. And it was certainly the kind of fault which would vanish the moment you turned back to the airfield. Leaving you with egg all over your face, and a very nasty interview with Groupie. That was always the way when a guy's nerve began to go . . . the slippery slope which ended with you lying on your bunk, gibbering like a baby under the bedclothes till they came to take you away and reduce you to the rank of AC2 and put you on cleaning the airfield bogs. Lack of Moral Fibre, they said at your court martial – LMF for short.

'*Leave* it,' I snarled at Mike.

We flew on, crossed the English coast. I could feel Mike watching that dial, over my shoulder. The rest of them were still like a funeral over the intercom.

Then Luke said, 'She always was keen to come before, skipper . . .'

And Hoppy said, 'We've done forty-two missions without a gripe. They owe us one . . .'

I turned back. Immediately, the bloody port engine settled down; and ran as sweet as a sewing machine, all the way home.

I was in Groupie's office next morning, having a strip torn off me, when we heard the bang, right through the brick walls. We ran out together. But across the airfield, on her dispersal pad, poor B-Baker was already a write-off.

The sergeant of my groundcrew had been revving up the port engine of his darling to demonstrate her innocence. When a prop blade snapped off clean at the shaft. Went through the cockpit, shaving a slice off his backside, and straight out the other side into the main petrol tank in the starboard wing. Which promptly caught fire. He got away with a well-singed skin, and one and a half buttocks. He was lucky; he was on the ground at the time. In the air, we wouldn't have had a prayer . . .

We never worked out how Dinah *knew*. There were those clever-cuts who reckoned she'd felt the different vibes from the duff propellor through the pads of her paws, the moment she got on board.

We reckoned she just *knew*.

Like she knew about O-Oboe.

I mean, she was always prowling around the aircraft on their dispersal pads. As I said before, she could jump as if she could almost fly. A two-metre jump to a wing root was nothing to her. She would chat up the groundcrews as they serviced the engines, and never say no to grub (though she got no fatter). Then she would go for a trot along the top of the fuselage, or wash herself in the occasional bleak glimpse of February sun, on top of a cockpit canopy. I mean, any crate, not just our brand-new B-Baker. The other crews in the squadron liked that; they reckoned she was spreading her luck round a bit. And certainly, in her first two months with the squadron, we lost no planes at all. (Though of course the snow and fog cut our bombing missions down a lot in those two months.)

But it was different with O-Oboe. Next to us, Dinah was fonder of Pip Percival's crew than any other. She was always running round O-Oboe. It was parked next to us at dispersals.

It happened after breakfast one morning. O-Oboe's groundcrew sergeant came into my little squadron office, looking . . . upset.

'I think Dinah's ill, sir. She's sitting up on O-Oboe, an' she won't come down, even for bacon.'

I got Luke, and we went across in my jeep. When we were still quite a way from O-Oboe, Luke whistled and said, 'Christ, look at that!'

He meant O-Oboe. Through the mist, she looked like a ghost. She looked . . . cold. She looked as if her wheels weren't really touching the ground. She looked like you could walk straight through her.

You probably think I'm talking nonsense. Surely on a misty morning, *all* the planes would look like that? But our new B-Baker next to O-Oboe looked just misty and oily and *solid*. We both knew what that ghostly look meant. O-Oboe was for the chop, on her next mission. We all got very twitchy about things like that. There were bunks where every guy who dared sleep in them got the chop straight away. There were Nissen huts where whole crews who dared live in them got the chop straight away. After a while, nobody would sleep in those particular bunks. After a while, a wise wing commander would turn that Nissen hut over to storing NAAFI supplies. There was even a beautiful WAAF on the station, all of whose boyfriends got the chop. Nobody would go near her. In the end, in despair, she got herself pregnant by a local farmer; as he married her, it was a happier ending than most . . .

Anyway, we knew O-Oboe was for it. And on top of O-Oboe, on the cockpit canopy, Dinah was sitting. Not washing herself as usual, but sitting hunched-up, eyes shut, ears down, forehead wrinkled. We called up to her; she never stirred. She must have been there for hours; there were beads of mist on the tips of her fur.

Luke climbed slitheringly up and got her. He wouldn't have done it for anything but Dinah. Nobody even wants to *touch* an aircraft that's due for the chop . . .

She was shivering. We took her into the squadron office and warmed her at the stove, and checked that all her legs worked and she wasn't hurt. We warmed up the milk ration, and she drank that. Her nose was cold and wet. She seemed quite normal. So we let her out . . .

She went straight back to O-Oboe, sitting in the same place.

Luke fetched her back four more times. And each time she went back. In the end, Luke said, 'She's not ill. She's just *grieving*. For O-Oboe.'

After that, we kept her shut up in a cupboard, with a blanket, till take-off. But it was too late. Word had got around. Nobody looked at O-Oboe's crew during the briefing. A sort of space opened up around them, at ops breakfast (which, confusingly, we eat at night, just before take-off). You could tell they knew they'd had it.

They didn't come back. Crews who know they're for the chop never come back.

After that, the groundcrews took against Dinah. When she appeared round their aircraft when they were servicing it, they shooed her away. She didn't understand, and kept coming back. They began throwing things at her. From being the queen of the wing, she'd become the angel of death. The first we knew of it was when she came into my office limping, with one ear torn, and her back soaked with dirty engine oil. Luke spent a whole day cleaning her up. But we didn't dare let her out of my office any more; till it was time to go on a mission.

And the new Wingco told me she'd have to go. Our losses were starting to climb again, because the weather was better, and we were flying more missions. But the wing as a whole blamed Dinah; Dinah had turned against them, and was bringing bad luck. Some bastard tried running her down with a jeep in the dark, as she was actually following us across the runway to B-Baker . . .

Luke took her to live with his aunty in Doncaster; I drove them across in the jeep. We sneaked out and left her lying asleep by a roaring fire, with a saucer of milk by her nose. We were sad, but she'd be safe there, and she'd done her bit for the War Effort.

Half an hour after we left, she vanished through aunty's open bathroom window. Two nights later, she turned up at dispersal, in time for the flight. Forty miles of strange countryside she'd crossed, in two days. And spot on time for the op.

It was to be her last op. The funny thing was, she walked aboard as calm as ever . . .

A new target. The U-boat pens at L'Orient, on the French coast. Should have been an easy one – over the sea all the way, after going as far as Land's End to confuse the German radar. Then into the top end of the Bay of Biscay, and on to L'Orient at zero height from the sea.

Jerry had Junkers 88s out over the bay, waiting for us. Ours came in from above, for a change. If Dinah hadn't made the most incredible leap off Luke's knee to touch the top of his turret, he'd never have seen the one that nearly got us. But Luke didn't waste his chance. The bastard made off for home with one engine stopped, and glycol steaming from the other; I doubt he made it.

He was Dinah's fourth and last. The flak was hell over L'Orient; they were waiting for us. Thirty seconds before bombs-gone we took a 35mm cannonshell amidships. Bob was badly hurt; and Hoppy a bit, and Hoppy's radio set burst into flames. I never knew where our bombs went; probably into the local fish and chip shop. It was just good, with a fire aboard, to know they were gone. We went skidding on over France, with me shouting, 'Bail out, bail out!' and trying to make enough height so that the parachutes would open, before the plane blew up or broke in half.

Because, above all, aircrew are terrified of fire. I mean, it's one thing to die; it's another thing to burn slowly . . .

So it's all the more credit to Hoppy and Bob that they stayed and fought the blaze, fanned by a gale blowing in through the shell holes. Hoppy tried to rip the wireless set loose and throw it through the window, with his mittened hands. That's why he hasn't got much in the way of hands any more. In the end, the set burned its way through its mountings and out through the side of the crate, and all we were left with was a hurricane blowing through the fuselage, and two badly injured blokes . . . I went down to zero feet again and got out over the Bay as quickly as possible.

I was so busy trying to keep the crate in the air, and Mike was so busy getting morphine into Bob and Hoppy that we were nearly back over England before we realised that Luke hadn't said a word. I sent Mike back to look . . .

The rear turret was turned hard left. The armoured doors were open. Of Luke and Dinah there was no sign . . .

Luke had bailed out when I told him to. He was even more frightened of fire than the rest of us.

I got B-Baker down on a Coastal Command field near Land's End; but the fire had weakened the fuselage, and she broke in half on impact. Goodbye, B-Baker. Goodbye, Bob and Hoppy, for a long stay in hospital (though Bob made a good recovery eventually). Goodbye to my bomb aimer and front gunner, a kid called Harris who doesn't really come into this story. He'd bailed out through the front hatch when I told him, and finished the war in Stalag Luft XII. And goodbye, Luke and Dinah. Or so I thought.

Wingco put Bob and Hoppy in for the Air Force Cross, and sent me and Mike home for a month's leave to get over it. It was the end of April, and the nights were getting too short for raids into Germany. The crates were being changed from black night-camouflage to brown-and-green day-camouflage, and the crews were getting new training, for day-bombing and no one seemed to want two bomb-happy odds-and-sods. It's not usual for the Air Ministry to be so generous, but we'd nearly finished two tours of duty. Anyway, I had a nice time at home, doing up my parents' garden, which had gone to pot with the old man being on war work. And watching a bit of scratch county cricket, while the world got ready for D-Day without me.

I was weeding away in the back garden, hands all soil, when my mother said there was someone to see me.

It was Luke, shy and grinning as ever. Just looking a bit thin, that's all.

'Dinah?' I asked, dread in my heart, after I'd finished banging him on the back.

He grinned again. 'She's still catching up,' he said. And he told me all about it.

He'd got down safely in the chute, with Dinah clutched tight in his arms, though he almost lost her with the jerk when the chute opened. But she'd shot off immediately, when she heard people coming, on the ground.

Fortunately, they'd been decent French people, and they'd passed him on to the underground network that got British fliers safely out of the country.

He'd admitted he hadn't enjoyed the network much. Flying crates was one thing. Walking and cycling through Occupied France, with a beret on his head, and civvy clothes was another. He'd kept his air-force tunic on, under his overcoat, but he was still scared the Jerries would shoot him as a spy if they caught him. And the endless waiting in the dark in barns and cellars . . .

It was Dinah who'd kept him going. She'd followed him all the way across France. When things got roughest, when he'd had to follow his guide past German patrols, she'd suddenly appear, poking her white head over a wall, or trotting along the road in front. Sometimes, when he had a long wait in some cellar or barn, she'd slip in to visit him. He was scared for her, too. Because the French were pretty hungry by that time, and were eating cats as a treat at Christmas. He said there wasn't another cat to be seen anywhere, and when people were offered rabbit pie in restaurants they made silent 'miaow' noises with their mouths.

But she'd stayed with him; as far as the Spanish frontier. And then the really incredible thing had happened.

The night they'd crossed into Spain, in the foothills of the

Pyrenees, they'd been driven to earth by a last border patrol of German soldiers accompanied by the local Vichy policemen. Luke had lain with his cheek pressed into the earth, while the patrol passed. But the last Jerry had lingered; been suspicious of the clump of bushes Luke was lying in. Had seemed to sense, beyond all sense, that there was something alive in there. And then Luke, unable to hold his breath any longer, had taken a deep one, and made a dead twig lying underneath him snap. The Jerry had taken two paces towards the bushes, raised his rifle, called to the others . . .

When out had stepped Dinah, with even a damned mouse in her mouth.

Luke said the Jerry must've been a cat lover. He made a great fuss of Dinah, stroked her, called her 'liebling'. The other Jerries had laughed at him, then called him after them, saying they hadn't got all night.

And so Luke had passed into Spain, and then the greater safety of Portugal. And still Dinah had been with him, at a distance.

He'd told the whole story to the British Consul in Lisbon, sure of getting Dinah a lift in the stripped-down bomber that flew the guys home.

The consul had been very snotty, and talked about rabies regulations, and refused.

Luke needn't have worried. They were halfway up Biscay before she emerged from the piled-up blankets of the crew's rest bed. And the crew, being good blokes, agreed to let her slip off at Hendon.

I looked at my watch. My parents lived 'somewhere in the home counties' as we used to say for security purposes in those days. And Hendon was only thirty miles away.

'She'll find me,' said Luke. 'You'll see!'

'Better stay here with us till she does. We don't want her having to walk all the way to East Doddingham. She'll be tired.'

I don't think either of us had the slightest doubt . . .

Early the second morning, she dropped on to Luke's bed through the open dormer window.

She should have come back to East Doddingham in triumph. You'd have thought they'd have put her story in the papers. But our old Groupie had gone where good groupies go, planning new forward air bases in the France that was soon to be liberated. There was a new Groupie that knew not Dinah. And the smell of Victory was in the air already, and with it that smell of peacetime bullshit that was the scourge of the RAF.

On the air station where she'd been queen, where they'd begged for a tuft of her fur for luck, or a carefully-hoarded dropped whisker, Dinah had become no more than a rabies risk. We offered to have a whip-round in the Wing, to pay for her to stay in quarantine. But such nonsense was not to be tolerated; there was a war to win. Dinah must be destroyed.

There wasn't time for anything subtle. We met the RAF policeman, as he carried Dinah out in a dirty great cage from the guardroom. It was quite simple. I knocked him cold, and Luke took the cage and ran.

They didn't court martial me, for striking an other-rank. Perhaps they were scared the story of Dinah would come out. They diagnosed me as suffering from combat fatigue, and I flew a desk for the rest of the war.

We had our first crew reunion in 1948. It took Hoppy that long to arrange it, when they finally stopped operating on what was left of his hands. Everybody but Luke was there. The Air Ministry was not helpful about Luke. They had finally caught up with him in 1945, when he returned home for his mother's funeral. He'd spent some time in the glasshouse, then got a dishonourable discharge.

We found him in 1950. He'd managed to get to Northern Ireland with Dinah; she'd stowed away on the Belfast-

Laugharne ferry, following him as he knew she would. They walked together in the freedom of the Irish Republic. He'd found work as a farm hand, till his mother died.

He'd not seen Dinah since; though there'd been talk of a white cat that hung around the glasshouse gate. But when he finally got out, she'd gone. Tired of waiting perhaps. Or knocked down by a lorry.

The following year we decided at the reunion to drive down to East Doddingham. We wished we hadn't. God, what a mess. The guardroom was roofless. The runways were crumbling, and being used by men on Sunday afternoons to teach their wives to drive. The field itself was back under turnips, and the hangars were being used as grain stores. The RAF had found East Doddingham expendable, as it had always found us.

But Luke swore he'd seen a glimpse of Dinah. A white head peeping above the parapet of what had once been B-Baker's dispersal. Nobody else saw her; but we pretended to believe him.

Funny thing is, we've gone down to East Doddingham for our reunion ever since. God knows why. It's a dump. The accommodation in the pub is awful, and the beer still tastes like piss, as it always did.

But every year, somebody reckons that they see Dinah. We never see her when we're all together. But there's always someone who goes for a last solitary sentimental stroll round the old field. And then they come back and say they've seen her. But she always vanishes immediately. She never comes across to say hello.

I saw a white cat myself, this year. Staring at me over the broken concrete with huge dark unfathomable eyes, set in a head like a beautiful skull. It *can't* be her; she'd be over forty years old, and no cat lives that long.

But maybe she went back to the field in 1945, when it was already running down, and nobody remained who remembered her (life was perilously short in the RAF). Maybe she lived in peace at last, and raised kittens. Maybe this was her daughter, or granddaughter.

Or maybe she was a ghost. Or maybe she just lives on in the fond memory and failing eyesight of ageing aircrew.

But she certainly wasn't a ghost in 1944.

Lightning Source UK Ltd.
Milton Keynes UK
UKHW041130141222
413910UK00004B/121